For Sissy

By A.H. Gilbert

Toad Song Publishing

FREE PREVIEW!

For a preview of A.H. Gilbert's Silver Falchion Award-nominated novel, *The Crandall Haunting*, read the first two chapters at the end of this book!

The Crandall Haunting

Where there's murder, there's revenge

When Emerson arrives for his new job as project manager of a Colorado casino resort, he doesn't realize he is putting himself in peril. But inexplicable things are happening at the Crandall construction site. This job means survival, so he accepts the challenges caused by the driven developer and his family, people who range from strange to downright dangerous. Then, there's the appealing but forbidden woman who is determined to ruin them. And Emerson has noticed the locals whispering that the Crandall might be cursed. But dealing with all this seems easy compared to his growing anxiety that something is out there, something worse than anything he has ever faced.

In this fast-paced paranormal tale of suspense, unforgivable acts cannot go unpunished. But who — or what – will deliver retribution? With the resort's grand opening just weeks away, Emerson can no longer deny it: The evil is real. As he learns the truth, will he reverse the course of destiny or become the next victim?

Acknowledgements

My special thanks go to Kara Henry and Brian Pappalardo, *beta* readers, whose thoughtful suggestions helped me greatly during the writing of this book.

Dedicated to Gibby, with all my love.

Do you want to know more about *For Sissy* or A.H. Gilbert?
Visit **ahgilbert.com**.

For Sissy

By A.H. Gilbert

Martin paused in his work.

Why did that little girl look familiar?

His hands were wet and sticky as he fumbled for his cigarettes in the dim room, which was illuminated only by the television and a single-bulb lamp in the corner. He lit one and sat back, squinting through the smoke at the TV. The local news was sharing a clip from its national affiliate about a trial, soon to start, in a county just outside of Denver. Martin didn't care about the trial – something about a hotel that had collapsed – but that girl caught his attention.

He knew her face.

Martin shuffled his feet, making room on the cluttered floor, the black plastic rustling under his sneakers. The shoes, once white, were now stained. He would throw them out shortly and get a new pair. He leaned against the stiff wooden chair, found the TV remote, stopped the news, and hit "Reverse." There she was. He hit "Play."

A tall, dark-haired man—presumably the girl's father—stared at the camera as he walked with her holding her hand as they attempted to hurry down the sidewalk, looking startled by the aggressive approach of the reporters with cameras. The shot lingered briefly on the child before going back to the man, who, the screen caption said, was the hotel's owner. Martin reversed the feed again and paused it on the best shot of the little girl.

A slow smile spread over his scarred face, which was pocked from the cystic acne that had tormented him until a few years ago.

Yes, it was the same girl.

Martin's dark brown eyes narrowed with focus as the realization settled in. He reversed the news story again and watched it with interest now, taking in all the details, such as when the trial was expected to start, and more importantly, the street and surroundings where the little girl was walking with her father.

The caption under the man's name said "Emerson Crandall." The little girl wasn't named, but he knew who she was. She was the one person who could identify him.

He finished the cigarette as he thought about what he needed to do next, then stubbed it out in an already-full ashtray. The filter was smeared red.

Reaching again for the saw Martin continued his work, methodically separating the dead woman's leg from her torso, cutting through the strong tendons at her hip, and then stuffing the leg, along with its partner, in an extra-strong, black, lawn-and-leaf bag.

Well, well. It looked like he would be applying for work in Denver.

~2~

A cell phone's ring jarred Emerson's frayed nerves, causing him to jump as though a gun had gone off next to his head. Detective Lotu looked at him curiously as he answered the call.

"Lotu," he said, his eyes on Emerson.

Emerson hadn't slept well for the last two nights. He stared dully at Lotu, watching his round, tawny face and wide mouth as the detective grunted a couple affirmative answers into the phone. Lotu hung up. Emerson's vision blurred, and he felt like he could just lean his head against the dingy yellow wall of the interrogation room and drift off. Then his body jerked involuntarily.

"You okay, man?" Lotu asked.

"Yeah."

"You seem a little jumpy."

The cheap, molded plastic chair in the interview room didn't fit Emerson's tall, lanky frame, and he shifted, uncomfortable. He realized that Lotu was waiting for more of a response.

"Yeah. I just didn't sleep well the last couple nights. It's catching up with me."

"Oh, sure. I see."

Emerson returned the detective's gaze, his vision blurring again slightly, his brain screaming for sleep. The other detective, Sheen, watched him warily, his expression confirming that Emerson was acting a little goofy. The detectives might be seeing his exhaustion as something else. Drugs? Mental illness? He had to focus. He sensed some change behind the large mirror, in the observation room it guarded, but when he looked that way, there was nothing. His gaze fell on his own reflection. He saw the wariness in his deep blue eyes, his dark, unkempt curls pushed back from his forehead impatiently, his long, straight eyebrows pressed low in a scowl, the muscle in his angled jaw pulsing as he clenched his teeth, his shoulders slouching defensively. The short beard he had allowed to grow, mainly because he hated shaving, looked scruffy.

The unexpected glimpse forced him to see himself as the two sheriff's detectives did, and he didn't like it. He looked like a slapped dog. He sat up straight, drawing a breath that opened his broad shoulders and stretched his hard torso. At six-foot-two, Emerson was much taller than Lotu, but only a little taller than Sheen. Sheen, a graying redhead, was built like a mountain gorilla with a broad chest, powerful arms and thick, muscular legs.

Sheen noticed the change in Emerson's posture and became alert, radiating aggressive energy. Emerson's exhaustion made him want to return that hostility. But he needed to suppress that and focus.

Lotu had opened the conversation by asking Emerson questions about his trips to New Mexico. Confused, Emerson let them know – several times – that he was never there. With that line of questioning going nowhere, Lotu circled to worn-out questions about Mrs. Stanton's death.

"Just to be sure we're square on all this, remind us. When did you learn that your father planned to kill Mrs. Stanton?"

"I never learned that," Emerson said, annoyed, but striving for civility. He thought of calling Jeff, the lawyer representing Emerson and all of Crandall Enterprises, but didn't want to bother him on a Sunday. Besides, the police could get nothing new from Emerson on this. They already knew it all.

Emerson found himself drumming his fingertips on his thigh, humming a tune that rattled around in his brain.

Lotu raised his eyebrows in little, pointed arches, his round head, receding hair and soft features making him look more like a friendly friar than a homicide investigator. Emerson refocused on the question, wishing he could catch a nap.

"I only learned much later that it was even possible that he had planned to kill her. I'm not even sure what did happen the night Mrs. Stanton died. I thought she froze to death, right?"

Why did he feel so guilty? He had nothing to do with Clara Stanton's death. But his tendency to accept blame made him feel responsible, especially when it came to his family's bad behavior.

"Really? All you needed to do was get rid of her, and then you and your father could go on and build the biggest casino resort in Colorado. You were on the brink of becoming a millionaire. Except you needed her land. She was in your way. And now look at you. You've got no job, you're probably broke, and if you're not, you will be after the lawyers get done with you. You're going to trial, and you'll most likely spend the rest of your life locked away at Canon City with the most dangerous felons in Colorado. What will happen to your daughter?"

The idea scared and angered Emerson as he thought about his seven-year-old daughter, Courtney. He knew he had to regain control, but his exhaustion was causing him to overreact. Sheen watched him steadily, looking like a mutt that was expecting him to drop a morsel of food. Emerson didn't like that look, or Sheen. He had pegged Sheen as a bully when they'd first met a couple months ago. He usually combatted bullies with his wit, rather than his fists. But he was too tired to have his usual filters. This was a bad day to come here, he realized, way too late.

He had heard about police constructing false cases against innocent people.

He stretched his head back, looking at the ceiling, and took a deep breath before finally responding. "The last I knew, nobody is being charged with homicide. Not me, not my father, not his company."

"Not yet, but I think there was a homicide. I'm betting the jury will, too. Even if you're not formally charged with it, they could try to nail you on the other charges. And there could always be a civil suit. You could get off a whole lot lighter if you cooperate."

Lotu let it sink in, then softened his tone. "Look Emerson, you're a good guy. We know that. We know you're not a murderer. All you want to do is make sure your daughter's safe. Is that how your father got you to help him kill them?"

His anger bubbled.

"Don't try to manipulate me," he said. "I'm exhausted, but I'm not stupid."

"Just answer the question," Sheen said.

Emerson appraised him moodily. He had trained himself to be mild and flexible in most circumstances. But to stay that way, he constantly cooled a deep, smoldering fury that he could never quite extinguish. It churned, deep inside.

Sheen took a small step closer. Emerson wondered what it would be like to pound that jowly pink face and the bulbous nose. Sheen smiled, his face reddening, with a look that said, "Bring it." Emerson shook the thought away and yawned abruptly.

"Mr. Crandall?" Lotu said. "You with me, man?"

"Yeah. Sorry." Emerson looked back at Lotu, still conscious of Sheen's heavy presence, too close. "Like I told you, I didn't know anything about what my father was doing at the time Mrs. Stanton died. I was in Syracuse, doing research. Invasive insects."

Sheen snorted derisively.

"For the government," Emerson added, wondering if that made it sound more credible or less. Impatiently, he reached for his phone, remembered it was off, per the detectives' instructions, and flipped it around in his hand a few times, staring at it blankly. His thoughts wandered back to that day in October when the Crandall resort was destroyed, and he learned about his father's treachery, the day that he and Maddie discovered the location of the diamonds that Clara Stanton had protected. These were some of the same thoughts that had forced him awake the past couple nights.

"Everything okay?" Lotu asked.

"What kind of name is Lotu, anyway?"

"It's short for Lotulelei." He pronounced it "Lo-too-lay-lay."
"It's Tongan. But people have trouble saying it."

Despite his patient answer, Lotu and Sheen grew more intense in their attention to him, as though he was acting just strange enough for them to prepare themselves for something unexpected.

"Huh," Emerson said. "Anyway, I hadn't talked to my father in probably six months. But my research grant was canceled, and all of a sudden Courtney came to stay with me, after her mother was hospitalized."

Emerson flipped his phone, glanced at the mirror, wondering who was in the room behind it.

"My father always told me he had a good job for me whenever I needed it, but I never wanted to work for him. But then, I needed a decent job for Courtney. So, I called him, planning to work for him for a while, just until I could find a good job in my field."

"Sounds like he had you just where he wanted you," Lotu said. "What would you have done for that income? What would you have done for that little daughter of yours? Would you have hurried along an old lady's death? Would you have made her lawyer disappear?"

Enough. Emerson stood up abruptly, accidentally knocking over the flimsy chair. Lotu jumped up too, in surprise, and Sheen stepped closer, getting ready to pounce if needed.

Emerson quickly raised both palms. "Sorry!" he said. "It was an accident." He picked up the chair and set it back in its proper position.

"Please sit down, Emerson," Lotu said, trying to sound calm.

Emerson didn't sit. He was sick of this room, the detectives, the questions hounding him for the past three months. He stretched, letting his fingers skim the low ceiling, then walked over to the mirror. Cupping his hands against it to cut the glare, he peered inside, spotting dark shapes that might have been humans.

"Hello in there," Emerson said.

"Sit down, Crandall," Sheen said. "We're not messing around."

Emerson turned and saw them both standing on guard. He remembered they were trained to take down suspects far bigger and angrier than him. He sighed, sitting again and leaning back, hands behind his head, staring at Lotu.

"You have me for five more minutes," he said. "I have to pick up my daughter at three-fifteen."

"Are you taking medication?" Lotu asked, now sitting down again, too. Sheen remained standing and inched closer to Emerson.

"No. Nothing. I'm good."

"Because I have to say, you don't seem good. You seem distracted, edgy even. You're not normally like this."

"I'm just ready to get out of here. I haven't slept for two nights. I feel like I've answered these questions a hundred times. But, go ahead, Detective 'Lo-too-lay-lay.' Let's get this over with."

He could tell his attempt at a cooperative smile came off as a sneer. But Lotu smiled, the dimple reappearing in the loose flesh of his cheek.

"Yeah, sure." The detective sipped his coffee, then slid the paper cup aside.

"So, what was the deal with your father? He just thought it was okay to kill people to get his way, or what?" Lotu suddenly sounded rude. "You just went along with whatever he said, no matter who got hurt?"

This question provided the breeze that flamed Emerson's fury.

"That's it." He started for the door.

Sheen stepped closer to him, not quite blocking him. Emerson could have stopped, but didn't, and his shoulder hit Sheen's. Knocked off course, Emerson's leg caught Lotu's small table, tipping the paper cup, spraying coffee onto Lotu's neck and white shirt.

Now Emerson felt his arm twisted painfully behind his back, and he fell forward as the cold steel of handcuffs snapped around his wrists. He was shoved to the floor on his stomach.

"Don't move!" Sheen's voice was near Emerson's ear, his elbow in his back.

Lotu, annoyed to find himself wet with cold coffee, stood at the ready. Two uniformed deputies rushed in.

"What do you think you're trying to pull?" Sheen said, pressing Emerson's face into the filthy, gray, concrete floor. "That's assaulting an officer."

"What are you talking about? You jumped in front of me," Emerson said, trying to swallow the rage, his voice muffled with his cheek against the gritty floor. His shoulders felt yanked out of their sockets. His hips were painful against the cold concrete.

"Let me up. I have to get my daughter."

Lotu wiped his neck with his handkerchief and frowned at the big, wet stain on his shirt.

"Nice going," he said mildly. "You just earned yourself a night at our place. What is wrong with you, Crandall?"

"I didn't do anything!" Emerson said, panicked. "Don't put me in jail! My daughter needs me!"

"You should have thought of your daughter before you attacked a sheriff's detective," Sheen said, sitting back and removing his sharp elbow from Emerson's spine. "Get him out of here."

The deputies grabbed Emerson roughly on either side and yanked him up, pulling him out the door.

"Stop it!"

"What has gotten into you, Emerson?" Lotu said calmly. "You never acted so strange before. You know better than to hit a sheriff's detective like that."

"I have to call her babysitter, please!" He looked to Lotu.

Lotu appraised him, frowning.

"Yeah, okay. Let him make the call."

"I want a copy of that recording," Emerson said.

Then the door closed, and Emerson was on his way to jail.

~3~

Martin checked into a cheap hotel near the airport. He needed to find a decent place to live, but this would work, short-term. He stepped into the room and spent a few minutes carefully hanging up his suit and shirts. Then he sat at the desk and pulled out a small, spiral-bound notebook. He was going to make a list. He liked lists.

1. Line up inspections: Paulson Plastics, Asian Supply, Benton's Real Estate.

He made his living as an insurance inspector, going to businesses to ensure they met his company's standards for safety. With his record of being reliable, thorough and fast, the national company for which he contracted was happy to assign him work here in Denver, when he told them he was moving. These three were his first Colorado assignments.

2. Locate Emerson Crandall. Learn his schedule. Follow him home.

He paused, looking it over. The three businesses were just so boring. And the urge was building. He knew he would not be able to hold that creature at bay for long. He didn't want it to distract him from his main goal, but none-the-less, he pulled out his tablet computer and checked the full list of inspection locations his employer provided. Partway down, he noticed the Salted Steak restaurant.

He tore up the list and started again.

1. Line up inspections: Paulson Plastics, Asian Supply, Salted Steak.

2. Locate Emerson Crandall. Learn his schedule. Follow him home.

3. Get the girl.

The urge was strong, getting stronger. Part of him knew he would deviate from that list, after he visited the Salted Steak. That part of him grew excited by this secret knowledge.

He reached for his wallet, opened it, and pulled out the photo. In it, Sissy was just seven, with her brown hair tied in pigtails, and big, dark eyes, no smile, but rather a sad and distant look. The background showed the apartment's cheap shag rug and wall paneling. It also included part of his mother, on the couch, still in her uniform. The photo cut her off, so he could see just the side of her head, face turned the other way, her shoulder and arm, part of her torso, one leg.

It was the only photo he had of her, of them. Sissy. His Sissy, gone so long now. Hers was a short life, ended in unspeakable tragedy. He kissed the photo and put it back in his wallet. He would never forget.

Everything he did, he told himself, he did for her.

~4~

When Lotu got to work the next morning, he considered what to do with Emerson. He really didn't feel like pursuing an assault charge against him, although he knew Sheen wouldn't mind. Emerson's strange behavior yesterday caused Sheen to move Emerson closer to the "dangerous whacko" category, but Lotu was more tolerant of human quirkiness. And in fairness, his offense was minor, almost accidental. Almost, but not quite.

It was true that Emerson never acted so badly before. In fact, Lotu rather liked the guy. He seemed solid, smart, responsible, sometimes funny. The distracted behavior was unexpected and uncharacteristic. Of course, considering that Emerson's father was likely a murderer, he couldn't count on Emerson to be completely stable. To his credit, Emerson managed to be a pretty normal guy. That flash of rage that both he and Sheen spotted in the interrogation, though, that was new. In his heart, Lotu knew Emerson was not involved in Clara Stanton's death, or the disappearance of Clara's lawyer, but the fury Emerson abruptly displayed, subtle though it was, made him second-guess his own instincts on the matter.

Lotu's cell phone chirped, and he checked the text message. It was from his wife, Tai, who was visiting her sister in the islands, leaving him the caretaker of their huge, fat Labrador retriever, Onike, or "Oinky," as he liked to call her. His wife sent a photo, showing her with her sister at the shore, surrounded by little, drawn-in hearts.

"Beautiful ladies! Miss you," he typed. It was true. He dreaded her long, bi-annual treks halfway around the world, and he suspected that Onike did, too. Last time, his daughter and grandkids came to stay with him while his wife was gone, but this time, it was just him and the dog. Luckily, his neighbor could let her out on nights when his job kept him out later than expected.

He refocused on Emerson. This mess made for a strange case already. Emerson's father, E. Rexham Crandall, had raised more than a billion dollars to build the Crandall Resort and Casino, but the whole thing literally collapsed during an earthquake just before its grand opening, injuring dozens of people. It looked like, among other issues, the hotel was constructed with cheap materials. Rexham Crandall might have gotten away with this, with normal use, but the earthquake was powerful – unusual for that location. When it destroyed the hotel, the lawsuits followed, leading to a more thorough investigation of the structure. That's when the code violations were discovered. On top of this, a young woman named Maddie Cunningham had emerged with some interesting, but circumstantial, evidence that Emerson's father killed at least one person to get the property – her aunt. Now, besides the civil lawsuits lining up from the injured guests and employees, the Crandall investors and Miss Cunningham had convinced the District Attorney to investigate criminal charges, homicide and theft.

That's where Lotu and Sheen came in. They were investigating the homicide charge, while another investigator from their division was chasing the theft. With Rexham Crandall dead, however, the DA made it clear that, unless they could find a living accomplice, he would not file the homicide charge. For Maddie Cunningham, a guilty verdict for theft by Crandall's corporation would return her aunt's land to her. For the investors, they could recoup their losses. However, Lotu believed that Maddie was correct in stating a murder was committed, and he dearly wanted to find that living accomplice.

Unfortunately, they struck out. Emerson was really the only one they could look at, but even with the credible tip they just received, they didn't get anything new from him yesterday. The only thing unexpected was that brief display of menace, buried in a normally calm and collected young man under a lot of pressure. Most people might not have noticed that flash of rage, or put any credence in it, but both he and Sheen had honed their abilities to detect such threats, even in the most unassuming personas.

The other detective team found some success in loosely linking Emerson to the theft charge. But Lotu really didn't suspect Emerson of being guilty of anything except naivety for not knowing what kind of a mess he had gotten himself into when he left his chosen career – studying insects, of all things – to make a better salary working for his father. But, Lotu had been wrong before, and he still wanted to be sure that Emerson was guilty of nothing more than being a dupe. After yesterday's interview, he was a little worried about Emerson's mental health. Crazy people were capable of anything.

He sighed and glanced across his cluttered desk. He didn't like it so messy, and he tried to make the piles look a little neater. Sheen's desk, by comparison, was spotless. Sheen possessed that rare and valued trait of being able to manage paper immediately, organizing it and tucking it away in its proper place, or destroying it when it was no longer needed. That was the same way Sheen approached people. He observed them, identified and categorized them as innocent, guilty, sane, crazy, with little cross-referencing of one trait to the next. He was likely to try to find proof of his determination without looking back. And he was often successful. Lotu, however, saw the overlap in people, the messiness in the personalities he met. He knew a person could appear to be a good father, husband and businessman by ninety-nine percent of the community, but be seen, for instance, as a serial killer by the one percent he was slicing up.

But the one percent of rage he saw in Emerson yesterday was not enough to call him a criminal, even though he appreciated the fact that Sheen would be watching Emerson closely. He and Sheen worked well together for their differences. Likewise, he knew Sheen would not approve of the decision he was about to make.

He picked up his phone and punched in the extension to the guard's office.

"Hey, Johnny," he said, when his call was answered. "It's Lotu.

I'm good, thanks. How you doing? How's your new baby? Oh, that's good. Hey, you can let Emerson Crandall go. I'm not going to press charges. He'll be seeing plenty of me, even without adding felony assault to the list."

Emerson stepped out of the investigation building, blinking as his eyes adjusted to the chilly, February sunshine, and hurried to his car. The black sedan his father had given him last March was parked behind the Sheriff's building. He climbed in and drove away fast, feeling like someone would try to stop him at any moment.

He was immensely relieved to be out of that small, cold, stinky cell. That one night in jail had felt like a life sentence while he was trapped, chewed by anxiety, knowing Courtney would be scared and confused by it, and that it would add to her fear of being abandoned. At the same time, he knew that the babysitter, Mrs. Guevera, would take perfect care of her, and she was safe. That was the thought that finally allowed him to get some sleep. Not even the cold of the cell, the thin blanketless mattress, or the drunken arguing that came from other, unseen inmates could rouse him. In fact, the guard had to shake him awake, after 9 a.m., to tell him he was released.

He felt completely renewed and energized and remembered his interview with the detectives as if someone else had taken over his body. It was shocking what sleep deprivation could do to a person's personality and responses.

Now, he just wanted to see Courtney and make sure she was okay, but she wouldn't be out of school for several hours. He didn't want to burst in on her second-grade class just to satisfy his own compulsion. He already talked to Mrs. Guevera, and she reassured him that Courtney had slept pretty well and seemed okay, albeit it worried about him.

He headed in the direction of her school, his stomach rumbling. Noticing a clean-looking diner, called Buck's Spot, he pulled into the lot. He picked a booth and slid across the dark red, fake-leather-covered bench. Since it was around 10 a.m. – between breakfast and lunch – the place was almost empty. The neat, little restaurant wore that classic diner design, with rows of booths across the front windows, then another row inside. Finally, a long counter with attached stools stretched in front of the cook's window. One couple sat at a booth down the aisle, and an elderly man sipped coffee at the counter, his egg-yolk smeared plate shoved aside as he read the newspaper.

The waitress who approached looked about Emerson's age – early thirties – with long dark hair pulled back in a ponytail, escaped strands falling loose by her face. She gave him a big smile when she brought his coffee, but he was too preoccupied to notice. He ordered pancakes, scrambled eggs and bacon.

He sighed, deciding to try to stop worrying about the Crandall Resort case and all the rest of it. He viewed it as some long torture to endure, one he would eventually outlast. He tried to remain optimistic, looking forward to the time he could leave it, and Colorado, behind.

His primary focus was ensuring Courtney had as normal a life as possible, considering their circumstances. He had socked away his pay while working for his father, and had a fair amount saved, but it wouldn't last long unless he found a way to start replenishing it. That was hard to do while he helped settle the disaster that was once the Crandall Resort. For now, he was just trying to keep his expenses low, while keeping her safe.

He wasn't entirely happy with his housing. He had decided to move closer to Denver with Courtney after the resort debacle, even though the trial was taking place in the next county. Its county seat, Creeley Junction, was a tiny town, and he wanted to get Courtney in Denver-area schools. Plus, he knew if he moved to Creeley Junction, he would stand out among the locals, both as a newcomer, and for his role in the trial. At least in Denver, he could melt into the bustle of the bigger city, enjoying a measure of anonymity. Plus, his lawyer worked there.

Still, it was expensive. They were renting a rough, basement apartment in a section of town that was half industrial, half residential. When they were there, usually at night, the neighborhood had a barren, vacant feeling. But the rent was reasonable and the home owner, an elderly woman, left them alone and liked them to do the same to her. As for child care, he had found Mrs. Guevera through a reference from someone he had trusted, at the resort. She was steadfast and amazingly tolerant of his erratic schedule, over which he had little control.

Of course, spending a night in jail because he had appeared to deliberately knock shoulders with one cop and dump coffee on another, well, that was within his control. Unless he wanted to spend more time in jail, he had to get a hold of himself.

That forced him to think about his newest concern. His knocking into Detective Sheen's shoulder seemed like a little thing, albeit, ill-advised. But Emerson was mortified by it. He was generally an amicable, tolerant person, and a kind one. He listened to others, respected their viewpoints, tried not to judge. However, becoming even-tempered was something he worked on. He knew that under his layers of patience and kindness, he hid a seething core. This rage was built into his DNA, inherited from his father. He had witnessed, and sometimes been the brunt of, his father's rage. He had observed his father summoning that fury to intimidate and manipulate others, including his mother. He was sure it was rage that had driven her off, when he was young. Emerson was capable of that same rage, and he had proven that in terrible ways. That's why, when he was a young teenager, and long after she was gone, he made the conscious decision to change it, to suppress it so completely that it would no longer be part of him. And, he was successful. Almost. Sometimes, like a sleeping volcano, that hot fury pushed to the surface. This time, he could blame the exhaustion for its appearance, but that didn't really satisfy him. He worried that he was losing control of it.

He had pretended that his knocking shoulders with Sheen was an innocent accident, that the detectives were being unfair, misinterpreting it. But he didn't fool them. They saw it for what it was: a deliberate act of aggression, disguised as a mistake. Before he fell asleep in that stinking county jail cell, Emerson had allowed himself to stew in self-righteous injustice. But now, in the light of day and after a good night's sleep, he admitted the truth: that he hadn't completely abolished that rage, and it could still control him, given the right circumstances. He needed to work on getting it back in its cage, so the feeling of furious control didn't become an addiction.

"Whatever you're thinking, it doesn't look like the right thought to have before you enjoy this amazing breakfast," said the waitress, setting down his heaping plates, one holding the bacon and eggs, the other containing pancakes so big they hung over the plate's edge.

He looked up at her, surprised by her presence and comment, realizing he was scowling. She grinned. She had a thin face with a magnificent, expressive mouth, full of big, white, even teeth. She wore a purplish brown lipstick that flattered her caramel skin. When she smiled, her deep brown eyes became little crescents. She set down a small pitcher of syrup by his plate, along with a handful of foil-topped butter packets from her pocket.

Her smile, not to mention the sight and fragrant heat of the food, snapped him out of his moody self-evaluation. He looked back at her, feeling silly.

"Sorry," he said. "Deep in thought."

"Do you have everything you need?" She smiled again, cocking an eyebrow almost imperceptibly, not in a hurry.

Now, he noticed her in a different way. She was pretty, friendly. His eyes moved almost involuntarily from her face to her body in the smallest of glances, and he noticed her slim figure was hidden behind a frumpy, maroon, uniform dress. Pretty, yes, but he knew waitresses always turned on the charm with customers to help beef-up their tips, and her behavior was most likely just that. He was not feeling particularly trusting of strange, beautiful women, anyway. Plus, he might be misinterpreting her altogether, which he felt was likely. Having just spent a night in jail for the first time in his life, he couldn't imagine there was much about him that would attract the kind of interest he thought, for a nanosecond, she might be offering. He felt coated in a layer of jail grunge.

And honestly, his heart still dwelt on Maddie, as hopeless an infatuation as there ever was.

"Yes, thanks. It looks delicious," he said, smiling slightly and nodding, then turning to the food.

He ate as if he had lived in jail for a week on rations of hardtack and water. During his meal, he listened to a voice message from Jeff, who apologized that he was unable to get to the sheriff's station, because he was with his teenage daughters, skiing in Aspen, and had no cell while on the slopes. He had not gotten the babysitter's call until evening. Jeff had then sent about ten texts of instructions and concern, along with a promise to get one of his colleagues to the station with bail in the morning, all of which Emerson now halted with a quick text, telling Jeff he was released with no charges. Why Jeff had bothered with all that hyperactive communication when he must have known the police had confiscated his phone, Emerson didn't know.

When he finished his breakfast, he placed his knife and fork together on the plate and pushed it aside. He still had time before he could pick up Courtney. He sat back and sipped his coffee, gazing out the window at the traffic on Route 6.

One thing was certain: Courtney would never see that rage. The pattern of fury and bullying he had inherited from his father stopped here. It would not go forward. He had so successfully fought it that not she, nor anyone else he held close – small number though that was – had any inkling of the darkness he had successfully conquered.

That's why it was so shocking and disheartening that Detective Sheen had easily identified Emerson's hidden weakness and picked that scab until it bled.

~5~

Martin waited at the hostess station of the Salted Steak. He watched a young waitress setting up tables for the dinner rush. She was lovely, about twenty-three, long, dark hair tied up, working quickly but carefully, making sure everything met the restaurant's high standards. She had said hello, but now ignored him. He wasn't surprised. He knew his scarred face was repellent to pretty girls, and he was ashamed of it. He had a thick beard, now, but the scars went higher up his face than the hair. Likewise, he had grown his bangs, and they were long enough to cover his forehead, but he could feel the scars, glaring through. He didn't like so much hair on his face and over his eyes, preferring a short, neat cut. But that girl was out there. She had seen him when he wore his hair short, his face shaven. He had to make the best of it, meticulously styling the bangs with gel, so they laid just right, and combing, trimming and oiling his beard until it gleamed. He knew the long hair didn't match the rest of his quiet, professional persona, but other than this quirk, he thought he looked sharp in his dark suit and tie. In fact, he cut a better figure than most men he had seen on his walk from the parking garage to the restaurant. He took good care of his body, worked it. He was strong and hard. He found it obvious that his body was grander in looks and strength to other men's. Martin, in fact, considered himself better in all ways.

Why did pretty women refuse to see this? It seemed that others neglected to notice his superiority, a fact that troubled and angered him.

His gaze hardened as he watched the waitress. She was probably a whore like the rest of them, but he knew she wouldn't put out for him. Anybody else. Everybody else. But not him.

Another waitress came in, tying her lacy apron in a bow at her back and murmuring something to the first one. She looked over at him and smiled but didn't offer to help him. They must know who he was, how important he was. He saw them exchange a look and smile. Were they laughing at him? He narrowed his eyes. He could show them what happened when women laughed at him. He and Sissy could show them. Sweet revenge. He felt the excitement, the urge. That other part of himself, hidden behind the version he let most people see. Except for the lucky few.

"Mr. Pulga?"

Martin had a hard time looking away from the waitresses, but as he did, his face changed from seething disdain to a charming smile.

"Yes. Mr. Waters?" He shook the man's hand. This man, too, wore a suit and tie. His graying hair was neat, and his mustache trim, his look altogether befitting the owner of one of Denver's best restaurants.

"No problem finding us?"

"Oh, no. No problem."

"Well, very good. Now, where shall we start?"

"The kitchen," Martin said. He pulled a digital tablet from his courier bag, turned it on and pulled up the inspection form.

He regarded his job as boring necessity, but he congratulated himself on choosing his profession well. This line of work allowed him to move around whenever he wanted. It was also a job that did not require long-term, workplace relationships. That was important, he had learned. He knew he could be charming for a while, but he had noticed that the longer he knew someone, the more they seemed to avoid him.

That reminded him. He needed to check the Milwaukee news to see if that last one had been found. One thing he knew: They would never find the other half of her head.

Emerson didn't think he could go on much longer. He was gasping, heart pounding, sweat dripping into his eyes. But Jeff was relentless.

Wop. The racquetball sprang from Jeff's racket, hitting low on the wall, squeaking off the floor, staying down and flying to the right. Emerson dove at it, flat out, racket extended, missed, landed hard on the glossy wooden floor, just shy of the wall. The friction of the slick floor burned his knees.

Jeff threw up his arms and jogged in a circle around Emerson.

"Victory is ours!" He started singing, 'Hail, hail Freedonia!' in an absurd falsetto.

"Don't be a sore winner," said Emerson, still lying on the floor, glad it was over.

Jeff held out his hand, which Emerson took, and yanked, pulling him up.

"Good game," Emerson said.

"You too, buddy," Jeff said. "You're getting better."

"I didn't know I needed to practice up on my racquet sports before hiring you."

"You should have," Jeff said. "And if we're still at trial come spring, I'll whip your ass in tennis, too."

Nearly forty with intense energy, his lawyer had kept his five-foot, nine-inch body trim and lean. He claimed it was because he was newly divorced and had to prepare to become a "chick magnet" again. But Emerson doubted that he was the type to ever let his body get soft, even when he had been comfortably settled into life as both a father and a husband.

"No doubt," Emerson said. "But we better not still be at trial in the spring."

Since they had to meet regularly to prepare for the case, Jeff had sized-up Emerson and, early on, suggested they get together before meetings for racquetball. He was rabid about the game and had already worn out most of his friends and coworkers. Through the racquetball and the trial preparation, Emerson had discovered that he liked Jeff and looked forward to the games, although he had not won yet.

"How come you haven't challenged me to hoops, one-on-one?" Emerson had sprouted to his full height at age thirteen and, from then on, was constantly recruited onto basketball teams for school, clubs and casual games.

"No thanks. I have to maintain my huge ego to be able to win your case."

They both laughed and headed for the locker room.

A little later, showered, dressed, and in Jeff's case, shaved, they headed out for breakfast to discuss their strategy. Jeff picked a restaurant in downtown, between the racquet club and Jeff's office. It was famous for its steaks, but also offered bagels and light breakfasts in the morning, along with some of Denver's best coffee. Although many places in Denver made that claim.

"Okay, first things first," Jeff said, stirring his oatmeal. "Repeat after me: I will not speak to the cops without my lawyer. I will not speak to the cops without my lawyer."

Emerson smiled. "It was no big deal."

"You got your dumb ass tossed in jail. That's a very big deal before a trial in which I'm trying to keep your ass out of jail."

Emerson conceded the point with a small nod.

"Say it."

"I will not speak to the cops without my lawyer."

"Okay, next thing.," Jeff spooned oatmeal into his mouth, then pushed his bowl out of the way, flipped open a folder, thumbed through it and reached for a thin laptop, opening it and switching it on. Emerson munched a toasted English muffin that dripped peanut butter, watching.

"The DA has made a final decision that there is not enough evidence to go forward with the homicide charge."

Emerson didn't know how to feel about this. Obviously, he didn't want to be personally involved in a homicide trial, but on the other hand, he suspected his father had had a hand in Mrs. Stanton's death, and probably did something to her lawyer, who went missing while on a vacation to New Mexico and was never found. He knew Maddie would be upset by the district attorney's decision, probably furious, because she wanted justice and revenge. And he leaned with her. He knew he was on the hot seat for the moment, but one side of him had faith that he would not be found guilty in any of the charges, because he was innocent. But the other side also realized that the prosecution was going to try very hard to put a face to those theft charges. And that face was his.

"First step is meeting to present our evidence to the judge. She will then decide if there is enough to go to trial. I will try to show there isn't, but she will definitely decide there is enough. Because there is enough."

"Okay."

"As you know, we rejected their plea bargain, because it involved a guilty plea from you, which we want to avoid." Jeff focused on his laptop, sifting through his folders of notes. "And they didn't go for our counter, which would have gotten you off the hook. Out for blood, this bunch. So, we'll have to go to trial. With the felony theft charges, we'll go with a jury. That'll work out better than just a judge. I have a good record in front of juries, and you have a natural appeal that will help them think favorably toward you."

Emerson reacted with a surprised laugh.

Jeff looked up, eyeing him as though appraising a painting, his light brown eyes skimming over Emerson's face and body.

"You do, trust me, with those eyes and that jaw and your dopey expression. Get a few little old ladies and single moms in the jury and you'll have an immediate set of allies. But you'll need to get a haircut and lose that hobo beard and mustache."

Emerson was used to taking direction on his personal appearance from his father – insults and all – and accepted this with a shrug.

"I'm going to defend the whole of Crandall Enterprises, as you know. But, considering the evidence and the fact that juries are notoriously tough on corporate crime, our best bet is to protect you at all costs, and keep you from being associated with any of the activity that could lead to conviction. Of course, there's always the chance we might get a plea offer we like better. But, in absence of that, we've already established that you don't really care what happens to Crandall Enterprises, so my main job is to save your skin. Right?"

"Right."

"Okay, so let's review the charges against you first, and see if we can uncover any surprises we haven't already answered."

After two hours, and with much more work to do, they set another date for later that week. Emerson told himself to brush up on racquetball strategy before then.

Neither of them noticed the bearded man who passed the window twice, smoking and glancing in at them with interest both times.

~7~

In his rental car on the dark street, Martin watched Emerson help his daughter out of the black sedan. They were heading into the worn, but well-kept, home across from a warehouse.

His vision was better than 20/20 – another indication of his magnificence – but he used binoculars to focus on her, just to be sure. In addition to his extraordinary vision, he could remember when and where he first saw someone, although he did not usually recall names. He decided names must not be important, or he would certainly remember them. He remembered important things, filed them away in his excellent brain, for future use.

Looking at her now confirmed it. It was she, the same girl who had seen him that night in Springfield, when he was in the alley with that slut. That was another one who wouldn't give him the time of day, he remembered. What was wrong with these women? Why didn't they recognize his exceptional quality as a mate? In the end, they understood they deserved punishment. Especially waitresses. They were supposed to serve him. Serve meant serve, in all ways. He watched how they flirted with other men, but when they saw him, they never looked past his scars. They didn't see his fine, strong body, his handsome, dark eyes, or recognize his extreme intellect. They just saw his scars and rejected him. Then they flirted with other men, far lesser men. Irresponsible. They must be punished.

He took a breath, tried to calm down and remind himself of the other reason: For Sissy, they had to die.

His cigarette smoke filled the car, and he cracked his window. The smoke rushed out, pulled away by a cold breeze.

Yes, this was the same girl; he was certain. He focused his binoculars on her pale face. She was quiet, not talking. Her dark hair had come loose from its clip on one side. Just like Sissy. Then, as he watched, the little girl's face started to change. He only had a moment before they disappeared into the apartment, but he was sure. At the last minute, she turned toward him, looked right into the car.

Sissy!

There was his little sister, whom he had worked so hard to protect, but in the end, couldn't. He couldn't. And his mother had just sat there and let her die a horrible, unspeakable death. She turned his way, glaring at him.

"You're worthless!" Sissy yelled. "Worthless!"

Martin lowered the binoculars, looking over them, straining to see. He covered his ears, pressing hard, closing his eyes tight. Opening them, he tried to see her clearly. He couldn't focus on her now. She looked like the waves of heat shimmering up from a hot road in the summer. He put the binoculars back to his eyes. Okay, he could see clearly again. No, it was just that girl, the one who had seen him in Springfield that night. It wasn't his Sissy, after all. Then she disappeared into the building with her father.

He was upset. Why had Sissy yelled those things? This was new, and he hated it. And seeing her like that, so young, fresh and vibrant, but so angry at him, brought back the sorrow. Yet another part of him liked to see her, even though, lately, she had become so hurtful toward him. It was confusing. He didn't like confusion in his careful world.

His eyes clenched shut, and his mouth was open. A small rumble started in his chest, finding a way out, becoming louder, turning into a sob. Abruptly, Martin pounded his forehead into the steering wheel, once, twice. A welt formed. He pounded it again. The welt opened, and blood trickled into his eye. He hit his head again on the steering wheel, leaving a large red spot, a bit of blood splattering out onto the dashboard.

He started the car.
He had to go. He had to go now.

~ 8 ~

After the sign that said, "Ram Horn Canyon, 7," Martin accelerated up
a steep hill. This paved road wound through a scrappy, barren
landscape, bright in the afternoon light. Snow drifted deeply in some
spots, while others were hard, thin patches of white. Remnants of last
summer's weeds and ice-crusted evergreens scattered the terrain,
hunched in the cold, February wind. He crested the highest point in
the road, then started down, into the canyon itself. He chose a gravel
road off to the right and followed as it twisted along an edge of the
canyon, past trail heads and small cabins. He noticed an overgrown
dirt road, little more than a trail, carved by tire tracks. An old, hand-
painted wooden sign marked the entrance, its words half worn away
by weather: "Private Road." He turned in and followed it as it traced
around rocky outcrops, pocked with snow, into deeper woods, mostly
evergreens and aspens, the latter bare of leaves. At last, the road
ended at a small cabin. Like the sign, it was weathered with dull
wooden siding, grayed and dry, in need of staining or paint. One of the
wooden window shutters was loose, hanging by a hinge. The door's
padlock was rusty and small, and it broke away easily when he hit it
with the hammer he carried in his trunk toolbox. Martin glanced
around the empty woods and stepped inside.

It was a simple, one-room structure. Half was a rustic kitchen
with a small, propane, cook stove and a squatty table, and the other
half was a sitting area with a cot, its mattress dry-rotted and gnawed
by rodents. A couple of faded, throw rugs were the only covering on
the plywood floors. A centrally-placed wood stove could provide heat,
and several battery-charged lanterns hanging from nails would
brighten the place at night.

He knocked a hole in the wall, pulling the drywall away with the claw of his hammer, finding the stud, a six-by-six. It was a sturdy little structure, built for someone's vacations, hunting or ski trips, maybe, but obviously not visited for a couple of years. He checked his watch. The cabin was fifty minutes from the heart of town on a clear day, but much slower in bad weather, he knew.

Part of him knew something else. That part knew he needed to try to stay focused on his main reason for moving here, and that was to get that girl before she had a chance to identify him. Ever since that night, last March, he was irked that someone out there had seen him, caught him, literally, red-handed. She was the only person still alive that had ever seen him at work – at his real work, not the monotonous day job. Yes, she was young, but he knew that young people could possess amazing memories. And she definitely saw him that night. He had looked right into her eyes as she took in the scene, staring at him, not really understanding what she was seeing.

Martin remembered that night with a shudder of excitement, but also disgust. He had been so new at his work then. He was sloppy. He would never do now what he did then. He wouldn't cut a woman in an alley, now. He would make sure she was far away from any other eyes before starting his work. But back then, he was still learning. His skills were not developed to the mastery he had now achieved, thanks to Sissy. When she had started showing up, he had soared to a level that was sheer artistry. Someday they would place him among the greatest of all time, which is where he deserved to be. And this cabin would help get him there. It was perfect.

He went out to his car, returning with a wireless drill, a couple of large eye bolts and a length of chain, and attached the bolts to the stud. He made one more trip to the car, lugging in a heavy vice. This, he clamped onto the wooden, kitchen table. When he was done, he put his own lock on the door hasp, and headed down to Denver.

He was familiar with the shift schedule at most restaurants and guessed she worked until 11 or 12. He glanced over to confirm he had a new roll of duct tape, sitting on the passenger seat. He still had some things to do, items to pick up, but he would make it there in time. Tonight, he would watch.

~9~

Emerson pulled up in front of the school, in a spot reserved for buses. Courtney started to unbuckle her seat belt, getting ready to climb out of the booster seat.

"Hold on a minute, kiddo. I have to tell you something."

She looked at him expectantly, her dark blue eyes worried against her pale skin, her almost-black hair pulled back neatly in two clips decorated with butterflies. The clips were only slightly uneven. He was getting better at hair.

"I have to go to court today."

"What's court? You mean, like in jail again?"

"No, not in jail." *I hope*, he thought. "Today, I'll go with Jeff, our lawyer, and we'll see the judge. The other side's lawyers will be there, too, and they'll talk about whether or not there will be a trial against Crandall Enterprises."

"Will Maddie be there?"

Hearing her name sent a squirt of adrenalin through him.

"I don't know. Maybe."

"Does she want you to go to jail?"

"No, of course not." He thought about that for a moment. "Well, I'm not sure, actually. Maybe."

"But you won't, right? Right? You won't go to jail?" He heard the panic creeping into her tone.

"No, of course not. I didn't do anything wrong."

"But you did the other night. You went to jail."

"That was a mistake."

"But my grandpa did something wrong?"

He sighed. "Well, that's what they will decide in court."

"But did he?"

He thought of all he had seen and learned that made it seem likely that his father had indeed done something wrong. In fact, a lot of things. His hand went involuntarily to the little jar in his suit coat pocket, feeling its small, hard shape through the fabric.

"I guess I'll find that out with the rest of them."

"Can I come?"

"Nope."

"Where will I go?"

"You'll be in school for most of it. And if the court goes later than that, Mrs. Guevera will be here to get you."

"Will you text me?"

He looked at her in surprise, eyebrows raised. Then he laughed.

"You're funny."

She was pushing him for a cell phone, which he had refused. A phone was expensive, and he thought seven was too young to start obsessing with a thing like that. He went around to her side and helped her out of the booster seat, lifting her high with a hug and a kiss. He set her down and gave her a little shove.

"Be great today," he said.

"Okay." She ran down the front walk and up the school steps, mixing in with the other kids and teachers. At the door, she turned and waved. He waved back, feeling a surge of regret, wishing he could give her a more stable world.

A school bus rumbled up and honked. He hurried to the driver's door and checked to see that she had gone inside. Before climbing behind the wheel, he took a moment to scan all around him. The bus honked again, but he finished looking before he got in the car. He wasn't trying to be obnoxious. He just suddenly had the feeling that someone was watching them.

***

Martin stood in the doll section, searching the shelves. He had found the right brand of dolls, but they didn't have the dark-haired one. He examined the boxes, looking behind the ones on display, in case the dark-haired one might have been pushed out of sight. He even considered some of the other brands. But none of the others looked right. He wanted the one that looked like Sissy. Really, nothing else would do. He was getting upset.

He walked through the aisles until he found a clerk who was restocking a rack of small, toy cars.

"Excuse me," Martin said, approaching him. "I'm looking for a particular doll."

"Oh, okay." The clerk, a plump youth of about eighteen, stood and set the little packages in a cart full of toys. "Which one?"

"The dark-haired Tappitsee doll in a blue and white party dress."

They walked to the doll aisle, where the clerk commenced the same examination of the shelves that Martin had just done. Martin grew agitated, knowing that it was pointless to keep searching here.

"Do you have any in the back?"

"I'll check, but usually we try to have all the inventory on the shelves." The clerk started down the aisle. "I'll be back in a couple minutes."

Martin followed him to the storeroom door and waited, frustration growing. He shifted his weight from side to side, checked his watch and tried to look through the dark window into the warehouse. Finally, the clerk emerged, a box in his hands.

"I think we got lucky," he said, handing it to Martin. "We just got these in yesterday and no one had a chance to unpack them yet."

Martin looked at the box and smiled. The doll was about fifteen-inches tall, with straight brown hair that was too thick and bulky to look real, but still, it was the right color and length. Its head was large and round, like a young girl's, with a pretty face and round dark eyes with eyelashes made of synthetic hair. He had always liked that detail. The hair was parted on the side and pulled back with a blue ribbon into a single pony tail on the side of its head. It wore a short dress, the blouse part sequined white, and the skirt a shiny blue material that matched the hair ribbon. The outfit was flouncy and so like the one Sissy used to wear. Martin grinned at the clerk, elated.

"That's the one! Thanks a lot."

"You're welcome. Glad we had it."

"It's for my Sissy," Martin said. He pulled out his wallet and opened it to the photo, showing Sissy to the clerk.

The clerk looked at it closely. "Oh, sure."

"She loves this doll." Martin looked at the picture. "I'll be seeing her soon."

"Well, great. I hope she enjoys it." He headed back to his cart. "Have a good day."

When Martin returned to his car, he opened the box and carefully cut the doll from its plastic ties. He took the blue ribbon out of the doll's hair and cut it in half with his pocket knife. Parting the hair down the back, he carefully retied the ribbon into two pigtails at each side of the doll's head. He and Sissy preferred it that way.

~ 10 ~

Emerson sat at an old, glossy wooden table with Jeff, who was
reviewing files and waiting for the last members of the prosecution to
arrive. Emerson's dark gray suit still fit him perfectly. It was one of
several his father had ordered, custom-made, for him. This was more
for his father's edification than for Emerson's, but he had to admit it
elevated his appearance of respectability significantly. Despite this,
Jeff looked at him critically before they entered the court and
reminded him that he must further transform to clean-shaven and
short-haired before the actual trial started.

Sitting at an identical table across the court was Albert
Kellerman, a man Emerson didn't know, but who was one of the major
investors in the Crandall Resort. He was in his late-fifties, about
eighty pounds overweight, with a loose, jowly face and heavily bagged,
angry eyes. He glared at Emerson a couple of times, looking like he
had a lot to say, and none of it pleasant. Now, his noisy breathing and
the slight rustling of paper were the only sounds as everyone tensely
waited for the proceedings to begin.

The door opened at the back of the court and fast, quiet steps
approached. Emerson knew it was her, and his heart jumped. He
turned around to see Maddie coming down the aisle, straight and
serious. Her honey-colored hair was braided on both sides of her
head, the two strands meeting at the back, where they formed a bigger
braid that hung past her shoulders. Her summer freckles had faded,
but they still sprayed faintly across her high cheekbones and straight
nose, adding a sweet, girlish touch to her serious face, softening the
guarded look in her golden-green eyes.

Emerson was impressed, as always. She looked confident and

poised in her short, forest green jacket, rust blouse and stretchy, black pants. He noticed her shoes were flat. He knew her well enough to know she wouldn't be handicapped with heels. She seemed always ready to take off running.

She glanced at him, acknowledging him with a small smile, and sat at the other table. He kept watching as she murmured to her lawyer, who was a hungry-looking woman in a dark red suit and rimless glasses, not much older than Maddie. The two consulted quietly, then Maddie looked back at Emerson with a challenging gaze, eyebrows raised, still wearing the small smile.

Oops, staring too long.

He quickly looked away, glanced at the American flag near the front of the court, studied the Colorado emblem on the wall – a complicated thing featuring tools, an eye and Latin – and finally settled on chewing his cuticle.

"All rise," said the bailiff, as the chamber door opened and the judge approached a tall desk, perched on a dais to give her added height.

Here we go, he thought, his stomach fluttering.

It was worse than he expected. The State of Colorado was the plaintiff The case incorporated the charges filed by Maddie, as well as by Kellerman and the other Crandall Resort investors. Since Emerson was the project manager during construction, his figurative fingerprints were all over the material orders and receipts. However, after the catastrophe had occurred, he'd discovered the orders he'd signed and the invoices his father had received and approved did not match. His father had changed some of the orders, purchasing inferior materials, instead of the ones Emerson had intended. He hoped Jeff could convince a jury of his innocence.

His anxiety bubbled in his guts, and for a moment, he felt his heart start to pound. It was almost a panic overcoming him, and he shut his eyes, taking a deep breath, fighting it back. He had tried to be lackadaisical about this lawsuit, as something he just had to endure for a while. But he couldn't always protect himself against his own fear that he would end up in jail, and Courtney would end up … who knows where? What happened to children orphaned by death and jail? He had no family members who could step in and protect her. He was all she had. And beyond Courtney, how would he cope with being jailed? He didn't even allow himself to imagine how he would survive.

He felt a hand on his arm and opened his eyes. Jeff was looking at him in concern, then he smiled cockily at Emerson and nodded, his expression clearly saying, "Don't worry. I've got this."

Emerson sighed and felt his heart thudding heavily, but slower.

As the charges were agonizingly masticated by the lawyers, the day became a blur to Emerson, just one terrible accusation after another. He slumped in his seat and let Jeff do his job. When it was over, the judge declared that there was sufficient evidence to proceed, with all the theft charges included in one trial: The State of Colorado versus Crandall Enterprises. Besides this trial, civil cases were already being filed by guests and employees who were injured in the hotel.

Great. Emerson saw himself spending the rest of his life in courtrooms, or in jail, or going back and forth between the two.

When the hearing ended, Jeff seemed pleased. He smiled at Emerson, then noticed his glum expression.

"Don't worry," Jeff said. "We were able to get a couple charges knocked right out for lack of evidence. It will simplify things and work in our favor."

It still seemed bad to Emerson, but he felt too despondent to ask for more information.

"It's good," Jeff said patiently, as if talking to a child. "I've already helped you."

Emerson knew Jeff was trying to sound upbeat and nodded when he suggested they meet the next morning for continued preparation.

He looked over at Maddie. She looked fairly miserable herself.

She glanced at him with a concerned expression. Obviously, she was realizing now what this meant for him, he noted with slight satisfaction. He wanted to talk to her, knowing it would be inappropriate. Still, he got up and approached her, causing their lawyers and the armed deputy at the door to go on alert. She looked up at him in surprise. He reached into his pocket and pulled out the small glass jar, setting it on the table in front of her. Light reflected brightly off its contents – sparkling pink. He had found the jar in her aunt's safe, after he stumbled on it the night the hotel collapsed and had forgotten it until much later. He had waited for a chance to give it back to her, but in his imagination, it was a very different meeting.

She looked at the jar and then up at him, startled, quizzical. She certainly recognized what they were, since they both had learned, that night in early October, that the land where the resort had stood contained rare, pink diamonds. It was a secret they now both protected.

"They were with your aunt's letter," he said. He had smashed open her aunt's hidden safe that same, chaotic night the resort crumbled, trying to find out the truth about her death. There, he found her aunt's letter to Maddie, pointing suspicion at his father, as well as the little jar of gems. Maddie just looked at them steadily, frowning, not meeting his eyes.

He left the courtroom feeling sad, more at her lack of enthusiasm about him than about the fact that his life would be sheer hell for the foreseeable future.

"Crandall!" A gruff voice came from behind him.

He turned to see Kellerman coming out of the courtroom with an awkward, painful, rocking gait, looking angry, smelling heavily of aftershave and cigars, his suit too tight over his belly, his thick neck overlapping his collar. Emerson said nothing as he approached.

"You should be ashamed, what your father did to me. I'm going to see to it the name of Crandall is fed to the dogs," Kellerman wheezed. A pair of women coming down the hall paused in surprise, looking at the two of them sharply.

"Think about changing your name after this, because you Crandalls will be done in the development world. Nobody's going to trust investing in your projects."

Emerson was not naturally aggressive, but he was no pussycat either – except with Maddie, and Courtney, of course. He worked out regularly, and his rangy frame belied the strong, well-developed muscles of his chest and shoulders. In reality, he was ashamed, and he really didn't care how the name of Crandall was perceived in the development world. On the other hand, he didn't like this fat old man threatening him. He felt that flash of rage, knew what he might do if he let it loose. But he suppressed it easily. It wasn't hard, when he'd had a good night's sleep. Instead, he simply straightened to his full height and glared down at the shorter Kellerman. It surprised Kellerman, and, true to the bully he was, he stepped back. He turned and scuttled away, in the opposite direction.

"I'll get back every penny," he said as he went. "After that, I'll take you to the bank. Sue the shit out of you."

Stand in line, Emerson thought.

The two women, probably county employees, glanced at Emerson as they passed, eyebrows raised. The fury that surfaced briefly may have been evident, but it was aimed more at his father than at Kellerman. He watched Kellerman until he disappeared into the elevator at the end of the hall, then turned and took the stairs down to the parking lot. As he went, he removed the sticky paper name badge he had received when he entered the courthouse that morning, crumpled it and tossed it in the garbage can by the door.

He had a looming sense that he should enjoy his freedom while he could.

Martin watched Kellerman and Emerson's exchange with fascination. He practically had a ringside seat, perched on a bench outside the court, reading the local sports news on his phone. His bangs were slicked back off his face and hidden by a Broncos cap. He was wearing a puffy blue coat, the same as hundreds of men in Denver at that time of the winter.

While Martin was devoid of many of the emotions that controlled others, he was a master of reading them in people. This was a skill necessary for him to slip through society without causing alarm. He had also learned to mimic them when needed.

He recognized the self-important and heavy-handed Kellerman with little interest. What he found more interesting was the anger he saw flare in Emerson, betraying him for just the briefest moment. Emerson quickly hid it, before responding to Kellerman. Martin saw that, by the time Emerson stood up straight and stared down Kellerman, the rage was gone and, in its place, stood a normal, self-protective man who was prepared to avert any aggravation from Kellerman. It was a subtle difference, that rage versus the confident challenge, and Martin admired Emerson's ability to contain the emotion that could have caused him to lose control of the situation. He doubted that the thick Kellerman had even realized the potential Emerson could unleash, but Martin spotted it, and to him, it served as a warning.

He was glad he saw it, because it showed him that Emerson might not be the easy mark he had originally thought. He would have to approach that animal with caution. In fact, it might be smarter to get him out of the way before he could go after the little girl, or at least make sure Emerson was not nearby when he grabbed her. He would like to do that without confronting him, in person. Immediately devising the threads of a plan, he glanced around and noted the two women who had halted in the hallway, witnessing the conversation with undisguised interest and alarm. Nice. Witnesses to the disagreement.

He was intrigued and perplexed by that flash of rage in Emerson. Martin kept himself physically powerful, for many reasons. He loved the way it looked, for one thing. Despite the terrible acne scars, he made his body beautiful. And of course, it was imperative for him to be strong to carry out his mission. He could easily overpower the unsuspecting women upon whom he preyed, without having to handle a weapon that could accidentally become a hindrance. Despite all this, something in him was cowed by the height and breadth of other men, especially when they were in reasonably good shape. And someone the size of Emerson, lean and long-muscled, with that goddamn clear skin and handsome face, seemed particularly daunting. He hated this fear, and he knew it wasn't rational. He practiced his art. He knew holds, take-downs, defensive and offensive moves. Most men didn't. They just acted with whatever limited street-fighting experience they had, bolstered by bravado and bluster. He surpassed them in his knowledge of hand-to-hand combat, impromptu weapons and strength.

Still, the physical presence of Emerson was intimidating to him. At the same time as he acknowledged it, he loathed himself for feeling it. And that flash of rage he saw, that was something else. That heightened Martin's anxiety about Emerson exponentially. It was like one lion recognizing another, he mused. But what to do about it, that was the question. Lions were good at defining their territories, live and let live. But sometimes, one would violate those boundaries, charge the other's pride, fight off the reigning leader, seize his lionesses, kill his cubs.

It wasn't Emerson Martin was after. It was his cub. But if he wasn't careful, his concern about Emerson might escalate. He knew himself. He became obsessive at times. He could grow scattered. He needed to stay focused on his reason for coming here. He had to get that girl out of the way, so he could continue to pursue his mission without concern.

In thinking about it, he became angry at the child. Why did she have to see him in the alley that night? Who did she think she was, seeing him like that, staring at him like that, making him feel like a freak? In the end, he had just dumped the body of that slut, without doing what he intended. Being seen by that girl had ruined the experience, and he just needed to get rid of it, like the garbage it was.

Martin, sitting in the courthouse hall, pressed his fist against his forehead. If only she were a little boy, it would be so much easier. Martin felt almost nothing for other people, other than loathing. He had no empathy, and although he knew it was the trait that made him the monster he was, it also allowed him to carry out his mission. But if there was any smidgeon of compassion in him, it was toward little girls. Because of his Sissy, his little Sissy, gone so long.

Martin emitted a short cry. But it wasn't for Courtney. It was for himself.

Right now, he felt so distracted, so anxious. He had to refocus, but he was more upset about this Emerson Crandall than he thought he would be. When he first saw him on the television, he didn't look like any problem for Martin. He just looked like any other man, unassuming, probably trusting, no threat. Just a hapless chump. But seeing him in person was different. Now he felt he needed to neutralize him before he could get to the little girl. He couldn't forget that flash of fury. He wanted Emerson out of the way, to change his focus, give him something else to worry about other than his daughter, maybe physically remove him without Martin having to confront him, face-to-face.

On his way out of the courthouse, Martin scooped Emerson's wadded badge out of the trash. He didn't know what he would do with it, but his criminal instincts told him it could come in handy.

~||~

The only thing wrong with this cheery, sunny afternoon in the canyon was that Emerson was lost. He pulled over on the side of the mountain lane, partly blocking a drive marked "Private Road." Jeff had warned him that a cell connection was iffy up here in the canyon, but the fact that his phone had died made that point irrelevant. So, he had to resort to a paper map.

"Are we lost?" Courtney said.

She was in the booster seat, wearing a polka-dot sun hat, orange-rimmed sunglasses and hiking boots. Emerson wore a dark blue, safari hat with a Mets logo and sunglasses to shield him from the intense sun on the mountain trail. If they ever found the mountain trail.

"No," he said, turning the trail map around and trying to figure out where they were. Jeff had told him the hike to the top of the canyon was spectacular. He had his Field Guide to Colorado Birds and sunscreen at the ready on the passenger seat, but it had all come to a halt after they wound round these high, narrow roads, trying futilely to find the trail head.

"Then why are we stopped?" Courtney asked.

"Just double-checking."

A dark blue car emerged slowly from the private road, surprising him. The road looked pretty much unused. Their being parked so close must have seemed strange to the driver, too, because he gave them a long, sharp look. Emerson took in the glistening beard and long bangs, the dark brown eyes, scowling at him with a look that bordered on anger.

"Who is that?" Courtney asked, an edge in her voice.

The exchange of looks lasted only a moment before the driver pulled away, heading in the direction of Denver. Or, at least that's the direction Emerson thought he was heading, as he turned his attention back to his map.

"Who was that?" Courtney said again.

"Just some guy."

"What was he doing?"

"Don't know."

"What was he doing, Dad?" Courtney said again.

Something about her tone made him look at her in the rear-view mirror.

"I don't know, kiddo. He's just a guy. Maybe he's lost, too."

"What's down there?"

"Where?"

"That road."

"I'm not sure. Probably a hunting cabin."

"Is it his?"

Her insistence on discussing the man made him refocus, away from the map. He thought about it. That hipster-looking guy in a newer sedan did not match his image of the type of person who would own one of the hunting cabins they had seen up here. Where he came from, such cabins were often family affairs, owned by beer-bellied weekend warriors with rusty pick-up trucks who hosted hunting parties in them a couple times a year with lots of booze, flannel shirts, camo coveralls, bottles of doe urine and shotguns. The rituals were sacred, passed down, along with the cabin, through the generations.

"I doubt it."

"Let's go see what's down there."

He considered the idea, then dismissed it.

"Nope. That's trespassing. Anyway, I think I know where the trail head is."

He put the car in gear and headed away from Denver. This time, he was right on target to find the trail head, which turned out to be just a mile further up the road.

They had a long hike over the rough, arid canyon overlooks, wore themselves out in the crackling, February sunshine and headed back down the mountain for what Emerson expected to be a quiet evening at home.

Kellerman belched through the restaurant door to the sidewalk. The roast pork, mashed potatoes and grilled asparagus he had washed down with Cabernet in a Denver steak house left him contentedly stuffed. He had planned to watch the hockey game in the restaurant bar, but he was tired, and his lungs were troubling him, so he decided to head back to his hotel. He didn't love the hotel. It was the best in Creeley Junction, but that wasn't saying much, considering how small the county seat was. He liked the amenities that came with fancier places, and regretted his decision not to stay in Denver, although the hotel kept him close to the courthouse. His emphysema was getting worse, so the less moving around, the better.

He walked slowly along the sidewalk, the bells on the Daniels & Fisher tower chiming seven, its spired silhouette distinct among the more modern, angular buildings lining the mall. His walk had become more of a swagger with as much lateral movement as forward, his knees hurting with every labored step. He took the elevator to the second story on the parking garage and hit his key fob, heading toward the tail lights through dimly lit lines of cars. He squeezed between his car and the truck next to it, plopped into the driver's seat, backed out and headed to the street. Traffic was heavy downtown, becoming lighter as he drove to the highway. He crossed into Creeley County and caught the red at the last traffic light before the highway ramp, cursed to himself at the slow pace, and stopped. His was the only car on the road, here. He reached for the radio and didn't notice when a man moved in the backseat.

Martin had waited for this opportunity, watching for sparse traffic, ready for a stop. As soon as Kellerman looked down, Martin sat up and, in one smooth movement, leaned forward and drove a fillet knife into his carotid artery. Blood sprayed Martin's hand and face as Kellerman cried out and reached up in surprise. Before he could clasp the knife, Martin sliced upward, ensuring the wound would never close.

He loved fillet knives. He had purchased this one, used, at the Good Will store in Milwaukee.

He sat back comfortably, watching Kellerman grasping at his neck and struggling for a moment. When Kellerman started to droop, Martin reached forward and yanked the knife out of his neck. Kellerman's mouth bubbled blood and phlegm as his clenched body now relaxed, and he slumped sideways, the artery no longer spraying, his eyes glaring sightlessly at the dashboard clock.

While planning this, Martin had wondered how it would feel to kill Kellerman. This was so different from the passion that drove him in his real work that he wasn't sure if he would sense any excitement or gratification. Now he knew. He didn't. The hunt was exhilarating, finding Kellerman's car, hiding in the shadow of the backseat while his unknowing prey was just inches away, and finally, the blow itself. But instead of the urgency and sense of release and relief he got from his preferred work, this made him feel almost nothing, just a little debased, because he knew it was not accepted by society to drive a knife into someone's neck. He was so put off by his disappointment that he almost forgot the most important part of all this. But just in time, before exiting the car, he pulled the wadded, sticky, name label out of his pocket and kicked it under Kellerman's seat.

He climbed out the backseat as the stoplight was turning green and walked into the shadows of the overpass. Another car was approaching, about a block away, from the other direction. Martin was certain he was invisible from its lights. It cruised through the intersection, the driver casting a mildly curious glance in Kellerman's window. Martin watched as its brake lights tapped briefly, then it sped off toward downtown. He knew he had to go. He climbed up the other side of the overpass and hustled onto some train tracks. He pulled out a packet of wet, disposable cloths as he went and wiped the blood off his face and hands, stripping off his outer shirt. Underneath, his T-shirt was still clean. By the time he reached his own car, he was reasonably clear of the red spray, so that in the dim lights of downtown, no one would have a clue that he had just stabbed a man and let him bleed out without even a look back.

He drove to Emerson's apartment house. He almost expected to find Emerson's car unlocked but was not perturbed to find it secured. He used the same cheap tool he carried to break into Kellerman's car, and opened it in seconds without damaging anything. People were fools to think that locks kept out criminals. He sat in the driver's seat for a minute, trying to decide the most natural place to hide the knife. It couldn't be the glove compartment, where Emerson would find it. He stuck it under the driver's seat. Most people didn't store things there, so he thought the chance of Emerson finding it before the police searched his vehicle were slim. Even if Emerson did find it and dispose of it, it was likely that some of Kellerman's blood would be left behind.

Martin liked the thought of how Emerson would feel if he found the knife: The confusion, suspicion, the knowledge that someone was after him, but not knowing who it was. That was fun. But it was even better to imagine what would happen when the police found it. And with that name badge under Kellerman's seat, it was a safe bet the police would find the knife.

He headed back toward downtown. He had more important business ahead of him. His disappointment in feeling such indifference about killing Kellerman only fed his real passion, and he couldn't let it wait any longer. He needed that deliciousness.

When the young waitress stepped through the back door of the Salted Steak, she was still wearing her uniform. She didn't notice the man in the shadows until she had unlocked her car. Surprised, she emitted a small, "Oh!" Then she recognized him as the inspector who had visited the restaurant a couple days earlier, before the dinner rush completely occupied her attention.

"Oh, sorry," he said with a big, friendly smile, which improved his weird, hairy, scar-faced appearance somewhat. "My rental car has a flat. You don't happen to have a tire gauge in your glove compartment, by any chance?"

She relaxed. "Oh, yeah, I think I have one."

She opened her door and reached across the seat.

He was on her. He hooked his right arm around her throat, clamping his left hand over her mouth. After her initial struggle, she went limp, her breathing cut off. He covered her mouth with the duct tape patch he had already prepared. Working with the speed that comes with practice, he taped her hands and feet, found her key, rolled her roughly into the back seat and took off into the night.

He really liked it when they were still wearing their uniforms.

~12~

Emerson re-read the text. It was just one line, but it was the first time Maddie had ever initiated contact with him.

"Thanks for returning Aunt Clara's diamonds."

He was on the couch that came with the small apartment. The sofa also served as his bed, as he opted to give Courtney the one tiny bedroom.

He had lived better recently, while working for his father, but for most of his adult life, living in a state bordering poverty was pretty normal. This apartment was a converted basement in a well-kept, ranch-style house. One of their neighboring structures was a rundown duplex with a brown patch of lawn. The other was a chain-linked storage yard, guarded by a fierce black dog that liked to wait until passersby were half-way along before leaping at the fence. The snarling, slobbering creature startled Emerson nightly until he finally remembered to walk on the other side of the dark street. It was not what he wanted for Courtney, but the fact was it was cheap, and cheap was all he could do right now.

The furnished basement apartment was assembled, long ago, by the landlady's son as a teenager, in what must have been a bid for privacy and independence. It was clumsy, with hasty paint in the hall and bedroom, and bad paneling in the main room that looked like it was salvaged and reused. The son was now middle-aged, living in Oregon with his wife and teenage kids. His elderly mother, a quiet and serious woman with the unexpected name of Lala Orchard, now made use of the space for income. She was not keen on having children there, so when attempting to convince her, Emerson had applied all his charms in a way he hoped would appeal to an elderly grandmother. Despite this, it was the double deposit he offered to pay that coaxed her to rent it to them. Considering the grim news about the Crandall court case and his recent night in jail, he suspected she now liked Courtney much better than she did him.

After reading Maddie's message once more, he typed, "You're welcome! I always meant to give them back but didn't get a chance."

No. Too guilty.

He tried again. "You're welcome. I hope they'll be helpful."

No. Too presumptuous, and sounded like he thought it was a gift, which it wasn't. Not stealing them from her wasn't the same as returning them to her.

"You're welcome. I was glad to see you today, even though the setting sucked."

No. Just, no.

Finally, he typed, "Sure thing."

He hit "send."

He watched the phone for those telling dots that would mean she was typing a reply, but there was nothing. After a while, he set it down, his feelings of hope mixed with doubt.

He was tired, but his mind was too busy for sleep, so he turned on the TV to watch the end of the Nuggets game, then a sports news show, hoping it would quiet his brain before bed. With the trial approaching, he couldn't afford any more sleepless nights. When it was nearly midnight, he was startled by a sharp scream from Courtney. He stepped swiftly through the short hallway that led to the bedroom and lifted her. She was yelling and crying herself awake, and he hurried out of the room with her.

At seven, Courtney had normal, childhood proportions, a biggish head and tiny, shapeless body. But she was taller than kids her age, taking after her father. She had the porcelain Crandall skin and blue eyes, a straight nose, the beginnings of angulation in her face, and a long, regal neck. Her dark hair was snarled now, sticking to her wet face as she awoke from her fright. She felt him holding her and relaxed a little.

Nightmares plagued the poor kid, and it was small wonder. Her mother had been killed by a hit-and-run driver less than a year ago, and Courtney had been abruptly deposited with Emerson, who hadn't even known of her existence until that moment. Her arrival, coupled with his losing his research grant on an invasive caterpillar, had forced him to accept the job with his father and move with Courtney from Upstate New York to Stony Valley, Colorado. Since then, four members of their family had died in accidents at the resort, including her grandfather. It was all upsetting, especially for a child. It was no wonder the kid had nightmares. Emerson did too.

Now, she cried.

"Mom!" The word was muffled against his chest. Her fear transformed into sorrow, and she sobbed into him as he held her. For all the nightmares, she hadn't dreamt about her mother for quite a while.

"It's all right, kiddo," he murmured, rubbing her back gently.

After a while, she pushed away, and he plucked a tissue from a box near the couch, wiping her face dry.

"You better now?"

"I saw him," she said. She was frightened, and, as she remembered her dream, her tears started again.

"Who?"

"The man who killed my mom."

He was surprised. She had never mentioned this before. Had she been there when the still-unidentified driver hit her mother?

"You saw him?"

She nodded, and began the convulsive, hiccupy breathing that sometimes occurred when she cried hard. He pulled her back against him, hugging her and wondering about it. Why had he never thought about the possibility that she saw her mother hit? He always assumed she was with her babysitter at the time.

His grief for her overwhelmed him for a moment and he held

her tighter.

"I'm so sorry, baby. I didn't know you were there."

She cried and hiccupped for a while. Finally, she sat back again.

"I just remembered."

That made sense. It was so traumatic that she had buried it. But, inevitably, it resurfaced.

"Do you want to tell me about it?"

She considered it, then started crying again. He heard Mrs. Orchard's footsteps overhead and wondered if they had awakened her.

"My mom and me were walking home. It was dark, and we were in a hurry, so we took a shortcut. But then..." She stopped, dissolving into tears again.

He didn't want to push her, but he felt he needed to hear this.

"Tell me what you saw," he said quietly.

"We were in a place I didn't like. Mom was scared. I think we might have been lost."

"It's okay now."

"And then, we passed a place between the buildings, and we saw a man. Then he saw us. And we started running. And he yelled. And we kept going, and I thought we got away from him, but then, we were about to cross a street, and he was in a car. My mom told me to run, and then he drove at her and ..." That was it. She started sobbing again and wouldn't say anything else.

He leaned back in the couch, holding her. Eventually, she fell asleep and he set her gently on the cushion next to him.

This was new information, and he wasn't sure how much might be real, and how much lingered from her nightmare. His heart broke for his daughter. She was too young to experience such a sad and scary situation.

A sudden, loud knocking on Mrs. Orchard's front door caused him to jump, then listen. He heard it again, then Mrs. Orchard's soft shuffle as she went to open it. He could hear a man's voice, then Mrs.

Orchard's, and the sound of several heavy footsteps approaching the basement door, the only entrance to his apartment. A knock. Jumping up, he took the stairs three at a time. He opened the door to find Detectives Lotu and Sheen, along with two uniformed deputies.

"Hello, Emerson," Detective Lotu said in a friendly way. But otherwise, nothing about this group was friendly. "We need to ask you to come to the station with us."

"Daddy?" Courtney sat up, wide awake. "Daddy? Who are they?"

Emerson saw Mrs. Orchard standing in her kitchen behind the deputies. Her arms were crossed over her yellow, terry robe and she glared at him.

Yup, she definitely would like Courtney more than him, after this.

He glanced from her to Detective Lotu, then to Courtney, who was now standing at the bottom of the stairs, looking at the strangers with anxiety. Emerson suddenly felt angry.

"Why? What are you doing bursting in here like this? What's so important that it can't wait until tomorrow?"

"We need to talk to you about Albert Kellerman."

~13~

"**K**ellerman? What about him?"

"We just have some questions."

"Am I under arrest?" Emerson asked, annoyed.

"No, we just need to speak to you."

Courtney was watching, eyes big.

"Well, it's not a good time. She's had a rough night and she has school tomorrow."

"Do you have someone to watch her while we speak to you?"

"Do you see anyone?"

"What about the landlady?"

"No way."

"Is there someplace where we can speak out of her hearing?" Lotu was trying to help him protect Courtney from whatever they needed to talk to him about, Emerson realized.

"How much time are we talking about?"

"I don't know."

Emerson gave him an exasperated look.

"I tell you what," Lotu said. "Let's go out to the car. We can talk out there. Deputy Quinn will wait here with your daughter."

Deputy Quinn stepped forward and Emerson appraised him. He was about thirty-five, a little overweight with a short, reddish mustache. Under Emerson's scrutiny, his eyes softened, and he nodded.

"I don't know Deputy Quinn," Emerson said.

Quinn reached out his hand. "Deputy Tony Quinn. I've been a member of the Sheriff's Department here for twelve years. I have won two medals for outstanding valor and one for community service."

Emerson continued to gaze at him, undecided.

"And I have three children, ages ten, eight and five. Two daughters and a son."

Emerson finally stepped back. "Come on."

He walked ahead of Deputy Quinn downstairs. "Courtney, this is Deputy Quinn. He's going to wait with you for a few minutes while the detectives talk to me about something."

"Are you going to jail again?"

"No."

Emerson turned the television to the cartoon channel and handed Courtney the remote.

"I'll be right outside, in the car. If you get scared, come get me."

"Okay."

"Oh, this is my favorite cartoon!" Deputy Quinn said with enthusiasm, then, surprisingly, started singing. He rattled off the cartoon's familiar jingle, grinning in a silly way at Courtney and winning a bit more of Emerson's approval. Courtney gave Deputy Quinn a small smile of appreciation, but overall, looked miserable and tired.

Emerson went glumly to the detectives' car. Sheen opened the back door for him. He would rather have talked outside, but the wind brought below-freezing gusts, so he slid in. Even though it was unmarked on the outside, inside, it was built for prisoners. He sat behind a cage-like separation between him and the front seat. There were no door handles that would allow him to open the door and launch himself out on the road. Not that he would do that, at least, not tonight. Lotu thumped in next to him, and Sheen and the other uniformed deputy got in the front. Ahead of them, a white and blue Lakewood police car idled.

Well, this ought to give the neighborhood something to talk about. Mrs. Orchard must be thrilled.

Emerson briefly considered calling Jeff, who would be beyond annoyed if he didn't, but he thought this would amount to nothing, and he wasn't keen to drag him out of bed, too.

"Sorry to disturb you tonight," Lotu said.

"Ask me your questions and let me get out of here."

"We need to know what you did today, or, I should say, yesterday," Lotu said, glancing at the dashboard clock, which showed it was now past midnight.

"Why? What happened to Kellerman?"

"Just answer the question," Sheen said.

Emerson glowered at him, but said, "I met my lawyer from ten to one, then I picked up Courtney at the babysitter's and we went for a canyon hike. Then we ate at a diner, stopped at one store and went home."

"Where's the babysitter?"

"Over on South Harlan."

"Address?"

Emerson found it in his phone, read it off.

"Where'd you hike?"

"The Rim Trail."

"That the one up off 77?"

"I think so. I got lost trying to find it."

"How long were you up there?"

"Couple hours, plus drive time."

"Then you did what?"

"Went to eat."

"What diner, did you say?"

"Buck's Spot on 6."

"Oh yeah, I like that place," Lotu said. "Good breakfasts. What time was it?"

He thought about it. He remembered noticing the same waitress who had served him breakfast the other morning and wondering what kind of shift she worked to be there serving meals at both ten in the morning and six at night.

"Six."

"What did you order?"

"Really?"

"Yeah."

"Why does that matter?"

"Why don't you want to tell us?"

"Because it seems irrelevant."

"Not to us."

"Answer the question," Sheen said again.

Emerson hadn't forgotten the feel of Sheen's elbow in his back.

"I had a cheeseburger with bacon, carrots and fries."

"What did your daughter have?"

"Macaroni and cheese and carrots."

"What did you drink?"

"Oh, come on."

They looked at him, waiting.

"I had water. Courtney had chocolate milk."

"Any dessert?"

"We shared an ice cream sundae. Vanilla ice cream, hot fudge, sprinkles, no nuts, whipped cream, two cherries." Emerson looked out at the house. He could see his apartment light through the tiny basement window.

"Anybody see you?" Lotu asked.

"No, we went invisible for that meal."

"Cut it out, Crandall," Sheen said.

"Well, unless she worked really hard not to look at us, the waitress saw us."

"What was her name?"

He thought about it. He had noticed it this time. He sorted through the memory.

"Angela."

"What's she look like?"

"Long brown hair, tied back. Brown eyes. Maybe Hispanic."

"Will she remember you being there?"

He considered it. "Yeah, probably."

"Why do you think so?"

"Because she remembered what I had ordered the week before, when I stopped there for breakfast. She asked if I wanted pancakes again." It had surprised him, and it was that question that made him notice her name.

"When did you leave?"

"About six forty-five."

"Where'd you go next?"

"We stopped at the office store. Courtney needed some construction paper."

"Got a receipt?"

"I threw it out, but I can get a copy from my credit card."

"I would appreciate that, if you don't mind."

Emerson went to his phone, focusing on it for a couple minutes.

"Email?" he said. Lotu gave him an address.

"There. You have the diner receipt and the office store receipt as attachments."

"Where'd you go next?"

"Here."

"Did the landlady see you?"

"Yeah. She was in her living room. She saw us come in, and we said hello to each other before Courtney and I went downstairs."

"What time was that?"

"Nearly eight. I remember thinking I needed to get Courtney to bed as soon as I could, because she has school tomorrow." Reminded of this, he scowled at Lotu.

"Did you go back out?"

"Nope."

"Have you seen Albert Kellerman lately?"

"The last time I saw him was outside the courtroom a couple

days ago, just after the preliminary hearing."

"What did he say?"

"I don't remember. Nothing much."

"You don't remember," Sheen repeated, not believing him. Emerson shrugged and looked back at him steadily. He had a feeling it wouldn't be a good idea to tell them that Kellerman had threatened him. Let them figure that out.

They picked at him for a little while, trying to find out what he and Kellerman had said to each other after the hearing, but he kept saying that he didn't remember. Eventually, the two detectives looked at each other, communicating with their eyes as Emerson watched them. He could see they had nothing else.

"Can I go back to my daughter now?"

Lotu sighed. "I guess so."

Emerson thought of something. "Hey, do you guys use police sketch artists?"

The detectives perked up.

"Sometimes. Why?"

"Tonight, my daughter told me that she saw the man who killed her mother in a hit-and-run last spring."

"What hit and run? Where?" Sheen said with interest.

"Springfield, Ohio."

"Oh." They looked downcast again.

"Not anything we can help you with," Lotu said.

"Well, if I can use your sketch artist, we might be able to get him identified."

Sheen looked at Lotu, who thought about it. "Give us some more details, and we can contact the detectives in Springfield. Was this your wife?"

"No, an old girlfriend. We weren't in touch with each other at that time. Her name was Annie Hughes."

***

Martin returned to the cabin. He was still shocked that he had seen Emerson and his daughter so close to his secret workshop. Of course, once he got over the initial surprise, suspicion set in, and he turned back to follow them, but it was too late. He couldn't find their car. He didn't want to be late for his inspection, so he gave up the search and headed for Denver. It had rattled him, at first. Thank goodness he had altered his appearance so drastically.

Thinking about it later, he decided it must have been a coincidence. He had passed other families up here near the trails, and he noticed that Emerson and the girl were wearing hats and sunglasses, like so many other hikers. He was pretty sure she could not have recognized him, with his updated look. But it just made it more imperative that he take care of this problem.

As he entered the dark, silent cabin, he felt better. He knew she was waiting for him. He switched on a lantern.

Her eyes were closed.

"Look at me!" he demanded.

He shook her by the shoulders. Her head flopped on her thin neck. Her skin was cold, and she was keeping well, her blood drained out through gashes at her femoral arteries. It was a good job.

He stripped off all his clothes.

"Look at me!" He stood before the body, hearing the deep, guttural voice that seemed to come from someone else at these times. She remained slumped against the floor, eyes closed. He pulled his folding, razor knife from his pocket.

"You will look at me."

Opening the knife, he stretched out one of her eyelids, slicing it off neatly at the base. He popped it in his mouth and sucked it meditatively as he removed the other.

There. Now her dark eyes stared at him.

"You will look at me," he said. He sat her up against the wall and stood straight before her, turning so she would see all sides.

"Look at me," he said.

~14~

Courtney was tired the next morning, but she wanted to go to school, so Emerson drove her and watched until she was inside. Then he went back to the apartment to shower before going downtown to meet Jeff. He had begged off from racquetball this morning – too tired – but they still needed to work on their case. He was met at the door by a stern-faced Mrs. Orchard.

"Mr. Crandall, you need to leave," she said, firm, if a little nervous.

He was stunned and stared quietly into her dark eyes, which were surrounded by fine wrinkles. Her white hair was thin, and she had a couple darker spots on her light brown skin, a small mole by her eye. While he gazed at her, his brain was scanning the different ways he could possibly get her to change her mind. He didn't bother asking her why, but that was the unspoken question she answered.

"You and your daughter are noisy and you're disturbing my sleep. The police come to my home and pound on my door, late at night. The neighbors are getting upset. You are being prosecuted for bad dealings at that resort up to Stony Valley. I don't need this kind of problem in my life."

Neither of us does, he thought. He looked at her a moment longer, trying to decide which way to go. Appeal to her maternal instincts? Offer more money? Just beg? She looked back, thin and frail, a foot shorter than he, her chin raised firmly, arms crossed over her mustard-colored sweater, waiting. He sighed. He respected her too much to try to manipulate her.

"When?"

Her firm expression relaxed a little and he was glad he hadn't fought with her.

"As soon as you can. You're paid through the end of the week."

He nodded and went downstairs, noticing he was running late. His exhaustion from the last few days hit him in the shower. He stood there for a long time, leaning against the wall in the tiny stall, the hot water streaming through rivulets of dark hair on his chest and stomach. He normally kept the sadness at bay, forcing it away with a combination of natural optimism or, occasionally, indignation. But for a moment, he let it wash over him, feeling the pain of all he and Courtney had experienced in the past few months. Then, he turned off the flow, shook his wet head of shaggy curls, and let the feelings of sadness disappear with the last of the shower water. Self-pity was fine for a moment, but he had to take care of Courtney and himself, and right now, that meant getting dressed and meeting his lawyer.

Jeff was already at a table, drinking coffee, when Emerson got to the restaurant. Electric with energy, Jeff was neat in a navy-blue suit that fit his athletic form perfectly. His dark, thinning hair was short, and he wore stylish, gray-rimmed glasses. His baby blue tie was decorated with little printed racquets and balls.

"You hear about Kellerman?" Jeff said, skipping a greeting.

"Well, in a way. I'm guessing he's dead, since the police questioned me about him last night."

"What?" Jeff was annoyed and shocked.

"Yeah, they came to my home, at midnight. They wanted to pull me down to the station, but I told them they'd have to put me in custody. I wasn't going to leave Courtney or have to get her to the babysitter at that hour."

"What did they say?" Jeff's aggravation was building.

Emerson filled him in and let him know about Kellerman's threats outside the courtroom.

"Well, did you kill him?"

"No," said Emerson, surprised.

"Okay, well, good. Let me tell you something. When the police ask to talk to you, you only tell them one thing: 'I'm calling my lawyer.' Then do it, and shut up."

"I don't see what harm it does to talk to them if I didn't do anything wrong."

"'I'm calling my lawyer,' and shut up," Jeff said again, firmly. "It can do a lot of harm. It sounds like they have a boner for you. That's not good. That means they are looking for ways to associate you with this crime. If they come by for anything, if they ask you anything, even if it's the time, don't answer. Just call me."

The waitress came by. Emerson looked at the menu, ordered an egg and sausage sandwich.

"Okay, some more bad news," Jeff said. "The judge ordered all of the Crandall Resort's assets to be frozen for assessment. Unfortunately, the prosecution included your personal assets in its list. That means your bank account is frozen, and your credit card. They also included your car."

"Great." Emerson had no money other than what was in that account, and he used the card for everything.

"They can't do this. Don't worry," Jeff told him. "We'll at least get you an allowance to provide for housing, childcare and food, and you'll be able to keep the car. I'll get that going today, and you'll have something by next week. Until then, I hope you have some cash."

"I don't."

"You're kidding, right?"

"Nope. I don't carry it."

Jeff sighed and shook his head. He reached for his wallet, pulled out four fifties, handed them to Emerson.

"Don't spend it all in one place, junior."

Jeff cut their meeting short, because he had to meet with the judge and the other lawyers to figure out what to do, considering that one of the parties to the lawsuit, a key witness, was now dead.

Emerson didn't know where to go. He didn't feel like going

back to the apartment, with Mrs. Orchard scowling around. He had his gym bag in his car, so he changed his clothes and went for a run, choosing a route along the High Line Canal. This path also went past the area where Maddie happened to live. As he got near, he swung off the canal path and headed toward her apartment complex. It consisted of a couple of buildings, long with gray vinyl siding, attractive but unremarkable, except that this was a better home than Mrs. Orchard's basement, and in a much nicer neighborhood. She occupied the townhouse at the farthest end from the street.

Like him, she had moved to Denver from Stony Valley, to be nearer to court. In his case, he had to move anyway, since he no longer had any right to stay on the property where the resort once stood. It was likely, after the case was tried, the courts would determine that the property belonged to Maddie. Not to mention that, since the hotel was gone, the only portion of the property still inhabitable was a small caretaker's home at the horse stable, and that's where she lived, until she moved to Denver.

He stood by a wooden privacy fence in the shadows near the parking lot. Her apartment curtains were open, and he didn't see her car. He wasn't sure why he was even here. He longed to see her, sure, but the chances of her wanting to see him were almost nil. That one little text didn't mean she was inviting him to show up at her door like some creep.

He was about to go on with his run when he saw her silver car pulling into the lot, then parking. She got out, a full, reusable canvas grocery bag hanging off her arm. He jogged up the sidewalk, intercepting her near her door. She stopped, looking at him apprehensively.

"Hey," he said, wondering briefly how bad he smelled through all the sweat.

"Hey." She didn't look particularly friendly, but wasn't openly hostile, either. She just gazed at him somewhat skeptically, her greenish eyes looking him up and down as she shifted the heavy bag to her other arm.

Now he realized he didn't even have a plausible excuse prepared to explain his being there.

"Can I carry that for you?" He felt like an idiot.

"You ran all the way here just to carry my grocery bag twenty yards?"

"Um." He looked at her eyes, which had an attractive, slight downward slope, and at her golden hair, her pale pink lips. She was dressed in a T-shirt and jeans, flat leather shoes, no make-up. Simple and beautiful.

"Yeah!" he said with enthusiasm.

He reached for it and was thrilled to hear her laugh a little, and relieved when she handed it to him. His heart pounded harder now than it had when he was running.

"All right. Come on."

She led the way up the front steps into the townhouse. Glancing around, he saw a staircase to the second story that stretched away from the door. The main floor was a big, open area, with a living room connected to a dining room, to the kitchen, no walls separating the space. Light flooded in through the high windows. The quiet shades of pale pink, gray and tan in the rugs, furniture and walls made the place bright and inviting.

"You can put those there." She nodded to the kitchen counter. She paused, looking at him for a moment. She seemed to reach a decision.

"I think I owe you a cup of coffee."

He looked at her, inquisitive, then remembered the day they first met, when he had offered her coffee in his construction trailer home, and Courtney had surprised Maddie with the bad news that her aunt was dead.

"Yeah, that's the other reason I'm here," he said, grinning. "To get that coffee you owe me."

She turned on the coffee maker and started putting the

groceries away. He watched with interest, taking note of the fresh fruit, tofu, whole grain bread, almond milk, organic chocolate bar and, incongruously, bacon.

Once she had prepared two cups of coffee, both black, she invited him to sit at the tall breakfast table that overlooked the canal.

"So, what's up?" she said, perching on the high-backed stool, looking at ease in that way he admired.

He raised his eyebrows, pretending not to know what she was asking.

"I don't really believe you ran here just to carry my groceries and get a cup of coffee, so what's up? What are you doing here?"

He sipped his coffee, trying to read her expression. She just watched him expectantly.

Finally, he said, "Actually, those are two more reasons than I really had to come here. I was just jogging this way and got the urge to come by."

Before he realized what he was doing, he had told her about getting questioned in the police car after Kellerman's death, being kicked out of Mrs. Orchard's basement and having his meager assets frozen.

She listened with growing concern. When he finished, she watched his face for a few seconds. He sighed, waiting for a response, shocked when a tear rolled down her cheek.

"Oh no," he said. "Don't! What did I say? I'm sorry."

He quickly got up, found the napkins and handed her one. She took it, dabbed her eyes, wiped her nose and let out a big, shaky breath.

"I didn't mean this to happen," she said. The tears started again, and her words became garbled. "It's your father I'm after. I didn't realize it would end up on you so much."

"Hey, hey." He moved off his chair, pressing a fresh napkin against her wet cheek, coming in close. It made her cry harder. Fortunately, he had learned very well, thanks to Courtney, how to handle a crying female. Sure, Maddie was a woman, but he suspected the basics were the same. He pulled her into him, wrapping her with his arms and shoulders, pressing her gently against his chest. She didn't resist.

"It's not your fault," he said, stroking her hair with his fingers. "You didn't do anything wrong. Neither of us did. It was him. He did all this."

With her finally in his arms, he followed his instincts and pressed his face to hers, kissing her cheek, finding her lips. They were warm and wet, and he had to hold back from going crazy as all his passions revved up. He knew he had to let her decide where this would go. She kissed back, a wonderful surprise, and he pressed into her, eager. But then, not unexpectedly, she pushed him gently away. She stepped back and sighed, wiped her eyes again.

"I'm leaving," she said.

It felt like the worst thing she could have uttered, especially after such a good kiss. He didn't want to widen the space between them. But, with this news, he stepped back, still hot and throbbing all over from their moment of passion.

"Where? Why?"

"I have a chance to join a research group, working for the Pampas Cat. In Chile."

He retreated further, back to his chair, sitting heavily and staring at her, dejected. Maddie had recently completed her doctoral degree through her field studies on the Andes Cat. Her work took her to some of the most remote parts of the world, where humans were still the minority among wildlife. Her work on the Andes Cat had laid out protections for them in the face of development and contributed to saving the species. Besides being smart, independent and gorgeous, she was highly regarded in her field of endangered felines. And now, she was heading to another, far-off place to continue her work.

"Chile?" he said, numbly.

"It's a great opportunity," she said, but not enthusiastically.

"But don't you need to be here, for the legal stuff?"

"I don't have to be here much," she said, shrugging. "My lawyer will take care of most everything. She'll let me know if I have to show up."

"How? Carrier pigeon?" She would probably be working far from any normal communication systems.

"No. I've made arrangements."

He realized again that, unlike him, she was not hurting for cash. He had learned that pink diamonds were valuable. The millions his father had paid for her aunt's land would, most likely, be returned to investors, but if Maddie sold even a single diamond, she could make hundreds of thousands of dollars, maybe more. The price of one would be more than enough to ensure a decent communication network to whatever wild place she would be working.

He was crestfallen.

"I'm sure it's a great opportunity," he mumbled, looking out the window. He watched a couple holding hands on a walk by the canal, a pointy-eared, red and white dog bouncing around them happily. His world now seeming impossibly dreary.

He was a scientist himself, having spent most of his career trying to find a way to prevent the spread of invasive insects in the United States. It wasn't until the double-whammy hit him – his research was canceled by the government and a previously unknown daughter appeared in his world – that he decided to temporarily abandon his chosen work. That decision to come to work for his father was the worst he'd ever made, and every day the repercussions got worse. And now, the one bright bit of hope – that Maddie might start to return his adoration – was fading away, or rather, flying away, to a remote region, probably filled with all kinds of rugged, handsome male colleagues.

He looked back at her, and found she was watching him.

"I have to go," she said, as though she owed him an explanation, which she didn't. "I can't stand it here. This place makes me think of my aunt and what happened to her. I feel like I could have prevented it, and now it's too late. I can never turn back time and help her."

"You couldn't have done anything," he murmured.

"How do you know?" she snapped, anger flaring. "I might have been able to, if I were only here, taking care of her. She was old, frail. Even without Crandall trying to hurt her, she needed help."

Her eyes filled up again, but this time, he stayed on his side of the table. He thought about it. If she was staying in Stony Valley, Maddie probably could have prevented her aunt's death by hypothermia last March. At least she would have checked on her that night of the storm. But, if his father had made sure her aunt froze to death that night, Maddie herself may have ended up his victim, as well. He wanted to help her feel better.

"You couldn't have known she was in trouble. And you were thousands of miles away, doing important work."

"And this legal stuff," she went on. "I hate it. I hate it reminding me every day that I could have stopped it from happening." She wiped her face, the tears flowing. Her next words came out between sobs, making them hard to understand. "And I hate watching what it does to you, and to Courtney.,"

He reached across the table, offering his hand. She took it, continued crying, dabbing her eyes with the soggy napkin.

After a while, he said, "When do you leave?"

"Saturday." Three days away.

She looked at him, an idea in her expression. "Look, I've paid for this place for the rest of the month. That's more than three weeks. You can take it."

That was a kind offer. It didn't balance out the misery he was feeling, but it was a good thing.

"Thanks," he said. "I will. I appreciate it."

She nodded. Then her phone rang. She looked down at the number. "Oh crap. My lawyer. I forgot I was supposed to meet her."

She looked at him apologetically. "I have to go."

"Okay." He got up and crossed the living room in a few strides. He was sad and frustrated and just wanted to leave now. He put his hand on the door knob.

"Emerson," she said.

Hearing her say his name made him feel soft inside, hopeful. He turned back and looked at her. She was standing in the bright living room, the light shining on her hair and clear, freckled face.

"I'll call you before I go, so I can give you the key."

A charge of optimism shot through him, but immediately faded when he remembered that such a meeting would be followed by her flying four thousand miles away, for an unknown period.

"Okay. Thanks." He went through the door and down the steps. He started running again.

~|5~

Martin parked near the school, then walked to the edge of the playground, wearing sunglasses, a baseball cap and a scarf pulled up around his mouth. The cold wind justified the scarf, although that was not his real reason for using it. He spotted the security camera and kept his head down, moving away. Big, metal waste and recycling bins at the back of the school told him he was near the maintenance and janitorial area, which was right where he wanted to be. It was about 9 a.m. and he was due at Campbell's office building at 1 p.m. for an inspection, so he had all morning. The temperature was hovering around freezing, but he ignored the cold. He believed his elevated strength and physique kept him from feeling the elements the same way common men did.

At 9:27, the door near the bins opened and a man came out, carrying a large pile of cardboard. Feeling with his foot, the man found a reddish rock the size of a slightly flattened softball and pushed it into the door, keeping it cracked open. He walked to the recycling bin, his vision partly blocked by the tall pile of cardboard. Martin noticed he wore lightweight, slate gray coveralls with his identification badge evident, hanging on an orange lanyard. Balancing the load, the man opened the bin, dumped the cardboard and went back inside. He left the stone in the door. After a couple minutes, he reappeared, carrying a huge, clear bag filled with plastic bottles. This, too, he deposited in a recycling bin. Martin observed his simple, sturdy leather walking shoes. He watched as the man made a third trip, with metal cans from the cafeteria, gallon-sized things that would hold large quantities of vegetables, fruit, tomato sauce, beans. By 9:33, the man had made his last trip, knocked the rock out of the door and vanished into the building.

Martin walked back to his car, satisfied. He would be back. He needed to return there, see how often recyclables were dumped, whether this man worked every day, and, more important, if the rock was part of the ritual, no matter who was doing the work.

He was feeling the pressure of time. He felt lucky that the little girl hadn't identified him yet. He figured it was due to the shock of the event, and maybe she didn't even remember what happened. But he knew that bad memories had a way of coming back. It had happened to him. So, while he didn't think he needed to rush at this point, he did want to make sure he understood his options, as quickly as possible.

This option was low on his list of possibilities. Grabbing her from the school was risky, but he had to evaluate his other choices, so he would work to make sure that this one became viable. He would have to make a list.

~16~

Emerson was agonizingly aware that Maddie was leaving today. He wished he had asked what time she was flying, so he would have a better idea of when she might call him to come get the key.

As Saturday morning slid toward afternoon, he started to get uneasy. Courtney was busy with her microscope in the morning but had just told him she was hungry. He was, too. He didn't want to be in the middle of a meal when Maddie asked him to come over.

He picked up his phone again, stared at her number, and finally decided to call.

"Hey," she said. "I was just getting ready to call. I'm heading out soon. Do you want me to just leave the key someplace where you can find it?"

"No!" What was the matter with her? Did that kiss mean nothing? "I can come get it. What time is your flight?"

"Four-eleven."

"Oh, you have some time then. Any chance we can buy you lunch before you go? Courtney was just saying she's hungry." Someplace cheap, he added to himself. "She'd probably like to see you before you go."

"Who?" Courtney said.

"Well..." Maddie hesitated.

"Who, Daddy?"

"Maddie."

"Maddie?" Courtney looked excited. "I want to see Maddie!"

"Hear that?" He knew she wouldn't turn down Courtney.

"All right, then. There's a decent diner near the wildlife refuge. It's kind of on the way to the airport." She gave him the address. "I just realized, you better pick me up. I don't want to take my car to the airport. Hey, you want to help me sell it? I've been trying, but no serious offers yet."

"Sure!"

"Okay, I'll leave it at the apartment, and if you sell it, good. You can just give the check to my lawyer."

"Sounds like a plan."

She was outside her apartment when they got there, sitting on the steps in comfy-looking yoga pants and an oversized blouse.

"Maddie!" Courtney yelled.

Emerson jumped out to carry her duffel bag, although she was already halfway to the car with it.

"Hi," he said softly, his voice deep and warm.

"Hi." She looked a little guarded but smiled. His heart gave a big thud.

He put the bag in the trunk. She had already climbed in the passenger seat when he slid behind the wheel. She wore a musky scent, reminding him of the first time he had seen her.

Courtney launched into a series of questions, engaging Maddie completely on route, and this continued when they got to the restaurant. Courtney had met Maddie at the same time he had, when he was project manager on the resort, staying in a trailer on the property that had belonged to Maddie's aunt. Maddie ended up working in the riding stable there, where Courtney was taking riding lessons. They had seen each other quite a bit, even though Maddie had avoided Emerson, and Courtney admired her.

Other than claiming to serve local food, and having hipster-looking wait staff, the diner was pretty much like any other with its selection of breakfasts and sandwiches.

Courtney asked Maddie about the horses at the Crandall Resort, and Maddie explained how she had found good homes for them, and that it was especially hard to rehome Bop, her favorite.

Emerson was content remaining mostly silent, listening to

their cheerful chatter without comment and watching Maddie's grace. Neither he nor Courtney was naturally talkative, but Courtney lit up around Maddie, and it amused him to see her working in her seven-year-old way to keep the conversation going.

Maddie good-naturedly went along with the chatter, seeming to genuinely like Courtney. Plus, Emerson knew that it was probably as much of a relief to her as it was to him to have Courtney picking up the lead in the conversation. If he got the floor he might end up begging her not to go, which would be overstepping his boundaries and would not be very manly.

After breakfast, they climbed back in the car and drove the twenty minutes to the airport. They found the right terminal and pulled to the curb. He jumped out to get her bag, as she opened Courtney's door and gave Courtney a hug. He waited at the back of the car, trunk open, deliberately using it as a visual barrier from Courtney. Maddie emerged around the side of the car to find him standing there, waiting. He was subconsciously blocking her bag in the trunk with his tall frame.

As usual, he wanted to say so many things, but hadn't prepared a single sentence. He felt that mix of hope and dread he knew so well. He hoped for a decent good-bye, but dreaded not getting one, and even more, he dreaded her leaving and that he might never see her again. She probably would not have to appear in court at all, if her lawyer did her job well, and she seemed like the type who would.

Maddie looked at him expectantly, seeming more intent on getting her bag and leaving than he had hoped. He scrutinized her face, and he could see she had put a mental barricade between them. She was pretending that kiss hadn't happened. He knew she had so many reasons to avoid him, and really, to completely dislike him. He wouldn't blame her for wanting nothing to do with him for the rest of their lives. Most of what had happened, once their circles had intersected last spring, had been horrible. But that didn't change the fact that there was something else going on between them. If she could only let all the rest of that fall away, he knew it could be amazing. But she didn't need to do anything like that if she didn't want to, and he wouldn't blame her. By all appearances, his father had killed her aunt and stolen her land. She probably regarded Emerson as a bad bet, even though he thought he was due more credit for saving her life twice last fall and preventing his rotten cousin from hurting her in a way he didn't want to think about.

He remembered that day, briefly. His cousin, Derek, all tweaked out on booze and pills, had pinned her down in a burning stable at the resort. Emerson had managed to get her out after fighting off Derek, not to mention letting all those horses loose to escape the blaze. Derek hadn't been so lucky, not that Emerson was sorry about him. Later, Emerson had pulled her out of a dangerous crevasse during the earthquake that brought down the resort. Of course, that was where they spotted the seam of diamonds. Those diamonds were still down there, as they had been for a billion years, and only Emerson and Maddie knew where they were. He had never said a word. That land, and the diamonds, would probably revert to her aunt's estate, and so, to Maddie, when the trial was done. Jeff had pretty much guaranteed that, and Emerson was glad.

This all went through his mind in that moment, as their eyes met. She reached for the satchel, and he blocked her gently.

"I'll get it," he said, but instead, held her wrist, sliding his hand into hers. She kept looking at the bag for a moment, but then glanced up at him with a sad and slightly defiant expression. But then he felt her hand grasp his – the signal he was waiting for. He reached down to kiss her, and to his delight, she met his lips with hers. The kiss turned into a kiss and hug, their bodies pressed fully together, something he didn't want to stop. Finally, she pushed away.

It was an unbearably rare and wonderful moment, he knew.

"That was a hell of a kiss," he said, smiling at her with a heat he couldn't suppress.

Her expression was serious, and she seemed to think about it for a second.

"You know what?" she finally said, with a little smile. "That was a hell of a kiss."

Wonderfully, her face turned pink and her tough veneer was suddenly cracking before his delighted eyes. She tried reaching for her bag again, but he caught both hands and pulled her into a big, close hug, holding her hands behind her back teasingly, kissing the top of her sweet-smelling hair, then reaching for her lips again. She relaxed into him, and he let her hands go so she could press them into his lower back as they kissed. When she pulled out of it this time, he was ready to get on his knees and beg her to stay. But he did so only in his imagination.

"Time to go," she said, still blushing from her forehead down her neck.

Regretfully accepting the inevitable, this time he did pull the bag out of the trunk and carried it to the sidewalk, feeling like he wanted to carry it all the way to Chile for her. Instead, he helped her drape its wide, canvas strap on her shoulder and transferred its heft. She looked at him one more time. He didn't need to get on his knees. He knew what his expression was telling her. But she turned without another word and stepped through the sliding airport doors into the busy crowd of travelers.

And then she was gone.

Emerson sat atop a cold boulder, its slanted striations showing the layers of sediment that had formed it three hundred million years before, and its odd placement a testament to the powerful water that had once rushed across this prairie. The barren flats showed the gold of weedy winter stubble, splotched white with a recent snowfall, and pale tans and grays where the wind had scoured the surface. He had scrabbled his way to the top of its thirty-foot height and now sat in an indentation, smoothed by thousands of other bodies that had perched there, leaning his back against the knobby rock slab, his face in the sun.

The icy landscape matched his brooding mood. Grumpy with the impatience of inertia, forced on him by the quirky schedule of legal proceedings leading up to the trial, between which days of nothing happened, he had taken to driving the hills around Creeley Junction. Some days, he went straight to the hiking trails and set off, burning his frustration through a fast pace along slippery, pebble-strewn paths that took him past breathtaking views from high atop the hills. Sometimes, he found the quiet of an aspen grove, where the jay's calls were answered only by the wind in the branches. Other days, he sought the drama of valleys such as this, with the improbable red boulders scattered around, jarring the monotony of the smooth grasslands.

Often, he planned his escape. Where would they go after he could leave this behind? That was, of course, assuming he was not sentenced to jail. This thought caused a thin slice of fear to creep up his spine, for himself partly, but more for Courtney and what would befall her without him, a ward of the state, with no one to protect her.

His mind slipped into the worst possible scenarios; Courtney hurt, abused, on the streets as soon as she could escape the foster system, a drug addict, a prostitute, dead. This pessimistic vision vanished when he saw his freedom assured, a "not guilty" verdict and their moving from this area that was so unlucky for them, and on to a brighter future, with him successfully employed, Courtney a model student, acing her classes, going on to college, becoming the scientist who cured cancer, or the first woman on Mars. And he and Maddie eventually becoming grandparents. A place inside him ached, feeling emptiness where his hopes about Maddie once glimmered.

Today, though, his brain chewed on his other anxiety: The recent emergence of his rage. Despite careful and deliberate conditioning, it had crept to the surface. Sheen had seen it, maybe Lotu. And then it had almost escaped in his brief confrontation with Kellerman, that lout at whom he would normally laugh, or simply ignore.

When he was young, it chewed away at his insides. But for his entire adult life, he had been successful in quelling it. In fact, he truly thought he had completely extinguished it. But obviously, that was not the case. The stress of this past year, starting with acquiring Courtney, then having to endure his father and the events at the resort, and now the aggravating aftermath, all this must have chipped at the joints of the vault in which he had stashed it. A thin crack had appeared, and the rage, like some white-hot, molten metal, was trying to ooze out.

He could not let that happen. He knew what his rage had once done.

Although he tried not to dwell on it, he couldn't help but see his mother. It wasn't just the sadness in her face he now saw, it was the fear. Strangely, he couldn't remember what had made him so mad back then, but he remembered the feeling of it taking control, and the rush of pleasure that came over him as he learned that his fist could so easily penetrate the pale painted drywall in the living room. He remembered punching and kicking and roaring with more fury than a single eight-year-old should ever possess. And he knew she couldn't stop him, though she tried. Then he had broken her new vase. It was a gift from a glass blower at a show. It was handmade, white with flecks of color, and it was extra special because the gaffer had chosen her, out of the large crowd, to receive it. Emerson hadn't meant to include it in his fury but had accidentally sent it flying. When it hit, it cracked in half. He remembered the fear on her face, and that his father appeared then, too. His father did not even attempt to stop him, but just said calmly, "See what you've created? He's a monster, and it's all on you. You can't blame me for this one."

He remembered his parents fought after that, and he knew that fight was his fault.

That was it, the whole memory. As vivid as this scene was in his mind, so much else was gone. Not only could he not remember what ignited that rage, he couldn't remember anything else until the day he realized she had left him. He had come home from school and she wasn't there. He searched the house, surprised to see her empty closet and the cursive note he couldn't quite read. The next memory he had in this chain was staying with his horrible cousin Raffie and Aunt Irma for a while, until his father finally returned, gloomy and terrifying, utterly derailed. Then, the funeral, with his mother's body clad in a bright yellow casket, the damage from her suicide hidden first under the mortician's make-up and then, the darkness of the grave.

When he was old enough to seek real answers, his father forbade him from talking about it. Without any sense of clarity about the events that led to his furious outburst, her leaving and eventual death, all he knew was that he harbored a rage that could cause nothing but destruction and pain, and that it must not ever be allowed to escape. Over the years, he had come to recognize the similar seething in his father, but it was one that he had mastered. He used it like a trained grizzly, to scare, bully and manipulate. He turned it loose on Emerson at times.

Emerson saw the hatred and fear his father's anger left in its wake, and he knew he would never try to use his own rage to get his way, not after that night so long ago. He renewed his determination that Courtney, especially, would never see it. The cycle would stop with him. But now, this beast that, for years, had stayed confined in his darkest depths, had successfully snapped one link in the chains that held it, and sensing an opening, was ready to roar forth, wrecking everything in Emerson's path.

He was not going to let that happen.

When it was nearing time to pick up Courtney, Emerson started back down the narrow roads toward Denver. Without warning, a hawk flew directly in front of his car, coming in at a sharp angle from above. He knew in the second before he tried to brake that it was so focused on its prey at the side of the road it didn't notice his car. The dull thud told him he didn't stop in time.

"Damn it," he said. Although insects were once his livelihood, he had almost become an ornithologist. He liked birds. Now, he had probably killed this hawk, and he felt bad about it. The road was so empty he just stopped the car without pulling over, thinking the bird might have fallen near his tire and not wanting to cause further injury by running over it. He climbed out, leaving the driver's door open, and went around the front of his car.

The red-tailed hawk was either dead or unconscious, sprawled in the dust at the side of the road. He gingerly picked it up. It was surprisingly light and seemed so much bigger in his hands than when he saw them overhead. He noticed blood on his wrist and quickly checked the bird for the wound. One of its talons bent awkwardly, bleeding profusely. He quickly reset the toe in its proper position. Its head and neck seemed okay. As he was prodding it, the bird roused. It looked around dazedly. He started to look for a branch for it to clasp when the bird apparently realized it was in the hands of a huge predator. It squawked and flapped so abruptly he couldn't hold it. It leaped out of his hands, spraying him with blood. It landed clumsily on the ground a few feet away and held up its injured foot in pain. He reached for it again, intent on getting it away from the road. He was successful in scooping it up, only to feel its talons dig through his winter coat and into his arm, as it launched itself into the air, spraying him with more blood as it flew off across the canyon and disappeared.

"Ouch."

Emerson pulled up his coat sleeve and examined his arm. He was hoping for surface scrapes, but the talons had penetrated, leaving two, deep gashes. He would have to find someplace to wash the cuts. He remembered a gas station and convenience store nearby and got in his car. His memory proved correct, and he found the store at the intersection with route 77. It was an unkempt, privately owned business, normally not one he would want to patronize. He saw the single bathroom door, outside, at the back of the building. He hoped it was unlocked, since his coat and jeans were covered with blood and he didn't want to have to ask for the key, but of course, it wasn't. He went inside the store.

The dark-haired cashier was middle-aged and overweight, sitting on a stool and watching a game show on a television mounted over the cigarette shelves, behind the counter. She had a bored air with some authoritative heft, and he was pretty sure she was an owner. It wasn't exactly a thriving business that would host a bunch of employees, out here in the arid canyonlands.

She gave him a hard look now, not at all friendly.

"Hi. Can I get the bathroom key?"

For a moment, she hesitated, and he expected her to say, "Customers only."

"Sorry," he said. "I have an injury on my arm. I need to wash it."

She reached behind her for a key, chained to a 12-inch chunk of wood, and set it on the counter, then backed away.

Thinking that odd, he thanked her and headed to the

bathroom.

It was predictably horrible in there, dark and smelly, with toilet paper stuck on the bare, damp floor. The urinal held a cake of stinky, pale pink disinfectant and the toilet seat in the doorless stall was stained with urine from people who apparently decided to squat instead of sitting.

The mirror was small and cracked, but when he saw his image reflected in the dim light from a low-watt bulb, he realized why the woman had acted unfriendly. His face looked as though someone had dipped a paint brush in red and flicked it at him several times. His nose, cheeks, neck, brow, and even his eyelids, were bloody. He first turned his attention to his cuts. Of course, there was no soap, so he rinsed the injuries in the cold-only water for a few minutes, then washed his face. The hand dryer was an ancient, rough, cloth thing that one pulled around a reel endlessly and which, he was sure, was never washed. He figured it still held the grime from everyone who had washed their hands there since 1972, as well as any of their germs that could survive in that dank room. He skipped it, dried his face on his shirt and returned to the store.

He found a dusty container of rubbing alcohol on a shelf in a corner and grabbed it, along with a bottle of tepid drinking water from a cooler and went back to the counter.

Setting down the key, he said, "Sorry about that. I hit a hawk back on the road and when I went to check it, it sprayed me with blood."

The woman raised her eyebrows in response and rang up his purchases.

He pulled out his credit card, completely forgetting that the account was frozen.

"No cards," she said, pointing to a hand-written sign on a piece of cardboard taped to the register. It said, "Cash only."

"I don't carry cash." He pictured what was left of the cash Jeff lent him, sitting on the kitchen counter in the apartment.

"We don't take cards."

"Okay, well, sorry then." He looked at the items wistfully. He was going to just leave them on the counter and leave but decided to be a little more polite and return them to the shelf and cooler. She watched him closely as she removed the sales from the register, as though expecting him to try to slip them under his coat.

"Have a great day," he said as he left, biting back the sarcasm.

He decided to head back home, where he could properly clean up the injury. Knowing those talons caught and killed animals, he didn't want to risk the infection he was sure to get if he didn't disinfect the wounds soon. Not to mention that it might not be smart to drive around covered in blood in a community where half the population already thought he was a criminal.

~18~

Martin sat at the cheap desk in his hotel, reading the obituary. It had taken him a couple hours to work backward through Emerson's online presence to find his way to this tragedy in his early life. First, he had read the plentiful coverage of the Crandall Resort, from its initial permitting to its ultimate destruction. In between, he read about the police investigation into the death of Clara Stanton, her mysteriously missing lawyer, and Madeline Cunningham's pressing charges that led to the case now at trial. He found a men's business magazine that named Emerson and his father Entrepreneur Bachelors of the Month. Martin's jealousy flared.

Moving backward, he found some of Emerson's research on invasive insects, but there the trail went cold. It was only when he circled back to an article about a grant Emerson had received that he found mention of his mother's name.

And now, here he was at her obit. Dead "unexpectedly" near a cliff in a campground, tucked into the base of Mount Rainier. Why she had gone from her family in Buffalo, New York, all the way to Washington, Martin couldn't fathom. But it was obvious from the terse description of the death, with no cause offered for this young mother, just thirty, that she had taken her own life.

Well, now. That was interesting. Martin had never seen his own mother after being placed in the group home. He knew what it was like to be abandoned by the careless cow who was supposed to be there, to take care of him. He knew how that pain stayed with him, and how it grew, how it was always there, eating away at him. It wasn't hard to imagine the festering abscess his mother's death had gouged in Emerson.

And yet, here he was, appearing to lead a normal existence, striving to raise that little girl. Sure, his problems right now were a little out of the ordinary, but that only served to emphasize how well Emerson was able to rise to the challenge, to overcome the obstacles, to move past them. Whereas he, Martin, remained stuck, a bug in tar.

Still, he shared that similarity with Emerson. He knew that pain, that certainty, deep inside, that he was so horrible his mother couldn't bear to stay with him. She had created this monster, and once she did, she couldn't be bothered to stay around and help him when he most needed it. With only his own experience to go on, Martin assumed that he and Emerson shared that rage, that pain, that fragmentation. But Emerson was able to overcome it, whereas Martin, well, he knew he was trapped in a cycle of self-hatred and burning need. It didn't seem fair. So many things in his world were not fair.

Here he was, scarred, ugly, short and totally disregarded by men and women alike. And there Emerson was, tall, handsome, his face in the paper regularly showing the confidence that he would overcome all problems strewn in his path, stepping over them easily with his goddamned long legs and heading off into the rest of his life, all the while protecting that precious little girl. He would raise her to a beautiful, capable young woman, smart and secure.

His Sissy never had that chance. His Sissy, cut short in the most brutal way imaginable while his mother did nothing. She sat by and smiled, that stupid, stoned look on her face, the addiction stealing her soul and any chance he had of growing into a successful man.

Maybe there was a way to share that misery with Emerson, who must know that pain of loss so well. Why should he get through life so unscathed? Why should that little girl enjoy what Sissy never could? She would grow into a beautiful woman, the type who would never give him the time of day.

Martin now felt an interest that went beyond his need to snuff the kid just for self-protection. He didn't just want to kill her. He wanted to destroy them both.

~19~

Courtney was going to a birthday party on Sunday. Emerson might have been even more excited than she was, happy that she was participating in typical, childhood activities, despite, well, everything. He helped her pick out a present for the birthday boy, assisted her in wrapping it and making a card, then drove her to the boy's house. He found out from the mom that he should be back at 3 p.m., a conversation that almost made him feel like he was heading toward a normal existence, maybe for the first time ever.

Except, he brooded as he drove away from the nice, homey neighborhood and back to his musty, basement apartment for the last time, gathering up their few belongings to take to Maddie's townhouse for a mere three weeks, his existence was not normal. He was on trial, the scapegoat for his father's unethical corporation. He was an entomologist who hadn't been in a lab for nearly a year, and instead had lived in some kind of alternate universe for the past eight months, pretending he was a project manager for something that had turned into a huge catastrophe.

He cleaned the rug with Mrs. Orchard's back-up vacuum that she kept under the stairs for him, scrubbed the shower, sink and toilet, checked the place one more time, and called it good.

"Mrs. Orchard?" he called, after his last trip to the car.

"Yes?" She emerged at the top of the stairs, immaculate in a crisp royal blue blouse and white pants.

"That's it," he said. "I'm done. Do you want to check it over before I go?"

"Oh, yes. Sure."

She came down the stairs, holding the banister, stepping

carefully with a little stiffness. He suspected she was older than she looked. She walked through the couple of rooms, checking for damage and cleanliness. He sat on the stairs, waiting. She came out of the bathroom.

"Everything looks fine," she said. "Here you go. I already wrote out a check."

He took it, a rueful smile slipping onto his face as he realized he couldn't cash the deposit check with his bank account frozen. Too bad, because it would really help to have that money.

"Do you have a place, honey?" Mrs. Orchard's tone was unusually soft.

Did he have a place? Not really, but he knew she didn't mean it existentially.

"Oh, yeah. I'm taking care of an apartment for a few weeks for my...for a..." What should he call Maddie? Finally, he said, "For the woman who is suing my father's company."

He enjoyed the shock on Mrs. Orchard's face for a moment. Okay, that was a bit of childish revenge.

"Yeah, she's actually pretty nice. Well, I hope you get it rented soon. Thanks for letting us stay here for a little while."

He handed her the key, as she still tried to figure out if he was making a bad joke.

"Good luck to you," she finally said.

"Thanks. Same to you." He took the basement stairs three at a time and went out the front door.

As he got in the car, he felt sad, knowing that he could move to the nice apartment only because Maddie was gone. This reality settled over his shoulders, a heavy yoke of loneliness. Apparently, he wasn't worth staying around for.

He still had an hour before he needed to get Courtney, so he swung by Buck's Spot. Angela, the pretty waitress who seemed to work there twenty-four hours a day, greeted him with her big smile and led him to a table. She had put him in her section, he noticed, when she stopped back for his order.

"What is it this time?" she said. "Pancakes or a cheeseburger?"

He was hungry but didn't have much left from the cash Jeff had lent him. He looked up at her, thinking about it. She smiled at him, her brown eyes making the little half-moons, turning on that warmth he had noticed before. Maybe it wasn't just about getting a good tip, after all. He smiled back.

"I better stick with rye toast and a coffee," he said.

"You do keep me guessing," she said, lingering a moment before heading off to place the order. He watched her with interest. The unfortunate uniform dress was sewn from the worst kind of polyester, but it did cling to her hips nicely, and they weren't as thin as he had originally thought, but rather shapely in a good way.

She came back shortly with the toast and a coffee refill.

"You seem to work every shift," he said.

She chuckled. "I do seem to work every shift."

He noticed an intelligence in her to which he hadn't paid attention before.

"That's because I work every shift. I pick up all the shifts I can. Money, you know? It's kind of important."

He laughed a little. "You said it."

He looked at her appraisingly again. Clear, dark brown eyes, some make-up but not too much, that same brownish purple lipstick that went so well with her complexion.

"So, how come you never came here before?" she said.

"I haven't been around here. Well, I was up the road, but I didn't come to Denver."

"Stony Valley, right?"

Okay, so she recognized him. That was a realization he still wasn't used to, although he had received enough notoriety in the past eight months, with the public relations around the Resort, then the news coverage of the disaster, and now the trial, that many locals did.

"Yeah," he said, looking down, wondering if she thought he

was one of the bad guys.

"It's because you're so handsome, that's how I recognized you," she said.

He looked up in surprise and saw, for sure this time, that she was flirting with him.

"Oh, really?"

"Mm-hmm. I saw your picture online and said, 'Well, there's a handsome guy in a lot of trouble.' And then, the next thing I knew, you walked in here and ordered pancakes."

He grinned. She looked out the window.

"Hey, isn't that your car?"

He looked around. A flatbed tow truck had backed up to his black sedan. The driver was quickly attaching chains to the car's underside.

"Hey!" He ran outside. "What are you doing? Stop it!"

"This your car?" the driver said, not stopping what he was doing. He was already done with the chains, and he hit a big button on the side of his flatbed, activating a winch that slowly hauled the car onboard.

"Yes, it's my car," Emerson growled.

"Here you go." The driver handed him a document titled, "Order of Seizure."

"Call that number right there," he said, using a yellow highlighter to mark an 800 number at the bottom of the form, moving quickly through this conversation he probably had several times a day.

"Have a good afternoon."

In a whisk, he was in the truck cab and driving off with Emerson's car. Emerson watched it go, then sat on the curb. He wiped his fingers up his forehead and into his hair, grabbing a handful and pulling in frustration before letting go, looking up again and sighing. He stared numbly at the court's seizure order, not able to focus enough to read it.

Angela came out to the curb and sat next to him. Her seeing

this made his humiliation ten times worse. He hung his head.

"You know what?" she said. "Now, you look like a man who needs a ride, and lucky for you, my shift is ending in five minutes."

Now driving Maddie's car, he was late picking up Courtney.

"Sorry," he said to the birthday party mother. "I had, uh, car trouble."

"It's okay," she said. "They're just watching T.V. and decompressing." She held up a glass of wine. "Me, too."

"Daddy!" Courtney ran out and hugged him around the legs. "Look. I won a doll."

She showed him the dark-haired doll in a party dress, still in its box.

"Cool," he said, scooping her up. "Did you say thank you?"

"Thank you," Courtney said to the mother.

"You're welcome, Courtney. Come again."

"Thanks," Emerson smiled. "Bye."

Courtney immediately noticed the different car.

"If we get stopped by the police, and if the police officer asks, I'm going to tell him you're eight," Emerson warned her. Her booster seat had gone off on the flatbed with the rest of his car. "You will be soon, so go with it."

"You're going to lie to a policeman?"

"Yes. Just this once."

"Okay."

"How did you win the doll?"

"I won a game."

"What kind of game?"

"Who could stay on one foot the longest."

He chuckled. "That sounds like a fun game. You must take after me. Well-coordinated."

"What's coordinated?"

"It means you can put your body where you mean it to go.

You're not clumsy, but graceful, athletic."

"Oh. But really, Terrance fell down and he knocked over a bunch of people."

He snorted a laugh. "Well, you were still the last man standing."

"I'm not a man."

They were quiet for a couple minutes.

"But I don't really want a doll," she said. "In the other game, the prize was a bow and arrow. I wanted that."

"How come?"

"A bow and arrow is way cooler."

"I agree." He thought about it. "Well, here's an idea. Why don't you donate your doll to charity, so some little kid who wants a doll can have her? Then we can go pick you out a real bow and arrow, not a toy one, and you can learn to use it like a pro."

"Really?" She sounded keen on that.

"Sure."

"Will some other little kid want the doll?"

"Absolutely."

"Okay." She was quiet for a minute, then said, "Will being well-coordinated make me good at shooting arrows?"

"Sure it will. As long as Terrance doesn't come by and knock you over."

She laughed in delight. Then she fell quiet, gazing out the window. That was typical of her after she had been in a social situation, decompressing, as the mother had said. It gave him a chance to think about how nice Angela was, and to wonder how Maddie was doing after her long flight. He knew she had arrived, because he checked her flight on his phone.

When they got home, they saw their new neighbor sweeping his front steps.

"Hi," Emerson said, pausing by his door.

"Hey there," the man said. He looked about 45, dark-skinned, receding black hair, close cropped. He was a big, hefty guy who probably once was solid muscle, but whose bulk had softened with age and laxity.

"You're the new guy," the man said in a friendly way.

"Yeah." Emerson started back down the steps, pushing Courtney a little to get her to go with him.

"Emerson Crandall," he said, extending his hand. "This is Courtney."

The man took his hand in his warm one and gave it a strong, friendly shake.

"Demond Skate."

"Who's that?" came a voice from inside.

"Come on out and meet our new neighbors, Mama."

A round, bent little lady came out on the porch, limping with a cane, wearing frameless glasses and a friendly smile.

"Hello, son," she said. "Are you the one involved in that hotel business up in Stony Valley?"

"Yes, unfortunately."

"I told you it was him," she said to her son, as if scoring a point. Then, she turned back to Emerson. "What all you think's going to happen with that one?"

"I wish I knew," Emerson said. "I can assure you, I didn't do any of the things they say I did. So, I'm hoping that, no matter what happens with my father's corporation, Courtney and I will be able to just get back to normal." Whatever that is, he thought.

"Okay, honey. You have a good night, now." She went back inside.

The man watched her go and then smiled and raised his eyebrows at Emerson, cocking his head in his mother's direction.

"She doesn't miss a thing, believe me. She's the neighborhood watchdog."

"Well, that's good by me. I like having someone keeping an eye on things."

"Me, too."

"Well, it was nice meeting you. We better go start supper."

"You too. If you need anything, just holler."

"Thanks. Same to you."

Emerson didn't notice the blue car, idling by the privacy fence in the darkening afternoon.

~20~

Lotu was looking at the lab report from Kellerman's car. No blood was found, other than Kellerman's, but it was a rental, so vacuumed frequently between customers. That was handy, because when the tech came up with a hair that wasn't Kellerman's, there was a reasonable chance it was left by the murderer. At first, the lab tech identified it as a pubic hair, but later settled on beard. When Lotu saw the lab's note on its length, he noticed it was longer than any he had ever seen on Emerson. He requested the DNA test, both the rapid one, the results of which the sheriff's department stored locally, and one at a certified lab that would be housed in the FBI's CODIS system. It was stupid to have multiple DNA data banks, but the rise of rapid DNA testing was moving faster than federal laws, so many law enforcement agencies were creating their own data banks, separate from CODIS.

Going forward, as he interviewed witnesses and suspects, he would be on the lookout for long beards.

"Why are you worried about that hair?" Sheen asked, coming up behind him and looking over his shoulder. "We got his name badge, for Chris'sake. That's pretty damned good evidence."

"Yeah, sure, the name badge.," Lotu swung his chair around and looked out at the drab, February street, busy with traffic almost all day.

"What's your problem?"

"Well, let's see. I'm Emerson Crandall and I leave the courthouse. I take off my name badge and wad it up. I don't see a garbage pail, so I stuff it...where? Pants pocket or jacket pocket?"

Sheen gave him an annoyed look. "Okay, I'll play. Let's say, jacket."

"Fine. Jacket. It's in my jacket pocket." Lotu stood up, walked to the window. "A few hours later, it's time to kill Kellerman. I break into his car, lie on the back seat. I'm Emerson Crandall, so I'm six-foot-two, and I have to cram myself in there, way down low and wait where he won't see me. Maybe that's when the label falls out of my pocket and goes under the seat."

He could see by Sheen's face that he knew where this was going.

"So, here comes Kellerman. I get lucky and he doesn't look in the back seat. We drive out of Denver, stop at the light. I sit up and 'Hello!' I drive a knife into his neck."

Sheen shook his head slightly, looking a little annoyed.

"Then I get out of the car and run off by foot. So, tell me, we know I did all this in my suit, since that's where I stuffed the label. I have to be in court the next day, and uh-oh! My custom-made suit's all covered with blood. Now I got to get it cleaned. I wonder if the dry cleaner might ask me about all that blood? And, also, am I still wearing my expensive, slippery, leather-bottomed shoes to make my getaway in the mud and snow, or did I switch to sneakers or maybe hikers? And as long as I was changing clothes, why didn't I change into jeans and a dark shirt, something I didn't care would get wrinkled, bloody and dirty, something I could move easily in? And if I did change my shoes and my jacket, why on earth would I take the crumpled name label out of my suit and put it in my change of clothes? If I remembered to take it out at all, why didn't I just put it in the garbage at that point?"

"He might have thrown out the suit," Sheen said.

Lotu looked at him steadily for a minute, smiling a little, eyebrows raised.

"We have his name label at the murder scene," Sheen said.

"That he probably threw out, after he left the courtroom, in one of the many garbage cans the courthouse has just inside its exit doors. Like ninety-nine percent of people do. I checked. Those cans are full of name badges. In fact, that's the reason they put the garbage cans there. Because so many people were wadding them up and tossing them on the vestibule floors when they left. I checked that, too."

"So, it's a plant, is that what you're saying?"

"Unless you think the scenario I just described makes perfect sense."

"I'm going for coffee." Sheen left, grumpily.

Lotu looked out the window, knowing Sheen just wanted to solve it as much as Lotu did. That's all they ever wanted, but it wasn't worth taking shortcuts.

It would sure be easy if Emerson left that name label in the car. Obviously, finding Kellerman's killer was not going to be that simple. Why was somebody out to make it look like Emerson killed Kellerman?

~21~

Lotu had seen too many mutilated corpses, but this was the worst.
The legs, hacked off at the hips, stretched along either side of the
torso, toes up. The femur was sawed as neatly as a T-bone, but the
skin and muscle around it were ragged, the muscles whitish-pink, the
skin purpling at the edges. At the other end, the toe nails were painted
a cheerful orange, and the contrast between the playful thought that
went into that color choice and the mangled mess this woman had
become caught him for a moment. He sighed, pressing his palm across
his closed mouth and down his chin.

Her neck, too, was sliced and hacked, its skin pulled back and
ragged, its lack of a head making the truncated torso look like some
wax museum's badly colored cast-off.

Laying a couple feet away, he saw what was left of the woman's
head. At first, he thought it was partly buried, but after further
examination, he realized he was only seeing half a head. The cut side
was against the ground. Lotu bent down and tried to make out her
features past the tangle of long, dark hair. He couldn't see much from
his vantage point, though, and it looked like it was a couple days since
she died. Even if her head was still whole, the purples, blues and
blacks that had replaced her pinks and ivories in life, along with the
flaccidity caused by the lax and lifeless muscles, would make it a
challenge to identify her now.

He thought about the placement of the head. Unlike the rest of
the body, so carefully posed, its position didn't seem to bear any
relationship to the rest of the corpse. It almost seemed as if the head
was dumped as an afterthought.

He saw a rough cut, opening her abdomen. The gash was about

eight inches, and it was made with brute force. Horribly, he could see something whitish sticking out of that opening. Scrutinizing it further, he realized it was part of a child's doll. He took a long look, but the ME would have to let him know what was going on in there.

Lotu rejoined Sheen, who was smoking up by their car. Sheen put out the cigarette, knowing Lotu hated them, and put the butt back in the pack.

"That's fucked up," Sheen said.

Lotu nodded.

The sleet, threatening them since they arrived, now started in earnest, a couple of little ice pellets at first, but then getting heavy and wet with the increasing wind. They hurried into the vehicle, Sheen behind the wheel. He started the car, but kept it parked, turning on the heat. The sleet hit the sides of the car loudly. The winds here in the canyon could get fast and cold, even during this February thaw. The crew by the corpse had set up a tent, but its sides were flapping in the wind, threatening to blow over.

The body, carefully dissected, was positioned with obvious deliberation. It was in a location where it was likely to be spotted, not right away, but probably within a few days, by hikers, or snowshoers or, in this case, cross-country skiers sliding along a crusty drift on the hillside.

Lotu sighed. They both knew what it meant. The killer was organized, and this was not his first kill.

Now, there was so much to do. They would need to identify her, and if she wasn't the one person who had gone missing from Denver recently – the waitress, Sarah Miller – that meant going through lengthy missing person files. They'd try to get the forensics done as quickly as possible, in hopes that the killer left DNA or fingerprints on something, and then hope they happened to have these identifiers in the databases. They'd have to start covering the area, speaking to people who might have seen or heard something that would help them find the killer.

Until this morning, Lotu had a relatively light load. Working the Crandall case had freed him from the county's other, few homicides, although Kellerman's death threw a monkey wrench in that one. He still had no suspects for that, other than Emerson. But the parking garage security cameras pinpointed the time Kellerman got in his car and left the lot, and a witness that had seen him slumped at the intersection. Emerson had proven that he was at the diner between those two times, thanks to his receipts and the waitress's statements. He couldn't place Emerson anywhere near Kellerman at the time of his death.

Of course, the two women who worked for the court had just given them some new information, about the disagreement between Emerson and Kellerman in the hallway. He was starting to think Kellerman's death might be a hit, but he couldn't believe Emerson would be that sophisticated, or that bad, or even that he wanted Kellerman dead at all. If Emerson killed Kellerman, it was nothing but base revenge, and Emerson didn't seem the type. He was in enough trouble without throwing a foolish murder into the mix. As it was, he'd probably get through all this okay, if he just stuck it out and cooperated. He didn't think Emerson had killed Kellerman. Still, its timing in relation to this Crandall lawsuit made the connection unavoidable, and he had requested the courthouse video, hoping to catch the altercation. But that was as far as it went, which was, basically, nowhere.

And now, the chief had requested he take this call, with Sheen, because of its weird nature – the dismemberment, the posing. They were good at their jobs, and the County would want this one taken care of quickly. However, he now needed to give the bad news to his chief, that this had all the hallmarks of a compulsive murder by an aberrant killer, someone acting with enough foresight to cover his tracks. They wouldn't solve this quickly. What's more, he also had to tell his chief that they had to prepare to warn the public – if not now, then after the next one. He was certain there would be a next one, given time, or a new moon, or a talking dog, or whatever it was that set this nut off.

Sheen gave Lotu a hard look.

"What's on your mind?" Lotu asked.

"My gut tells me to look at Crandall for this," Sheen said.

"Emerson Crandall? What are you smoking?"

"Hear me out. That guy is squirrely. There's something off about him. Remember how he acted in the interrogation the other day? Just before he knocked that coffee all over you, he was acting seriously goofy. And don't forget that flash of rage. It wouldn't surprise me if he's going schizo. I mean, we don't even know that he isn't taking medicine to control the voices in his head."

"Lack of sleep can make a person act weird. He said he hadn't been sleeping."

"He shows up in town, and suddenly we have a dead party to the suit that is suing the shit out of him, and now this freaky murder? I think the guy was barely holding it together, and something set him over the edge."

"I don't make him the type to do something like this."

Sheen thought about it for a moment.

"Well, let me ask you something," he said. "Do you think his father killed that old woman and her lawyer?"

Lotu chewed the side of his lip, looking out at the sleet, now coating the sparse, weedy landscape.

"That's how it looks," he said. "From what we've been able to find out about his father, he was capable of it. He had the time and the motive. We just couldn't put him there."

"The apple doesn't fall far from the tree."

Lotu thought about it. His instincts told him Emerson was not a killer, but he knew Sheen could sometimes see things in people he didn't. He also knew that in Sheen's view, the other day, Emerson had proven himself capable of abnormal behavior, even if it was due to exhaustion.

Finally, he said, "No, I don't see it. What his father did, and this?" He nodded toward the corpse. "It's different. It's two very different types of things. For this to be Emerson Crandall, that apple tree would have to be dropping watermelons."

"I'm just saying," Sheen said. "This girl? We know she's going to turn out to be the missing waitress, right? I'll bet you twenty bucks that Crandall ate at the Salted Steak recently."

"So did half the lawyers in Denver, and the tourists and the businessmen. It's the most popular steak place in downtown."

"That's true," Sheen said. "We need to get their security video and start looking at faces. Hey! He had noticed a van pulling up nearby, the name of a local television station painted on its side. Luckily, a uniformed deputy saw it, too, and hurried over, preventing the reporter and videographer from getting too close.

"That didn't take long," Sheen said. "It'll be the lead story tonight. Anyway, we need to look at Crandall."

"We'll put him on the list and see if anything turns up. I agree there might be something strange about him. But not this kind of strange." He waved again toward the body. "We have to have more of a reason than just you not liking him to question him."

"Well, I wouldn't want to go on vacation with him, but I don't really dislike the guy. I just don't like the looks of this. You know there's going to be more, and we don't have any idea who's doing it. I'm just pointing out that it started at the same time he showed up."

"Yeah, I know. He's on our list," Lotu said. "But we need a better list."

~22~

Emerson dropped off Courtney at school, still using Maddie's car, "For Sale" sign in the window and all. He decided to swing by the diner for breakfast. Angela grinned when she saw him, a big, happy, genuine smile, and he couldn't help but notice the intensity of her energy.

"Hello," he said, a rumbly warmth in his voice. He glanced at her body, still too hidden in the stupid uniform.

She led him to a table and brought him coffee without asking if he wanted it.

"So, how are you?" she said.

"Oh, I guess I'm doing okay," he said, smiling, trying not to think of the things that were conspiring to not make him do okay.

"I'm glad to hear it," she said. "I'm guessing today is a pancake day."

His bank account had not been unfrozen this morning, despite Jeff's promise. But he had succeeded in getting Jeff to cash the check for the double deposit that Mrs. Orchard had returned. Compared to the last time he saw Angela, he felt like a millionaire.

"Blueberry pancakes," he said. "With eggs over medium, bacon and hash."

"Oh really?" She gave him a saucy look. "You have a wonderful appetite today. I like a man who knows how to eat a really big meal."

She smiled at him, waiting. He took the bait.

"Oh? Why is that?"

"Because it means a bigger tip for me," she said.

They both laughed.

"I thought so. Is that all I am to you?" he said.

"Why? What do you want to be to me?" She said it in a light

and flirty way. Now, he saw where this could go. He was still a bit wary when he found himself getting attention from beautiful women. It wasn't long ago one tried to trap him into marriage based on the hopelessly misguided misconception that he was some kind of rich jetsetter. But he had found some confidence in himself from that experience, especially sexually, since that was pretty much the only thing comprising that relationship, and he used this bit of positive change to try to overcome his self-doubt and shyness.

As he examined Angela's smile and sensed her energy, he also realized he was angry at Maddie. The truth was, deep down, he was hurt, and that was the source of his anger. But today, he didn't think that deep. He just looked at the beautiful Angela smiling at him, emitting that energy, and pictured Maddie, as he often did, on a mountain, in a tent, in a sleeping bag with a handsome, Latino lover.

He remembered Angela's question now: What did he want to be to her?

"I'm not sure," he said. "It might be fun to figure that out."

She checked his expression to see if he meant it the way it sounded. Then she smiled again and turned a little pink. Emerson enjoyed watching it. She was pretty. He was suddenly curious about her – who she was, why she chose waitressing, whether she had a big, biker boyfriend who might appear at any moment.

She went swiftly to the cook's window to place the order, then busied herself at the empty tables nearby, straightening condiments and napkin holders, wiping at smears. He watched for a few minutes, working up his nerve.

Finally, he said, "Do you ever get a chance to take a break?" He nodded at the seat across from him.

Angela looked behind her. The cook was staring at her through the short-order window. She looked back at Emerson, rolling her eyes toward the cook.

"I can't," she said, regret in her voice. "That's the boss."

"Oh?" Emerson appraised him. He was fifty or so, looked a

little ragged, short-necked, with small, woodchuck eyes. Emerson didn't see him as a threat, but he could understand why Angela did.

"Got it," he said.

The cook slapped a bell twice, sharp and deliberate, still watching her as he set a plate on the hot table.

"Oh," she said. "Your pancakes!"

She hurried off, then returned with his breakfast.

"Here you go."

The meal looked and smelled delicious. She turned so her back was fully to the cook, who was still watching, Emerson noticed.

She said, "I can't really talk to you during my shift, but today, I get done at two."

"I have to pick up my daughter at three-fifteen," he said, a little surprised by her suggestion, but willing to go with the idea.

"Well," she said, looking out the window. "There's a really pretty park just a block away. Would you like to go for a walk at two?"

"That sounds good," he said.

She smiled, looking genuinely happy. How nice, he thought, somewhat vindictively, Maddie flipping through his thoughts, to see a woman who is happy to be meeting with him.

"Okay," she said. "Make it five after two. That will give me a chance to change." She noticed a couple of college-aged young men sliding into a booth on the other side of the diner and hurried off to greet them.

Emerson dug into the food, wondering where this might lead.

~23~

Emerson leaned against an oak tree, just inside the entrance to the park, watching Angela hurry down the street. She hadn't spotted him yet, and he could see her anxious, searching expression. Her face was interesting, because it could change. At times, it was smooth, open and youthful. At others, it seemed aged and care-worn, belying a heavy burden.

Now in her street clothes, jeans and high-heeled boots, her body was lean, but not skinny. She had a nice roundness at her hips and medium-sized breasts, moving with her rapid steps under a short, tight, winter jacket. She carried a hefty, fabric purse on her shoulder.

He stepped to the park entrance, gratified by the big smile that transformed her face from anxious to joyful when she saw him. There was none of the skepticism he was used to seeing whenever Maddie happened to glance his way.

"There you are!" she said. "I thought you might've stood me up."

"I would never do that," he said.

"Let's walk." She took his arm comfortably and they headed along the sidewalk, ambling in toward a large pond in the center of the park, partially iced over. He noticed she carried a light scent from the diner, something warm and delicious.

"So, tell me about your daughter's mother," she said.

He smiled, appreciating the tact she showed while asking a question that could be critical to wherever this first step might lead. He shook his head slightly.

"Courtney was the result of a short fling I had with her mother after I completed my master's degree."

"Well, since you describe her like that, like some kind of chemistry project, I'm guessing your master's degree is in a scientific area."

He laughed. "Sorry. Don't get me wrong. I'd do anything for Courtney. She's my daughter. But I didn't know about the pregnancy, or anything about her until last March." And it's been a very strange year since then, he thought. "Unfortunately, her mother was killed, so Courtney is with me now."

Angela gasped. "How horrible!"

"Yeah. Hit and run."

When he didn't elaborate, she said, "I can tell how important she is to you, just watching you together. I think you're a very good father."

"Thanks." It surprised him to realize how important those words were to him. No one had ever said that to him before. "What about you? Any kids? Pets? Big, biker boyfriend?"

She laughed. "No boyfriend, biker or otherwise. My son's father is from Los Angeles, and I haven't seen or heard from him in years. I don't know where, and I don't care, except for how it hurts my son. Oh, and yes, a son. He's 17, trying to be a man, you know? But he's still mostly a boy, and an angry one."

"What seventeen-year-old isn't angry?" Emerson said, surprised that she could have a late-teenaged son and estimating her age in his head.

She smiled in acknowledgement. They stopped at the edge of the pond.

"What's his name?"

"Lucas," she said.

"As in, 'light'?" Emerson asked.

"How did you know that?"

"There's a lot of Latin in the bug business."

"He is my bright light," she mused. "But he's frustrated that his father is gone, not interested in school, even though he's very smart. And he's found some friends I don't like at all."

"You must be worried about him."

"I am. I think he'll be okay, but I need to get him through this hard stage. I worry about him all the time. It's tough with my schedule, working all kinds of shifts and not always being there at night. My mother is in San Diego, but I have a sister here who helps with him."

A trio of mallard ducks puddled on the other side of the pond, tipping bottoms-up.

"It's hard to believe he's now the age I was when I had him. I thought I was such a grown-up back then, but now, it's obvious that I was still mostly a child, too."

Thirty-four. Cool.

"But having a baby will age you quickly," she said with a small smile.

He thought wistfully of his own simple existence, pre-Courtney.

The ducks noticed them and swam across an ice-free patch of water, quacking back and forth as if they were discussing their prospects with these humans.

"Oh!" Angela remembered something and pulled a couple of dinner rolls out of her purse. She gave one to Emerson and began to break hers into small pieces, tossing them to the ducks. He smiled at the fact that she had put a priority on the ducks in preparing for this walk.

"These were too dry to serve," Angela said, as though she felt guilty about taking them from the restaurant.

"Ah." He tossed some pieces to the ducks, his eyes automatically searching the water for aquatic insects, even though spotting any this time of year would be unusual.

They didn't have long before he had to leave to get Courtney. Before they parted, at the entrance to the park, Angela reached up and gave him a quick, sweet kiss on the lips. He really liked that part, and he liked what she said next.

"Thank you for the walk. It made me feel like I didn't have to be a mother or a waitress or anything at all for a little while. Just me."

***

Lotu and Sheen were waiting for Emerson when he pulled into the apartment parking lot with Courtney. He slowed, looking through the windshield at them as they waited, standing on Maddie's steps, Sheen with his arms crossed, scowling at Emerson, Lotu looking up from his phone.

"What do they want?" Courtney said.

"I don't know."

"Are they here to throw you in jail again?"

"No."

"How do you know?"

"I just do."

"But you didn't know they were going to throw you in jail the first time, right?"

"That's true."

"So how do you know they aren't going to throw you in jail again?"

"Stop saying 'throw you in jail,'" he said. "You might be putting a whammy on me."

"What's a whammy?"

He parked and helped her out of the used booster seat he had picked up at the Goodwill Store. She had rather liked not using one and objected to going back for this last month before she turned eight and would be legally freed from them, but he insisted.

He didn't say hello to the detectives when he approached, and they didn't say hello to him. Instead, he unlocked the door for Courtney, made sure she was inside and out of earshot, then turned to them and looked at Lotu.

Lotu cleared his throat and said, "Any idea why we're here?"

"You want to wish me a happy birthday?"

"Is it your birthday?"

"Nope."

Sheen made an annoyed noise and Emerson eyed him warily. He hadn't forgotten how quickly Sheen had thrown him to the ground at the station.

"We need to talk to you," Lotu said.

"I'm all ears."

"He means we need to question you," Sheen said, leaning into Emerson. "And we would prefer to do it at the station."

"Not again!" Emerson was exasperated.

"Daddy, no!" Courtney slipped through the front door and grabbed him around the legs. "Don't go to jail again!"

"Happy now?" Emerson said to Sheen, setting his hand on Courtney's head.

"We're not trying to upset anyone," Lotu said, nodding at Courtney, who still clung to Emerson, her face buried against his leg.

"Are you going to take me into custody?" Emerson said, thinking of Jeff.

"That's not necessary today, Emerson," Lotu said. "We can talk in the car. Would you like Deputy Quinn to sit with your daughter while we talk?"

"No, she should be okay for a couple minutes."

He thought about texting Jeff, but he hated to bother him on a Monday night, one of the evenings when Jeff got some precious time with his teenage daughters. Plus, Emerson hadn't done anything wrong, so he didn't see how talking to them would hurt, despite Jeff's pessimism. He would just talk to them long enough to find out what was going on.

Lotu began.

"You know a woman named Sarah Miller?"

"No."

"You ever eat at the Salted Steak?"

Emerson was about to say no, but then he remembered meeting Jeff there for coffee and an English Muffin. He felt a little surge of adrenalin.

"Yes," he said.

"Oh really? When was that?"

"Why don't you look at the video again? I'm sure you'll see the date on it."

"Why do you think there was a video?"

"Denver's famous for its security cameras, and I'm guessing the restaurant had some. And you had to have some reason to come here, asking these questions."

"Why don't you tell us about that day?"

He sighed and thought about it. He had met Jeff so many times at so many restaurants, it was hard to remember what happened when, or where.

"I think it was the day after the preliminary hearing, so that would've been February fifth or sixth. My lawyer's office is just down the block from there, so we met there for a coffee and quick breakfast, before we went to his office. Oh, wait. I remember. It might have been the day after Kellerman's death, because he had to leave to talk to the judge about it."

"What time was that?"

"Our meeting was at ten, so about then."

"Tell us about the person who waited on you."

He thought about it. He barely remembered anything about that part of the meeting.

"Female."

They waited.

"And?" Lotu said.

"That's all I got. I don't remember."

"You remember 'female' only?"

"Yep."

"Young? Old?"

"Young."

"Dark hair? Light hair? Skin? Shape?"

"I don't remember."

"Nothing else?"

"Nope."

"Have you ever been up northwest of Creeley Junction, up in the Canyon Park?"

He had hiked up there more than once. He felt a jolt of heat tingle through his body and was sure his face was flushing. He vaguely remembered a news report about the body of a missing waitress being found in the hills.

"Why? What's up in the canyon?" he said, trying to keep the same, confident tone, but hearing the worry creeping into his voice.

"Sure, sure. I know," Lotu said, watching him closely. "Plenty of people go up there, to hike, ski, rock climb. I'm sure there were lots of folks up there the last few days, with the thaw. Whereabouts do you like to go, when you go up there?"

Emerson's impulse was to answer him, be honest, but he remembered Jeff's firm warning.

"I guess I better call my lawyer."

"Oh, suddenly you need your lawyer? Well, that's fine, sure. But if you just let us know when you were up there, and where you went, it would be really helpful, and we'll be out of your hair."

"Well, you know I love to help you guys," Emerson said, thinking of the app he used to track his hikes – the route, the speed, the distance, the date. He had a phone full of his little tracking maps. These guys would sure love to see them. "But my lawyer doesn't like me to talk to you guys without him around."

"Oh, sure, we understand. You go ahead and call him. But could you just let us know when you went up there last, just so we can check you off the list and move on?"

"Let me see if he says it's okay to keep talking to you."

Emerson unlocked his phone, taking his time to look for Jeff in his contacts, still not really wanting to call him. He was hoping the detectives would back off at the threat.

"Okay, Emerson," Lotu said, looking a bit annoyed. "We'll say goodnight for now. But if you remember when you were up there, it would really help clear you."

By now Emerson had discerned that the missing waitress' body had been dumped in the canyon that he hiked regularly.

Before they got in their car, Emerson said, "Did you find my sketch artist?"

They looked at him in surprise, a little guiltily.

"No," Lotu said. "I'm sorry. I didn't get a chance to contact Springfield."

Emerson was not surprised. "Hey, there's a killer out there. You guys seem pretty intent on pinning something on me. Why don't you use your powers for good and try to catch a real bad guy?"

"We can't do anything in Springfield."

"Yes, we established that. But if you can help us get a sketch to them, they might be able to identify the driver who ran down my daughter's mother."

"We don't actually use a sketch artist much anymore. It's mostly computerized."

"Whatever. If you can hook us up, we might be able to help Springfield catch the man who killed Annie Hughes."

"Yeah, we got some things here we have to take care of," Lotu said, mildly sarcastic. "All right, Emerson, let us know if you remember when you hiked."

After Emerson went back inside, Sheen said, "What do you think about this Springfield hit and run he keeps talking about?"

Lotu sighed. "I'd like to help him."

"But?"

"Not our circus. Not our monkeys."

Over on the other side of town, a man knocked at Mrs. Orchard's door. She looked disapprovingly at the clock – 8:30 p.m. She tightened her robe, going to the door.

A dark-eyed, white man in a suit was standing on the steps. His long bangs were slicked back from his forehead, carefully gelled, and his close-cropped beard was neat and shiny.

"Hi. I'm here about the apartment you have for rent."

"Oh, I see," she said, looking him up and down. "Well, I only rent to people who have a good job."

"I do," he said, smiling. His smile improved his appearance.

"And no children."

"Nope, I'm single. I worked during the day, full time. I've been with the same company for six years. I can give you references. I just moved here. I need a place to live."

"Okay, then, come in. I'll show it to you."

The man stepped into the front hallway.

"This just come up for rent?" he asked.

"Yes," Mrs. Orchard said. "Right this way."

"Why is it for rent?"

"Oh, well, the man who lived here, he and his daughter were noisy, and they had visitors late at night. I need my peace and quiet." She looked back at him. "I don't allow visitors after 9 p.m. What kind of hours do you keep?"

"Oh, I go out at night, sometimes, but I won't bring anyone here. I like my privacy. And I'm very quiet. Did the man find a new place in town?"

"I'm not sure where he went. He is still in the area, I know that." She watched the news, following the Crandall case. "It's down these stairs."

"Well, his loss, my gain," the man said lightly. She looked back at him again before they started down the stairs. He smiled.

He wouldn't be bad looking if it weren't for those acne scars.

~24~

With Emerson all but admitting he was up in Creeley Canyon, Sheen seemed to feel recharged in his effort to link him to the murders. Lotu agreed it was interesting that he had obviously been up there but didn't want to admit it, and that the canyon question was the one that caused him to almost pull the trigger on calling his lawyer. Even though Lotu suspected the call to the lawyer was a bluff.

They parked in the tiny lot of a gas station and convenience store that was closed the last time they came up this way. It was a junky little place with high-priced gas and virtual extortion on the necessities a camping tourist might realize they were lacking. He was sure locals would avoid the place, and the population was sparse up here, as it was. Most owners of the little cabins visited seasonally – for hunting or ski trips – and the permanent residents here would buy supplies when they went to town. It was a quiet part of their county, from Lotu's perspective, except when people stumbled on a meth lab or discovered their cabins were burglarized while they were away.

When they walked in, the woman behind the counter turned her head from the television for a moment, gave them an expressionless nod, then went back to her show. Dust yellowed the shelved cans and boxes.

"Good morning," Lotu said. "I'm Detective Lotu. This is Detective Sheen."

The woman didn't look like she liked cops, but he was guessing she offered the same welcome to most of her customers. She had dark eyes with black hair showing strands of white. She carried about sixty pounds too many, and her round face was couched in a cowl of flesh. The tendrils of a tattoo stretched across her neck, trailing under her shirt, some kind of vine or thorns. Her expression was almost blank, with just a little hostility in her dark eyes.

"What can I do for you?" she said, not bothering to turn the sound down on the television.

"We're investigating the death of the woman whose body was found about a mile from here."

This information didn't change her empty expression. She just looked and waited.

He gave her the date Sarah Miller's body was found and the date that she was likely killed.

"Did you notice anything suspicious around those times? Maybe see anyone you didn't know?"

"I don't think anything is suspicious up here. You could say everything is suspicious. I just mind my own business."

"How about strangers?"

"The people who come in here are all strangers to me. I don't pay no attention. If they want to buy something, fine. If not, they can move on."

They showed her a picture of Sarah Miller. They could tell she had already seen it, on the television news, probably.

"Did you see her?"

"Nope."

"Anyone acting funny around the time she was missing? Cars at night when you wouldn't expect them? Anyone upset, or rushing, or with any injuries?" Lotu could be patient. He knew it took some people a little while to decide to open up. Sheen was quiet, moving around the store, looking at things, pretending not to listen, trying to ease the pressure on her.

Lotu could see she was trying to decide if she should bother to tell him what was on her mind.

"We're concerned that this guy is out here somewhere. We don't want a killer to be stalking these hills. He could be looking for his next victim. Maybe in an isolated place like this. If you saw something, it could help us put this creep away where he can't hurt anyone."

She sighed, looked out at the road. A car pulled up to the pump. The driver climbed out, tried to start the gas pump, failed, saw the "Pre-pay, cash only" sign, got back in his car and drove off.

She looked back at Lotu. "Well, there was one guy here last week who was kind of weird."

"Oh yeah? Why was he weird?"

"He was covered with blood."

Sheen stepped back to the counter. She had his attention now.

"He said he hit a hawk and needed to wash up. I thought it was kind of lame. Hawks don't usually get hit by cars. They're smart, great eyesight. But I gave him the key."

"Can you describe him?"

"Well, when I saw him, he looked familiar, and I thought at first he must've been in before. But then I realized he looked just like that guy from the news, from that casino that collapsed."

"Emerson Crandall?" Sheen said.

"Yeah. He looked like him. I could've sworn it was him. But it would be pretty weird for him to be up here, right?"

"Right. Is that actually recording?" Lotu nodded to the camera in the corner.

"Yeah, but it's ancient. I don't have good Wi-Fi up here, so that's just an old VHS. I change the tapes every day, cycle through, reuse them. I don't know why I bother, they're so old they're worn out. Hard to see anything on them. I have one at the pumps, too."

"Any chance you got this blood-covered guy on one of them?"

It took a while, but they left with two tapes. One contained a very blurry video showing someone that could be Emerson Crandall in the store. Or it could be Abraham Lincoln or any other tall, white guy with dark hair. The other showed the guy's car pulling up outside, but not the plate number, since he didn't pull up to the pump, where the plate would have been recorded.

"I told you we'd get something on him. We just need to get his car, check it for blood. If we're lucky, it will be Sarah's."

"What do you want?" Emerson slipped outside his apartment door, shutting it behind him.

"Hi Emerson. Can you tell us which car is yours?"

He nodded toward a light-colored hybrid.

"Which one, that silver one?"

"Yes."

It was not the same car as in the video. That one was black.

"That car registered to you?"

"No. It belongs to a friend. She's letting me use it."

"Do you have another one?"

Emerson looked annoyed. "Yeah, the one the court took. If you're looking for it, try the police impoundment lot."

"Is it a black sedan?"

"Yes. Why?"

How ironic that it was already where they needed it, Lotu thought.

"When did it get impounded?"

"A few days ago. I don't know. Jesus. Will you guys go bother somebody else for a while?" Emerson didn't show anger, just exasperation.

Sheen held up the warrant. "We're going to search the black one. And depending on what we find, we may be back for the silver one."

Emerson took the warrant, started reading it. "Why?"

He pressed a button on his phone and held it to his ear, still looking through the warrant.

"Hey Jeff, the police have a warrant to search my car." He paused. "OK." He took a few pictures of the warrant, sent them to his lawyer.

"Let's go," Sheen said to Lotu.

"Why are you searching it?" Emerson held out his phone, which he had placed on speaker, so his lawyer could hear it.

"We have a witness who told us she saw you covered in blood up in Creeley Canyon. We're going to check the car."

"Blood?" Emerson looked shocked. Then a memory seemed to click. He surprised them both by snorting a chuckle. "You're right. I was covered in blood."

"Emerson, shut up." His lawyer's voice came through the phone.

"It was the blood of *Buteo Jamaicensis*."

"Who is that?" Sheen said.

"Not who. What. It was a red-tailed hawk I hit with my car."

"OK, sure," Lotu said. "We'll be able to determine that fast enough. If that's the case, it will be fine."

"Please don't tear it apart," Emerson said. "I'm going to need it."

He abruptly went back inside, shutting the door without saying goodbye.

Sheen and Lotu looked at each other.

"I know," Sheen said. "He doesn't seem worried at all."

"I have a feeling we're going to find hawk's blood in that car."

"Even so, now we know he was up there, right before Sarah's body was found."

"That's true. But that's not enough."

"Well, maybe we'll find something else in the car. Now we have the warrant, we don't have to just look for blood. We could find hair, fingernails, saliva. If she was in there, we'll find something."

~25~

The criminal trial started, trapping Emerson for hours every day as he listened to the prosecution make accusations – most of them true – against his father and his father's enterprise, the Crandall Resort Hotel and Casino. He found it hard to stay focused, although Jeff expected it, since he sometimes needed Emerson to clarify a point that the prosecution was making, further preparing his defense.

Being at the trial forced Emerson to face what could happen to him. He had optimistically expected that he would never be found guilty on the charges because, simply, he *was* not guilty. But he was not so naïve that he didn't know that things could go sideways fast with a jury. The members of the jury were mainly retired and unemployed locals. Most of the people who had jobs had managed to find a way to get released from duty, although there were a couple of professionals on the jury who must have known their jobs were secure, despite their potentially prolonged absence while they served. Emerson suspected all these people would like nothing better than to punish someone for the corporate greed and unscrupulous behavior described to them. He already felt the ire of so many people in the community, who looked at him as the only remaining human from whom the wronged could carve their pound of flesh.

He couldn't bear imagining what would become of Courtney if he was sentenced to years in jail. The anxiety gnawed into him, hurting his stomach, giving him headaches, until he had to protect himself by letting his brain take him elsewhere, to try to assume the outcome would be the best. He just needed to regain his freedom, get his daughter and leave for friendlier climes.

The obvious absence of Maddie left a hole in the room and his heart. Her lawyer represented Maddie's interests with competence and a decided relish. With prolonged periods of sitting still, he had plenty of opportunity to daydream, but unfortunately his daydreams about Maddie overflowed with images of her enjoying her life, her work and her coworkers in a way that he couldn't even imagine for himself any longer. He was both happy for and jealous of her, and her freedom to simply perform her chosen work. He longed to go back to his entomology studies and research.

Today, the third day of the trial, he remembered the new, bright spot that was developing in his life. That walk in the park with Angela was fun. He liked her. Even though she worked hard all day in the restaurant carrying heavy trays and answering the sometimes unreasonable requests of customers, she was still filled with an energy and happiness he so appreciated right now, seeing as he was having a hard time feeling cheerful himself. As he was thinking about her during the trial, he decided to see if she might be able to get together the next time they were both free during the day. Her work schedule was all over the place, so it was a matter of finding those rare moments when their free time aligned.

At a break in the trial he sent her a text asking, simply, "Time this week for a walk?"

He had to wait for their lunch break to see her response. Angela wrote she had time the next afternoon at two. He replied that if court got out early, he would text her and they could meet again in the little park.

He got lucky. Court released early the next day, on the prosecution's request, for some reason Emerson didn't hear. He grabbed a quick lunch with Jeff then went to the park to meet Angela.

He sat on a bench near the park entrance, awaiting her arrival and watching the passers-by, fewer than there would be in the summer, but still a fair number. People who chose to live in Denver weren't scared inside by cold weather. His gaze had landed briefly on a bearded man passing by in a puffy, blue winter jacket. This guy looked somewhat familiar. It seemed Emerson had seen him before, that he was someone he was seeing repeatedly. He must work in downtown Creeley Junction, Emerson supposed. There were several business men and women he saw regularly, as their schedules aligned.

Angela appeared down the street, wearing tight blue jeans and a snug leather coat, zipped around her curves. Watching her walk toward him with a big smile made him feel energized in a way he hadn't for quite a while. Still, his natural lack of self-confidence with women shackled him, and he was hesitant to show his feelings, without an indication from her that she was sharing that energy.

She solved that problem for him quickly. They had wandered to a far corner of the park, a remote area amongst some scrappy shrubs with red branches and tiny purple buds that would burst into leaves in another couple months. They were happily chatting and, at that moment, she slipped her hand into his, pulled him gently against a tree and smacked a big, wet, warm kiss on his lips. It felt good. It progressed from lips to tongue and the next thing he knew they were at her apartment.

Once inside, they couldn't strip off their clothes fast enough. She was as hungry as he was, and this apparent sexual starvation on both sides made what followed a frenzy of skin and body fluids.

It was 3:10 before he roused from a snoozy, spooning session to realize that he needed to leave immediately to pick up Courtney, as he was now late. It made for an unfortunate, but characteristic, ending of their lovemaking, one he hoped would be excusable. She had to understand that, no matter what else was happening in his world, Courtney was still the most important part of it. But he anticipated that they would find more time to explore this new, passionate adventure.

Deputy Quinn was assigned the task of searching Emerson's impounded sedan. He asked a tech to go with him, since they knew there would be blood in it – hawk or human was yet to be proven. The car's interior was fairly neat, except near the child's booster seat, which was surrounded by the usual collection of crumbs and spills. A gym bag in the front passenger seat contained shorts, socks, shirt, jock, sneakers, and a racquet. A close look at the driver's area showed them they didn't even need to use chemicals to enhance the blood. They could see a smear on the seat, and a cell phone camera helped them find some on the back of the steering wheel. They took pictures and collected samples.

Quinn continued to dig around, checking in the side door pockets and glove compartment. When he reached under the driver's seat, his gloved hand clamped on some small tool. He wasn't expecting it to be anything interesting and, when he pulled it out, he was shocked to find himself holding a bloody filet knife.

Lotu had forgotten that Quinn was searching Emerson's car, so when he saw the text come through with the photo, he opened it without any expectations. Then he saw the bloody knife. He immediately called Quinn, got the details.

Sheen heard his surprised tone and tuned in.

"What?"

"Quinn found this under Emerson's driver seat."

Sheen squinted at the picture, took the phone, used his fingers to make the image bigger. Then he looked up at Lotu with a grin.

"Save your 'I told you so's' until the lab gets a chance to run it."

"Hey, Shelly said that Kellerman was killed with a thin, sharp blade, something like a filet knife," Sheen said, referring to the medical examiner. "What am I supposed to think?"

"Emerson's alibi for the time of the murder is strong, with witnesses and a paper trail."

Sheen looked back at the picture. "Yeah. And we have a video of Kellerman leaving the parking garage, so the timeline is defined. No question about it."

"Too bad we don't have a decent video of the killer getting in his car." The security camera at the parking garage had recorded a light going on in Kellerman's car, presumably when the killer opened the door to enter it, but no image of the intruder was captured. He – or she – was obviously skilled at avoiding cameras. And Emerson was out driving with Courtney at the time that light went on in Kellerman's car.

"Plus, who would be stupid enough to leave a murder weapon under his own car seat? Remember how blasé he was about our warrant to search the car?"

"The guy is weird. Maybe he has schizo episodes and then forgets about them."

"Yeah, and maybe he fileted a fish in his front seat. But I doubt it. Sounds more like another plant."

"Don't let him off that easy," Sheen said.

"You and I both know a lot of cops would close the case, based on this. But we're smarter than a lot of cops."

"Maybe you are. I just feel like throwing that smartass in jail."

Lotu smiled at Sheen's honesty. "We're investigators. Let's investigate."

Martin stayed back from the silver car with the "For Sale" sign in its back window, watching it signal, turn right. He turned right, following as it then turned left into a parking lot next to a townhouse development. He cruised by, turned around and pulled into the parking lot, finding an open spot by the security fence.

Although the sun was just below the horizon, the sky was still light enough for Martin to see them from a distance. Emerson Crandall and his daughter were climbing the steps of the last townhouse in the row. He watched as Emerson unlocked the door with a key and held it open for the little girl, then the bright apartment enveloped them as the door shut.

Martin waited until the last light had left the sky, watching the apartment. He prided himself on his patience, and although it was painfully boring, he waited. When it was fully dark, he quietly left the car. He went through the parking lot to Emerson's apartment, standing in the shadows and watching for a few minutes. Then he went around the building and slipped quietly up the back steps and tried the door. Locked. Okay, that was important information, but not unexpected.

He stood on the stairs controlling his breathing so it was slow and silent. Inside, he could hear the television's sounds of a cartoon with artificially childish voices, silly noises emphasizing the action. The father called out to his daughter, very close to Martin, causing him to stiffen. A cupboard shut. A dish tapped on the counter. The stove pilot clicked. He must be making supper.

Grabbing the girl from here was still high on his list of options. But only if he planned to kill her right away. If he wanted to take her first, then kill her later, this was not a good option. Unless he wanted to face the father, or kill him, too. He did not like the idea of fighting with Emerson Crandall over the life of his daughter.

He slipped off the porch and went soundlessly back to his car, pulling out and heading toward his apartment.

What was taking the police so long to arrest him?

~26~

Emerson heard the knock.

"Someone's at the door," Courtney called from the living room, where she was watching cartoons.

Emerson had just dumped macaroni into a pot of boiling water.

"Damn." As he crossed through the living room, he said, "Switch to the Nature Channel, please." He looked out the window by the front door and saw Lotu and Sheen. "Damn."

"Who is it?" Courtney asked.

"It's the detectives." He saw her frightened expression. "I'll be right out front. You stay inside, but you can look out and see me there if you want."

He pulled on his coat, walked out onto the steps, cast each of them an annoyed glance and headed toward their car, to bring the conversation out of Courtney's hearing. They followed him.

"Shall we get in out of the cold?" Lotu suggested, nodding at the car.

"No. Whatever it is, make it short. I'm cooking dinner."

Sheen held up a baggy containing a crumpled square of stiff paper. Emerson could make out a couple letters on it and remembered writing them on the label himself, as he did every day before being allowed to enter the second floor, where court was held.

"Yeah?" he said.

"Want to guess where we found it?" Sheen said.

"No."

"We found it under the front seat of Albert Kellerman's car," Lotu said.

The detectives watched Emerson closely. Surprised, he scrutinized the badge, confirming again to himself it was his handwriting.

"Okay," he said. He hadn't wanted to bother Jeff at dinnertime, but he would if he felt this was going in a bad direction. "Which one of you planted it there? Or did you have one of the deputies do it?"

"Were you ever in Kellerman's car?"

"No." They waited, giving him time to think about it. He looked toward the house. Had eight minutes passed yet?

"Hold on a second." He started back up to the house but felt Sheen's hand on his arm.

"Where are you going?"

He yanked his arm out of Sheen's grasp and stood up straight, looking down at him, fighting the anger that his anxiety was causing. "To turn off the pasta."

"Go ahead," Lotu said, alleviating the tension. But still, they followed him to the door. He wondered if they thought he was going to run for it or something. He saw his neighbor, Demond, watching from the window. Emerson rolled his eyes at him, shaking his head slightly. Demond waved and disappeared. Emerson stuck his head inside his door.

"Hey Courtney, will you turn off the pot on the stove?"

She jumped off the couch and headed for the kitchen.

Emerson and his escorts walked back to the car at the curb.

"How'd it get there?" Lotu said. They watched him, letting the seconds tick away. He knew they were trying to get him to start talking. Most people did, when facing stretches of silence, cops watching them. But Emerson was comfortable with silence.

"How did it get in his car?" Lotu asked again.

He thought of possibilities. He was in the habit of peeling off the labels and throwing them out, just before leaving the courthouse. Could he have missed the garbage can one day, and Kellerman picked it up by accident? Or on purpose?

"Maybe it got stuck on him?"

"And he just kept on going to his car with your name label stuck on him?" Sheen asked.

"It's the only thing I can think of. Either that, or a plant. But I'm not a smart detective like you."

"So, you were never in Kellerman's car after court?" Lotu asked. "Never sat in there to talk about the case? Never asked for a ride somewhere?"

"No." Emerson almost said he stayed as far from Kellerman as possible, but stopped, not wanting to give them a reason to ask more questions.

"Okay, Emerson," Lotu said. "Just one more thing." He nodded to Sheen, who reached in the car and pulled out another bag, this one containing the blood-cover filet knife.

"Jesus," Emerson said, turning so his body was between them and the row of townhouses. "What are you trying to do, freak out the whole neighborhood?"

"We asked if you wanted to get in the car," Sheen said.

"You didn't warn me you were going to start pulling out scary, bloody things in bags."

"You want to tell us how this 'bloody thing' got in your car?" Sheen said.

It took Emerson a moment to piece it together, remembering they had searched his black car at the impoundment. Now, he just put his head back, looking at the dark sky for a moment, and snorted a disgusted laugh.

"You guys are unbelievable," he said. They both looked at him, deadpan, apparently not finding this the least bit funny. "You're kidding, right?"

"No, Emerson," Lotu said. "It's not a joke. Our deputy found it under the driver's seat of your car."

"Okay," Emerson said, starting toward the house. "This is ridiculous."

Sheen moved in front of him, stopping him. "It's enough to place you under arrest, Crandall. You think that's funny?"

"Are you arresting me?" Emerson asked. He wanted to pull out his phone but was worried that Sheen might jump on him if he reached for something in his pocket. He didn't need to be pinned to the ground in front of the whole neighborhood.

Lotu moved next to Sheen. "We're not arresting you. We're just asking questions."

"Okay, then," Emerson said. "I didn't kill Albert Kellerman. I have never seen that knife before."

"How did it get in your car, Emerson?" Lotu asked. "Just tell us that."

He looked into the detective's brown eyes, so sincere, calm and intelligent.

"Somebody planted it," Emerson said. "That's the only way it could get there."

"Pretty unlikely, don't you agree?" Lotu said. "First the name label, then the knife?"

"Well, how likely is it that anyone would kill someone else, going to extremes to make sure they weren't seen, then leave the murder weapon under the seat of his own car?"

"Maybe you were in an altered state when you killed him, and that caused you to forget about it later," Sheen suggested. "You ever been to a psychiatrist, Crandall? You taking anything for mental illness? A little Haldol, maybe?"

Emerson looked at him in surprise. "This is where you're trying to go with it now?"

"Well, we've seen you when you get mad, Emerson. We didn't toss you in jail that night for nothing."

It hit a nerve. Emerson wanted to defend himself, but realized, just in time, that talking too much was not smart right now. It was time to call Jeff.

"I'm going to call my lawyer," he said to Lotu. "That means I have to reach in my pocket."

Lotu put up one palm. "Don't worry about it, Emerson. We'll be leaving. We just needed to ask you about these things. I mean, what are we supposed to think? First your name badge shows up in Kellerman's car, then a bloody knife, matching the ME's description of the wounds, shows up under your car seat?"

"You should be thinking the same thing I am: That someone planted them."

"But who, Emerson? Think about it. Think how serious this is. Who on this earth would want to do that to you? Who would go to the extreme of murdering a man in cold blood, then planting evidence pointing at you?"

Emerson was already wondering that. The thought chilled him. "I don't know. But I hope you find him, fast."

~27~

Emerson awoke suddenly, already sitting up. It took him a moment to understand where he was and what had awakened him, but then he heard Courtney's cry. Wearing just the gym shorts he slept in, he hurried to her room. When he opened her bedroom door, he was hit with the full volume of her wail, anguished.

"Hey, hey.," He pulled her up, rocked her awake. "You're okay, kiddo."

When she was awake, her cry turned to snuffling, and he blotted her face gently with the sheet.

"What happened?" he asked softly.

"I saw him," she mumbled. "That man again."

"The one who hit your mom?"

She nodded, her face pressed against his shoulder, crying for a little while before falling back to sleep.

Emerson lay her back in her bed and returned to his. Instead of dropping off to sleep, his brain tormented him with worry about these weird occurrences. The name label, the knife. Who would plant this highly incriminating evidence? Who wanted Emerson to take the blame for killing Kellerman? Maybe it was someone associated with his father, someone who wanted to kill off Kellerman and take out Emerson while he was at it. Maybe it was the police. Maybe it was some random whacko who followed the news and hated Emerson.

And now Courtney was having more frequent nightmares, focusing on the man who had killed her mother. In the past, her nightmares were sporadic, but now they were regular, honing in on the killer. Why now? What had happened to spur this sudden memory?

Sweating, he rolled from his back to his right side, yanked back the layer of blanket and punched the pillow to fluff it, agitated. He nestled his head into it, trying to feel more comfortable, encouraging his body to sleep. He started to feel drowsy, but then his subconscious seemed to send him an urgent thought: Were these things connected?

He was wide awake again. He had to try to do something. He knew he couldn't do much about the planted evidence, but maybe he could help Courtney. Maybe he could help the police identify the man who killed her mother.

Thinking about it the next morning, Emerson realized that Lotu was not going to let him use police resources to create a composite image of the man Courtney was seeing. He did a little research online and learned that one of Denver's retired police composite artists still lived in the area. He sent her a message through a social networking site, explaining what he wanted, and was pleased to get a quick response. In her note, she agreed to do it, but warned Emerson that the process could be very difficult for anyone and especially a child. He talked to Courtney about it, and she decided to give it a try. At 2 p.m. the next afternoon, they were at the artist's studio.

Jean Connor was a tall woman in her late fifties with shoulder-length straight white hair, the lean build of a runner and a quiet, intelligent demeanor. She offered them coffee and hot chocolate and seemed to hit it off with Courtney right away. After a few minutes of small talk, they moved to a bright window, where her drawing supplies were arranged on a small table.

"What's the thing that stood out the most about this man?" she asked.

"His eyes, and his skin," Courtney said.

"Okay, let's start with his eyes." For the next two hours, Jean collected minute memories about the face Courtney saw that night.

"Now, I'm going to show this drawing to you," Jean told her.

"If it's close, it might upset you. You ready?"

"Yes."

Jean turned the sketch pad around, and sure enough, Courtney started to cry. Emerson, sitting nearby, got up and gave her a little hug with one arm, then left it draped around her protectively.

"If you want to go on, then you'll need to tell me what doesn't look right about this drawing, so we can make it more accurate." Jean was kind, but matter-of-fact.

By the time they left, Emerson had paid Jean seventy-five dollars, and he carried an accurate drawing of the man that Courtney said had killed her mother. He photographed it and made a few copies at the nearest office store, then drove the thirty minutes to the Sheriff Investigator's building.

He and Courtney went through the metal detectors and on up to the third floor, where a surprised Lotu came out to meet them in the reception area.

"Well, well. We can never get you to come down here when we ask, but now you just show up uninvited. You're lucky to catch me. I wouldn't usually be here on a Saturday afternoon, but my wife's away and I didn't feel like hanging out at home with the dog."

Emerson handed him a copy of the drawing.

"Oh yeah?" Lotu said, giving it a perfunctory glance. "This him?"

"Yes," Courtney answered, looking serious, seeming a little intimidated by this busy sheriff's office, and the detective that she had seen a few times, never in happy circumstances. Then she surprised Emerson by adding, "That's the bad man you should be looking for, not my dad."

"Courtney," he warned gently. Even though she had probably seen him be rude to the detective, he didn't want her to start being disrespectful.

But Lotu regarded her, kind and serious. "I will give this to the police detectives in Springfield," he told her. "Unfortunately, there's not a lot more I can do from here."

Courtney looked surprised. "But he's here!"

Emerson was startled.

"What do you mean? Have you seen him here?" he said, alarmed.

"No. But I dreamed he was here. I dreamed my mom told me."

Emerson looked at her, considering it. "It may be you dreamt that because you are afraid of him. That kind of thing can happen."

"It seemed like she was trying to tell me, so I'd know to be careful."

Lotu thought about it, apparently coming to his own conclusion about her statement that he didn't share.

"Okay, well, can I keep this?" he asked.

"Yes," Emerson said.

"Thank you," Lotu said, more to Courtney than to him. "I hope it helps catch a bad man."

Courtney nodded, and Emerson said, "Hope so." He guided her toward the door.

Back in Maddie's car, he said, "You didn't tell me about that dream."

"I forgot."

He knew the dream was probably just the subconscious churning through her memory, but he found her statement disquieting. What if this man was now in Denver? Was it possible that his hitting Courtney's mother was something more than an accident?

Lotu took the drawing back to his desk. He recognized Jean's work. She had done her usual good job, even using colored pencil to show the brown eyes and blotchy cheeks, square jaw and small, thin mouth. He thought about what the little girl had said about the killer being here. Unlike Sheen, who scoffed at such things, he took statements like that seriously. In fact, the older he got, the more he appreciated the superstitions of his Tongan grandparents. He, himself, had sometimes been walking toward danger, when something told him to stop. In fact, that little voice had saved his life more than once. So, when he looked at the drawing and thought about Courtney's assertion, he didn't wholly dismiss the idea that this fierce-faced man might possibly be in Creeley County.

~28~

Martin pressed the doorbell of the drab brick building, located off highway 285.

"Yes?" It was a woman's voice, muffled and crackly through the speaker.

"Hi, I'm here to discuss insurance inspections."

"Do you have an appointment?"

"I spoke to a gentleman last week, but I don't have his name," Martin lied.

"Hold on."

He waited for about three minutes. Then the voice came back. "Come in."

The door buzzed, and he entered a plain lobby.

A lock clicked in a door to the inner office, and an older man appeared, big-bellied, small-eyed, white-mustached, not smiling, dressed in a security uniform.

"What can I do for you?"

"How ya' doing? I'm Terrance Palumbo." Martin shook the man's hand and gave him a card. "I'm an independent insurance inspector. Just wondering, when was the last time you had an inspection?" He was friendly, non-threatening, but the man looked unsure.

"I don't usually set those up. The insurance company does that."

"Oh sure, no problem. But, what I mean is, I'm offering my services to do a preliminary inspection, prior to the one the insurance company does, and the code guys."

"Oh?"

"Yeah. The best organizations do this, hire their own inspector to identify any potential risks that could threaten their coverage, and fix them, independent of the insurance company. That way, there is never any risk of a coverage lapse, or any code violations."

He glanced around the room. It had little in the way of decor, apparently not a place that was set up for visitors. There was one attempt at decoration, a chair and small table holding a silk plant and a framed artist's print of a trout. He looked at the man's name badge, which said "Timothy Keefe."

His brain somehow associated that name and fishing. He looked at the man for a moment, then the memory came back. It was something local he had read.

"Keefe? Hey, you're not related to that fisherman, are you?"

The man's stiff demeanor relaxed, and he smiled. "No, but I fished against him."

"Yeah?"

"Yeah, up to the Three Lakes ice tournament. Granby."

"How'd you do?"

"I did okay. Pulled up a 2.8-pound Brown. Thought I'd get him." Keefe grinned, waiting for Martin's response.

"Yeah?"

"His was 2.9."

"No kidding." Martin laughed. "Well, I guess a Keefe won that day, anyway; that's what counts, right?"

"Yeah, the wrong Keefe," the guard said, laughing, loving telling the story to fresh ears.

"You should've shoved a couple sinkers in your fish, being that close." Martin pantomimed turning his back, as if he were sneaking weights into an imagined fish. "Who me? Oh, I'm not doing anything!"

They laughed.

"So, what do you have going on here? You should let me help with your insurance and code inspections. For instance, it looks like you could use a lighted exit sign over there."

Keefe looked above the door. "Oh, we're just a small place. We all know how to get out."

Martin kept smiling. "Well, you know OSHA might look at it differently, and there's the fire code. Want me to look around? I could give you a few tips. No charge. You're with a security company, right?"

"Yeah, we're part of Randall Securities. What we do here is monitor the surveillance systems for the public schools. We only have a few people working here."

"Oh, really? Are they working in partial darkness? There could be some special safety concerns with that. I can give you some tips, and then maybe you can put in a good word for me at your headquarters. You have a lot of locations, right? Plus, if you make some of the changes that I recommend, you could get some points for initiative. Maybe they'll give you recognition and an afternoon off to go fishing."

"I doubt it!" Keefe smiled. "Well, okay, why not?" He opened the inside door with his badge and let Martin in.

Martin stepped through with confidence and looked around. Two people were sitting in front of three, large, wall-mounted monitors, each of which was divided into multiple, small pictures. Signs above each monitor identified its location, "Graybill Middle," "Sentinel High," and "Eastwick Elementary." The latter was Courtney Crandall's school. Martin, who had seen many security systems, knew that the smaller screens showed the views of cameras in the three schools. The two women watching the monitors turned and said hello to him, watching him curiously.

"We don't need it to be too dark in here," the man said.

"Yes, I see. Even so, you might want to put some reflective tape here, on this step down, just to be sure it's noticeable if someone has to leave quickly."

"Oh, I see what you mean."

"This is very impressive," Martin said, nodding up at the

screens.

"Yes, this is the security center for all the southside schools, elementary, middle and high. We have over one hundred and forty cameras in the area schools. This center watches seventy-two of them."

"Wow, that's a lot for three people."

"Oh, not really, look. Each screen shows twelve camera locations at a time, then automatically scrolls to the next twelve. If we notice anything unusual at any of the locations, we can just hit that camera." He used a mouse, chose one of the small squares that showed some movement, clicked on it, and that camera's view enlarged. They had a good view of a hallway, lockers, and one male student hurrying down the corridor.

"I see." Martin was familiar with such set-ups. They were only as good as the people watching them. Anything could happen, if someone looked down to respond to a text, get a cup of coffee, or go to the restroom. And he couldn't imagine a more boring job. Any distraction would be a relief and cause a lack of focus.

He gazed at the elementary school for a few moments, checking the camera locations.

"Interesting," he said. "So, at this building you have good coverage, it looks like."

"It's excellent. Every hallway. Every entrance. It's a safe place for kids."

The man took his time pointing out the locations of the cameras in that school, clicking on a couple of them to show a closer view. Martin already knew there was no camera at the janitor's entrance, although there was one with a wide angle that covered the whole back of the building.

By the time he left, Martin felt satisfied. He knew what he had to do to avoid the cameras as much as possible, but part of it would be counting on the security personnel's not noticing his appearance on camera. With such small screens showing so much activity at so many schools, he was not worried. It was virtually impossible to watch all those shots at once, and simple human movement wouldn't necessarily cause concern.

He also left Keefe with advice for improvements in their facility in advance of an insurance or code inspection and let him know he was available for a full audit, if that ended up desirable, once he touched based with the higher-ups.

Of course, with that phony business card, Martin would never get such a call.

He hadn't decided if he was going to snatch her at school – he was a careful man and liked to evaluate all his options. He considered himself a master of planning every little detail. He knew it would be easiest to grab her from the babysitter's, but only if he didn't care that it was noticed right away. The babysitter would see him and immediately sound the alarm. That would be the way to go if he decided he wanted to kill the girl immediately and get away.

But, if he planned to keep her alive for a while, he would need more time. To get that time with her, he needed to grab her when the father would be away for a while, or asleep. Or in jail. Or dead. But facing Emerson Crandall in a battle was the most difficult option.

The most interesting challenge was taking her from the school. If he did it early, and planned it skillfully, it would be hours before anyone even knew she was missing. It was a challenge, but one he liked. There was very little he couldn't do and very few people he couldn't outsmart.

~29~

Sheen was sifting through pages of tips. These were coming in steadily now, and the deputies at the phones recorded them in a shared drive. Sheen preferred the printed page, so he sorted them by date every day and printed the new ones, further sorted into a binder, according to priority. Some he considered credible, and they went behind his "Follow up" tab. Some had shreds of possibility, and they went into the "Maybe" section. His final tab was labeled "Martians," which was his personal description for tips that were too far-out to merit further investigation.

Lotu was searching online for news and other reports of crimes that could be similar to this murder. The crime presented plenty of distinctive characteristics, and he thought he might be able to find something similar that could help them identify the killer.

His cell phone buzzed, and he recognized the medical examiner's number.

"Hey, Shelly," he said, making his voice purr a little. He always had a soft spot for Dr. Shelly LeMoix.

Sheen looked up at him and rolled his eyes, then made a "jerk off" motion with his hand. Lotu showed him his middle finger without taking his hand off the phone.

"Hey Lotu," she said. "How ya' doing, friend?"

"I'm doing just fine. How are you doing?"

"Just fine, thanks. I have some perplexing information about your dismembered victim."

"Really? Let's hear it."

"I have just been examining the cuts. As you know, her body experienced a multitude of them, to separate her head and legs, and to open her abdomen."

"Yeah."

"Well, the perplexing thing is, there is some variety in the cuts, and in the blades that made them. I see mostly deep, strong cuts, some with a knife, like a heavy, chef's knife that would be used for butchering beef or deer. Could be a hunting knife. I'm not sure yet. Another tool that was used for the strong cuts was a bone saw."

"That makes sense."

"It does. But what doesn't make sense is that there is also evidence of little, lighter cuts, made with a smaller blade, more like a paring knife. Some of the first cuts across the throat, for instance, were made by a smaller knife, and a weaker touch. Likewise, for some of the first cuts at the hips. Also, I believe the smaller knife was made to open the abdomen. Once that knife got through, though, the larger knife was applied, and it must be sharp, because a strong hand opened the abdomen with a single swipe."

Lotu was stunned silent for a moment.

"Are you telling me there were two people cutting this girl?"

"I think it's possible. I'm going to have Dr. Lee take a look. I want a second opinion on what I'm seeing." Dr. Lee usually worked the night shift, and he and Shelly frequently conferred on some of the odder cases. "I'll be wrapping my examination today, but I'll leave it open until he gets a chance to review."

"Okay, well, you just threw a major monkey wrench into my day."

"Sorry, Lotu!" She laughed lightly. "I calls 'em like I sees 'em."

"I know you do, and I appreciate it. Hey, you coming over this way any time soon?" He turned his back on Sheen. "We haven't seen you in a while."

"Next time I'm down that way, I'll make sure it's near midday, so you can buy me lunch."

"That's a date."

When he hung up, Sheen said, "Does your wife know you have

a crush on the ME?"

"No, and shut up. It's not a crush. Anyway, wait 'til you hear this."

He filled Sheen in on what Shelly had told him.

"I don't believe it," Sheen said immediately. "There's no way in hell two people did this. It's too specialized for two people to be doing it. It's the work of one, single, fucked-up psycho who has to do things a certain way. There's no way two people could share this particular whacked-out fetish, or that they could get along well enough to work together on it."

"Yeah," Lotu said. "But it definitely is strange, and it means we may have to look at this from a different perspective. We may be looking for two psychos. One strong and one weak."

"I know we have to," Sheen said. "But I'm telling you, two people could never work together on something like this. It's too far out there for two people to harmonize."

"Harmonize? That's a big word for you."

Sheen threw a pen at him, and they settled into silence, each puzzling over what they had learned.

~30~

"If this guy comes after us, what can I do to protect myself and Courtney?" Emerson asked Jeff.

The waitress, a plain, soft woman in her forties, set down his salad. It looked good, tuna and sesame seeds.

"What do you mean? Like, physically?" Jeff asked, digging into his own salad. The seared tuna with romaine and rice noodles was Jonas' Greens and Beans' specialty. Jeff had recommended it.

"Yes. What kind of self-defense is okay?"

"Well, hopefully you're delusional and nothing like that is going to happen," Jeff said. "At least, not until we get a 'not guilty' verdict."

"No, I'm serious. What can I do in Colorado that's legal?"

"You can't 'do' anything without risk. If someone comes after you, the only safe thing to do, both physically and legally, is to get away. You can use only enough force necessary to escape. So, if somebody grabs you, you can use enough force to get away, and when you do, you can't turn back and, for example, punch him out before you start running. The only place the law offers some protection is if you're under attack in your home and it's clear the only chance you have to protect yourself is to use deadly force. It's called the Make My Day law."

Emerson snorted a laugh.

"Seriously. That's what it's called. But it has to be inside your home, you have to believe the intruder is going to use force, and you must be acting in self-defense. No shots in the back, no shooting from a window into the yard, no shooting through a closed door."

"Good to know."

"Listen, Emerson. I know the label and the knife plants are threatening, but I think the stress of all this is getting to you. Try to forget the Kellerman situation and police accusations and stay focused on the trial. I know it's upsetting. It seems like a hit to me, and the killer is trying to pin it on you. I don't know what Kellerman was into that could've brought this on, and I don't care. Mainly, I don't want you getting so paranoid that I find out you put a hole in some poor delivery guy who shows up to bring you a package after dark. Do you have a gun?"

"No."

"Well, that's a good thing. Keep it that way. Your job as a father and my client is to stay focused on this trial, do everything I say and get exonerated. That's the best way you can protect your little girl."

"First of all, I'm not paranoid. Half the town hates me, and the other half only doesn't because they are waiting to see what happens in the trial. And second, I'm seriously worried. Somebody planted my name label in a murdered man's car. Somebody planted the murder weapon under the seat of my car, and he either did it when it was right outside my door or while it was impounded at the police lot. What kind of balls does that take? Not to mention that Courtney says this guy who killed her mother is in Denver. I'm not saying she's right, and I'm not saying he's coming for Courtney. But in case he is, I'd like to know what I can do to protect her."

"Well, now you know," Jeff said, apparently satisfied for the moment that his client wasn't going Rambo on him. "Now, can we refocus here? We need to form your statements."

Martin followed Emerson to Jonas' Greens and Beans. Even though he had started tailing Emerson, periodically, from almost his first day in Denver, he often grew distracted and let Emerson slip away while he focused on other business. For instance, today, at the restaurant, where Emerson was eating with his lawyer, Martin became absorbed in watching the waitress. She was older and a little doughy and plain. She served him, yes, but he couldn't help but notice that she served everyone else in her station first, and was slow to get to him, to take his order, bring his meal, check on him, bring the bill. And she didn't smile much, barely making eye contact.

So, she was another one who didn't think he was worth her time. And she, plain, almost unattractive. She had the nerve to think that he was beneath her? Meanwhile she chatted and flirted with the other men who came in. Regulars, probably, local workers and business people, even a couple of cops. Sure, with them, she smiled and moved her hips and breasts in suggestive ways, but she didn't even look at him. Another one who would be sorry, who would know that she was wrong, so wrong. He was far greater than those men in every way, except for the scars, the damned scars that made her not want to flirt with him. She was so shallow, she couldn't see beyond the scars. Well, she would find out.

He was so bothered by the waitress, he didn't notice when Emerson left.

Emerson stepped out of the restaurant, trying to feel optimistic by Jeff's encouragement on their position in the trial. Yes, the Crandall Resort was going down. But the good news was, according to Jeff anyway, it looked like Emerson might only be convicted on one charge of theft, at worst, which could mean a light sentence of a year or two, cut short by good behavior. Try as he might, Emerson couldn't internalize that latter part as good news, no matter what.

"Don't let it happen, okay?" he said, before heading out to meet Angela. They were going to get an ice cream cone, then, whatever. He thought he'd better not try to jump on her as soon as he saw her, because he liked her. He thought it might be possible to have a real relationship with her, and he worried she might just think all he cared about was sex.

But that thought disappeared when she started teasing him with the way she licked that ice cream cone.

This time, their love making was less frenzied. He was able to slow down and take the time to appreciate her finer points, like her breasts, lips and hips, and that neatly trimmed area between her legs.

~31~

Time to go for it.

Martin, wearing his slate gray coveralls and the fake ID badge on its orange lanyard, waited until the janitor was at his farthest point from the door – the metal can recycling bin. This week, it took the janitor as long as one minute and four seconds and as little as fifty-one seconds to dump the metal containers and go back inside. Ample time. Martin slipped from around the corner and stepped inside. Once in there, he settled between the furnace and wall to watch what the janitor did next. When he came inside, the janitor removed the rock from the door and pushed the empty recyclable containers to the wall nearby where he aligned them under their individual signs, "Metal," "Cardboard," "Glass." Then he filled his wheeled mop bucket with water from a wall spigot, took a string mop from its hanger, put the mop in the bucket and wheeled it out a door that led to the school hallway.

He gave the janitor two minutes, then slipped out. He put his head out the hallway door. No one was around. Aware of the security cameras, he had slicked his long bangs away from his forehead. It changed his appearance considerably, so if the security people he had visited saw him, they would probably not recognize him as the insurance inspector with the eccentric hairdo. He straightened his fake ID and stepped out with confidence, walking down the hallway as if he worked there, in his sensible, brown work shoes. He found an empty classroom and slipped inside. This room, a music room, was situated at a "T" intersection. He could see three hallways from here, the one to the office and two to the classrooms. Noting the security camera at this intersection, he walked a little way down the hall. He could see the next security camera. He went back to the door to Maintenance. Since the doorway was receded, he could stand inside it, out of sight of the cameras.

Okay, he could work with this. He was starting to like this option. It presented a challenge, one that he could conquer. Really, there was nothing he couldn't do.

Why didn't they see that?

That night, Martin waited until the doughy waitress opened her car door. He approached her, smiling, charming in the way he could appear.

"Sorry to startle you. I have a flat on my rental car. You don't happen to have a tire gauge?"

She was a little more suspicious than the last one, trying to get in her car quickly. He had to jump in on top of her, clapping one hand on her mouth, closing the crook of his other elbow around her throat. She struggled and was successful in holding the car horn down for about five seconds before he wrenched her away, closing her windpipe until she blacked out. Apparently, no one seemed to think the honking was unusual. He taped her up quickly, rolling her in the back seat, and drove out of there.

He had already checked the location of the parking lot security cameras and made sure they never saw his face.

~32~

Martin had let this one live a little longer than usual. Right now, her head was lolling to the side, her eyes glazed, but she was still alive. Her hands were taped to her naked body with duct tape that went around her torso. Her legs were chained to the strong, metal bolt he had screwed through the wall stud.

 He wondered if he should keep her alive until after he captured the little girl. He couldn't decide. He didn't feel he had to impress the little girl like he did the waitresses. She was too young to scorn him. His Sissy had never been scornful of him. She had always been nice to him. She was the only person who had always been nice to him. He would have done anything for her. Except that he couldn't protect his Sissy from him, that man. The time that she needed him the most, he couldn't help her. His mother's boyfriend was just too strong. There was nothing Martin could have done.

The memory came back vividly. He remembered the man hitting Sissy, her crying, his taking her into the bedroom. His mother had worked the late shift at the diner, but by then she was stoned, he remembered, just smiling from the couch in the living room like she was watching a funny movie. She was passed out by the time his sister started to scream.

Martin shook his head. That was his sister. She was different from the girl he needed to get. He had to make sure he kept the two distinct in his mind.

He was getting confused. He had never claimed two women in such close succession before. Usually, he took care of one and then relished in the memory of the act for a while before the urge started to build again. This time, however, with that girl out there, a threat, he felt the urge surging in him. It was there almost all the time, right under the surface, never resting. It was as though the concern that he might be identified had amplified everything. He hadn't even finished with this woman, and yet he was already feeling the kernel of hunger for the next one. He had to slow down, enjoy watching her realize that he was the one and only person she should have served, but that now it was too late. She would come to understand why she needed to suffer, to die.

He pulled a small paring knife from his tool box, removed its protective sleeve, laid it next to her. Sissy would be here soon. That was one of the best parts of all this. It gave him a chance to be with Sissy again. And when they were together at these times, she didn't yell at him, call him worthless. She would be happy.

She had come to him for a few months. At first, she just appeared in dreams, whispering about how these whores had to die. But that one night, when the urge overwhelmed him, and he knew he had to answer it, that's when he first saw her again, outside of his dreams.

When she had initially appeared, it was magical. He had hovered over the woman, a waitress from Milwaukee, holding his knife, ready to cut, but unsure where to start. He was feeling he needed to do more, to make this a work of art, and a message of pure superiority and dominance. Back then, the Milwaukee woman was freshly dead, bleeding out at the neck. It didn't seem quite right anymore, just cutting their throats, but he didn't know what to do to change it, improve his craft.

He had dropped the knife, pressing his face into his hands, when he felt the change. He could tell she was there, his Sissy. She was with him. He could feel her.

That night, she told him what to do: Cut the femoral arteries. Slice the throat. Get rid of the head. Tear open the abdomen. Then, she planted in his mind the idea of the doll.

That was his pattern from then on. It was perfect. Death

through the legs, like the blood a girl expels when she becomes a woman, something Sissy never had the chance to do. Remove the legs. Remove the head. Cut open the abdomen. And then, later, during the critical positioning phase of his work, insert the doll. The doll was their special secret, a tribute to the girl Sissy had been, and a reminder of the fact that it was her own mother who failed to let her experience the life she could have. Should have.

After the fifth one, he had started to cut the head in half. He had come up with that on his own that night, after Sissy had gone away. It just seemed right.

Now, in the cabin, he could feel her coming. Before he struck that first blow, he could feel her there. She seemed to approve, to tell him that now he had started, he must never stop. It was Sissy that helped him realize that this was his true mission. This is why he was here, why he did this. For Sissy. He had learned that taking them always let him be with her again. It made answering the urge so much sweeter.

He went across the room, where a case of water stayed cool in the corner. He plucked a bottle from it, carried it over to the waitress, opened it, dumped it on her head. She moved her head, eyelids fluttering. He stripped off his clothes and stood before her, turning slowly.

"Look at me." Her eyes flickered opened, then she closed them tight.

"You must look at me." He opened his razor knife, reached for her eyelid. He had never done this when one was still alive. She screamed through her gag as he sliced off her eyelid. Blood poured into her gaping eye, down her face, as he placed the eyelid on his tongue. He reached for the other one.

This Crandall girl, though, she was a danger to him. He couldn't forget that. He had to grab her soon. He wouldn't do to her what he did with these women, of course. She was just a kid, but he did have to stop her. And she wasn't his sister. He knew that, but he had to constantly remind himself. She wasn't his sister. He would never kill his sister.

He could feel her here now. She whispered to him. Tears slipped down his cheeks.

"Sissy!" He went to his knees, gripping a little paring knife. He hoped she wouldn't yell at him. She yelled at him more and more, telling him he was worthless and stupid. He couldn't bear it when she did that. To keep her calm and happy, he made cuts the way she would, if she had the knife, small ones, precise, but not always deep.

"Here. Watch me. I'll cut her for you."

He made a little cut across the woman's throat, just a little, shallow cut, but it drew blood. The woman protested weakly.

"Shut up," he snarled, punching her nose with his other hand. "Let us work."

She seemed to pass out, but it was hard to tell with those eyes.

He turned to the legs, laying the edge of the small blade on one hip.

"Yes, yes, right here, just where you like it," he said gently.

Finally, he went for the abdomen. The woman was mostly gone now.

"There you go, Sissy," he whispered. "For my Sissy."

After that deep stab into the gut, he sensed Sissy was leaving him.

"No!" he said, tears coming again. "Don't go, Sissy! Please!" But it was too late. She was gone.

"My Sissy," he whispered.

He couldn't hold it in any longer. Still on his knees, sobbing, he fell to his side. Curling his legs up, he held the little knife to his face, kissing it, holding its cold, wet blade against his cheek, rocking gently. He would finish this one off, soon enough, with his own, powerful cuts, his strength cutting through her neck, hips, gut, so easily. But for now, he just wanted to think of Sissy, his little Sissy, and these moments they shared. It was so special, just theirs, only them, together, on this mission.

He began to touch himself.

~33~

Social media exploded with the news of the missing waitress from Jonas' Greens and Beans, beating mainstream media by several hours. Emerson read the reports skeptically, not believing most of it until he saw it appear on Denver's primary newspaper's website. When it did, that evening, he read it closely, running a hand across his rough cheek, the beard now replaced with a day's worth of stubble. Her name was Rozzy Wirth, and she was a 42-year-old divorced mother of teenaged twins. He had, of course, been at that restaurant the day she was abducted, and he knew the detectives would be after him. He wasn't sure if she was the one who'd waited on him. She did look familiar, but the picture on the news showed her relaxed, smiling at home, not dressed for waitressing, so he couldn't be sure.

He wondered how high on the police list he was and was not happy when his phone rang, a little after nine, with an unidentified number.

"Hi, Emerson." It was Lotu.

Emerson glanced out the window and saw Lotu and Sheen standing by their car in front of the apartment. Lotu waved. He checked on Courtney, who was sound asleep, grabbed his coat and went outside. He didn't say hello.

"Care to get in?"

"No." It was freezing out, but he hoped that would help keep things short.

"Where'd you have lunch Tuesday?"

"Jonas Beans and Greens. I was waited on by a short, slightly heavy, white woman of about forty, long, light brown hair, plain looking. I had a chilled, rice noodle salad with tuna and diet soda. I was with my lawyer, Jeffrey Rossi, whom I'm about to call."

"Hey, now, we're just talking. But you can call him anytime you want, of course."

Emerson looked toward the house, wishing he had grabbed his hat, and stuck his hands in his jeans pockets to keep them warm.

"After that I met a friend at an ice cream place in Lakewood and went back to her house for the afternoon. Would you like to know what we did?"

"That's not necessary," Lotu said, smiling.

"Unless you killed someone," Sheen said.

Emerson tried to ignore him.

"But what's her name?" Lotu said.

"Angela Flores."

"Got her number?"

"I'm not the telephone company," he said, noting their annoyed surprise. "I don't hand out my friends' phone numbers. I picked up Courtney a little after three and was with her the rest of the day. After I got her to school this morning, I went to court and was there until four. Afterward, I picked her up at the babysitter and we came back here and have been here ever since."

Emerson used to spend so much time alone, something he enjoyed. Ever since Courtney showed up, solitude was hard to find. But right now, he was grateful for that.

Lotu blew on his hands. "You sure we can't get in the car?"

"I'm sure, unless you want to put me in custody."

"Angela Flores?" Sheen said suddenly. "Isn't that the waitress from Buck's Spot?"

Emerson remembered they had already questioned her once about him, to verify his whereabouts after Kellerman was killed.

He gave a short nod.

"You move fast, huh, Crandall?" Sheen said. "Spending the afternoon in a waitress's apartment? Interesting."

"Any law against that?"

"Are you really seeing her?" Lotu asked, a little too keen.

"You could call it that."

"This new?"

"You know the timeline about as well as I do," Emerson said. "You figure it out."

"You got a thing for waitresses, do you?" Sheen said.

Emerson started to snap out a sarcastic response, but then he heard Jeff's warning voice in his head.

"Anything else you want to ask me?" He cast a cool glance at Sheen. "Any real questions, I mean, that might actually help you find the missing woman?"

"Did you see anyone at the restaurant that might've been acting funny?" Lotu said. "Anyone who seemed out of place?"

Emerson had tried to remember this already, ever since he saw the first social media reports on the missing waitress.

"The place was packed. We had to wait to get a table for a couple minutes. There were a lot of business people in suits with big, wet overcoats." He remembered that the place had smelled of hot food and wet wool. "There were some people who looked like tourists, too, maybe skiers."

"Do you think you can describe any of them?"

"Come on, guys. Denver is famous for its downtown surveillance system. It will give you a lot better information than I can. I'm sure Jonas' has social media accounts all over the place, too. Check the crowd photos."

"You're right. We're getting the recording, but it would help if you could tell us if anyone stood out as being out of place, weird, unusual."

"Unfortunately, no. I didn't notice anyone. Like I said, the place was packed. It was crowded with all the people, the coats, every table full. Service was a little slow because of it, but everybody seemed fine. And I really didn't pay much attention. I was at one of the last tables, my back was to the rest of the place. I was either looking at my lawyer or out the window. And I don't usually study other people that closely."

But he was going to get in the habit of it now, he thought.

"Okay, Emerson," Lotu said. "Thanks for talking with us. We'll leave you alone."

Emerson started to leave.

"Oh, one more thing," Lotu said. "Where'd you have lunch today?"

"That hot dog place near the courthouse. The one that serves the elk meat hotdogs with cheddar and jalapeno."

"Jack's?"

"Yeah, I think that's the name. You can call my lawyer to be sure. He's the one who recommended it."

"We will."

They wouldn't, he knew. He turned and went back inside, glad they didn't call him back again.

The sky, a bloated gray and streaked with steel, portended snow.

The birders stayed back at first, viewing the sight without having to digest the detail. It was just a plop of wax, the palest blue against the crust of white. Here on the canyon ridge, the wind had worked the snow, and it formed drifts, some strong enough to walk on without breaking through. Mostly, the ground was bare, pebbled and weedy. The body no longer held the heat that would allow it to sink into a snowy cocoon; it lay starkly atop an icy drift as if on a porcelain plate.

Finally, they moved closer. The torso retained only its arms and breasts to give it shape. The arms were gracefully positioned at her sides. Without a head to hold up, the neck was a loose, ragged flap of skin. The legs were all wrong, resting along the body, framing the torso. The feet lay by the shoulders, the thighs roughly hacked off near their hips. The toenail polish was fuchsia, matching the fingernails.

The partial head teetered where it had landed, sawed roughly in half, its whitish pink insides oozing onto the icy surface, the dark hair a tangle.

This was the reality, but it didn't make sense. It was all mixed up.

Forty yards away, an elk stepped out of the trees and snorted, startling them, then trotted with heavy dignity across the plateau, carrying its horns gingerly, as though they might topple off his broad head.

They watched the animal, then turned and looked again. They moved away as if to run, but stopped and turned back, gazing longer. A full minute of silence passed as they stood, holding each other protectively, long enough to finally believe it was what they thought. Then they became animated again, discussing what they should do. They backed away. They went in closer and took a picture. The man kept his phone out, checking the cell, finding a good spot. He made the call. Then they moved further back, toward the road, to wait. Although it would be a while, they were tense, impatient.

The deputy who first arrived was young but carried the gravitas of competence. He stopped about twenty feet away, conscientious, preserving the scene. He made a call, started taking pictures.

As he moved closer, he scrutinized the repositioned corpse. He could see the purple where its back met the snow, where what little remaining blood pooled. What was left of the face was not young, not old. In its lax and flaccid state, he could see it bore papery lines that would never have a chance to deepen. The wide, staring eyes were brown. He felt sad for her, and for the relative – a sister? Mother? Husband? – who would have to identify the body.

~34~

Sheen walked the fifteenth potential witness from Jonas' Beans & Greens to the lobby. Number 15 was the woman who owned an organic vitamin store in downtown. Although she had eaten lunch at Jonas' the day of the abduction, she provided nothing of value, just like the fourteen before her.

"Who's next?" Lotu said.

"Martin Pulga, insurance inspector. He inspected the Salted Steak a day before the first one was abducted."

"Oh, back to the Salted Steak? Good. Something new," Lotu said, bored and frustrated. He slumped over his notes, doodling. They were doing what they had to, but it wasn't getting them anywhere.

But when this man walked in, Lotu looked at him with surprise and sat up. This guy was different. That hair style – — the fancy beard and carefully groomed bangs – — bordered on eccentric. There were still a fair number of beards among the Denver hipsters, but the trend was dying. Plus, this guy didn't look anything like a hipster in his cheap, dark suit and boring, department store tie. Except for the hair, he looked very much like Lotu would expect from a thirtyish, insurance inspector. Lotu looked at him closely and realized the hair was covering copious acne scars. Okay, at least there was a reason. Still, a lot of people would have just gone with the beard and not the bangs, which looked too young on this guy. Within all the hair, the dark brown eyes smiled out at him.

"Hello," Lotu said, introducing himself.

"Hello, I'm Martin Pulga." He had a good handshake.

"Please, sit down. Would you like a coffee?"

"No thanks. I have an appointment this afternoon, so I don't want to take too long." Pulga sat in the cheap plastic chair, his eyes roving over the papers on Lotu's desk.

"Oh? What sort of appointment?"

"I'm an inspector for Brick and Board," he said. The nationwide insurance company was well known. "I inspect businesses to make sure customers are meeting our requirements and the code regulations and notify my company and the business if they need to make corrections. And I inspect the premises of potential customers to determine if we want to insure them."

"Got it," Lotu said. "That a good job?"

"Oh, yes. It pays well, and I can get as much work as I want. It doesn't always make me the most popular guy, but I do my best to make the process go smoothly." Pulga smiled and chuckled a little bit. Lotu saw he would be able to make an irritated business owner feel at ease during the potentially aggravating process of an insurance inspection. But still, he sensed something a little off about the guy. The smile, the chuckle, there was something artificial about them.

"Do you live in the area?"

Pulga looked back at Lotu's desk, seemed to focus on something, then looked quickly back at Lotu.

"Yes, over in Lakewood."

Lotu glanced at his desk, and saw some of the clippings, notes and part of Emerson's composite drawing were visible. He casually turned over the top page on the pile nearest Pulga, straightening it, as though he were just neatening it without much thought. He didn't need this guy reading his notes.

"Lived here long?"

"I just moved here."

"Really? Well, then, welcome. What brings you to our area?"

"Thanks. I have allergies. The doctor recommended I try a drier climate."

"This is a good place for it. Would you mind if we copied your driver's license? It helps us keep all the people we've interviewed straight."

"I didn't bring it."

"Oh, okay. You know you can't drive here without one, right?"

"Of course. I took a cab here. I don't like to drive in unfamiliar places, so I often just take cabs."

"That's unusual, for a man to not carry a driver's license, even if he's not driving," Sheen said, conversationally. Lotu could tell he was becoming interested in this Pulga guy.

"Yeah, I know. I had pulled it out of my wallet, so I could fill out the paperwork for a new one, for Colorado, and then I forgot the darn thing back at my apartment."

"Oh, sure. I see." Lotu wrote "license," subtly on his notes, so he wouldn't forget to pull this guy's.

"Where did you move from?"

"Milwaukee." He was still smiling, friendly, but he said, "Would you mind asking me what you need to, so I can make sure I get to my appointment on time?"

"Of course, sorry about that," Lotu said, also smiling. "I'm like one of those hound dogs, following his nose. I just follow questions anywhere they go." This wasn't true, of course. He asked questions for a reason. "But we asked you here because you were at the Salted Steak on January thirteenth. Can you tell us about that?"

"Is this about that waitress, the one that was found outside of town?"

"Well, we're looking into several things," Lotu said.

"I see. I hope I can help. That was one of my first inspections here. I had just arrived in town and was running a little late for my appointment. I don't like that. It's not like me. I arrived there about two p.m. and met the owner, Mr. Waters. I started the inspection right away. The place is in good shape and I was able to complete everything by five."

"I'm glad to hear that. It's my favorite steak place."

"Yes, I heard it's good," Pulga said. "Too expensive for my

budget, though.”

“So, you didn’t eat there?”

“No. I don’t think that would be proper, anyway. I like to keep business separate. I mean, I might go back in the future, but not the same day. They might try to comp me, and that wouldn’t be kosher. That’s a conflict of interest. I’m very careful about following the rules.”

“Sure, I understand. Did you notice this woman while you were there?”

Lotu showed him a large photo of Sarah Miller. He and Sheen watched Pulga closely as he looked the picture over.

“No, I don’t think so.”

“Look again.”

“No, I don’t think I’ve seen her.”

“Not at the restaurant? Take your time.”

“No.”

“Okay.” Lotu left the photo on the table in front of Pulga. “What did you do after the inspection?”

“I went back to my hotel room and completed my report and sent it in.”

“Where did you eat?”

“I just grabbed a burger from Odiburger and brought it back to my room.”

“What time was that?”

“I don’t know exactly. Maybe six.”

“Anyone see you that night?”

“Not after I got to my room. I didn’t go back out.”

“Hotel?”

“It was the Economy Family Motel, by the airport. A dump.”

Lotu paused, taking notes, looked over at Sheen.

“Is that everything? I better get going.”

“Yeah, sure. Just tell me your address, in case we have to be in touch.”

Pulga gave them his Lakewood address. It sounded vaguely

familiar to Lotu, but that wasn't unusual.

"Thanks again for your cooperation. Is it okay if we call you, if we think of anything else?"

"Sure, no problem."

Sheen walked him out, came back, looked at Lotu.

"Yeah, I know. Weird guy."

It wasn't what the guy said, so much. In fact, he came off as charming and polite. But there was just something about his behavior, a steely deadness behind that charm. And the missing driver's license was too convenient. Then, there was that long beard. Lotu wished they had just a bit of Martin Pulga's DNA.

"I'll run him," Sheen said.

"Yeah, and just for fun, I think I'll drive over to the hotel later and see if they keep their security cameras in working order."

~35~

Martin walked into a different toy store this time, one big enough to carry the Tappitsee Dolls.

He was pleased at how well he had handled the police interview. It was obvious that they never suspected a thing. He did wish he had updated his driver's license faster. He didn't like to carry the one that showed how he looked back in Springfield, when the girl saw him. Like his old mug shot. But his explanation was perfectly reasonable, and he had thought it up so quickly. Always two steps ahead.

He found the right dolls and pulled one down, admiring it. It was far better than the other versions of the Tappitsee Dolls, the blonds, redheads, Asians, Hispanics, African Americans. The simple dark-haired one in the party dress was the perfect doll.

At the register, the sales clerk, a young woman who could have been anywhere between sixteen and twenty-five, paused before scanning it.

"This one!" she said. She looked up at Martin, appraised him briefly, as though trying to decide what she should say. "This one hasn't been as popular lately."

"Oh?" Martin said with keen interest. "Why?"

"It's the same one they found." She looked around, saw a couple of young kids, decided they were out of earshot, but lowered her voice anyway. "It's the one they found at the scene of that murder, stuffed inside the body."

Martin looked surprised. "Really?" He looked at the doll as though having second thoughts about it.

"Yup."

Martin pretended to decide. "Well, my Sissy won't have heard about that," he said. "This is the one she likes."

He already had his wallet out, and now he proffered the photo. "See? It even looks like her."

The clerk examined the photo for longer than expected, then looked up at him.

"That's your sister?"

"Mm-hmm."

"I can see the resemblance. "

He laughed and smiled. "Yeah, the poor kid. Everyone always said we looked a lot alike."

"Well, I hope she enjoys it," said the clerk, giving him an odd look.

"Thank you." He smiled at her. She smiled back.

He left the store and went to his car. Once inside, he opened the box, carefully removing the blue ribbon, cutting it in two with his knife, parting the doll's hair and tying it in pigtails.

With no other customers in her line, the clerk went to the window to watch him walk to his car. By the time he got there, he was too far away to see clearly, but she could swear she saw him opening the box.

She pulled out her phone and texted her friend. "OMG. Creepy guy just bought the murder doll."

The local waitresses were getting nervous, taking precautions. So, Martin had to up his game. When the waitress from Jack's drove away after her shift, he was already in the back seat. Her name was Sasha Kolomer and she was a college student, studying petroleum engineering. Martin couldn't have cared less about that. For his purposes, she barely registered as human.

~36~

The Nuggets were playing silently on TV as Emerson looked at the composite drawing, thinking about his next steps. The police were obviously not going to do anything with it. But if Courtney was correct, the man was in Denver, for some reason. Why would he be here? Was he even here? Courtney was obviously remembering things she hadn't before. But that didn't mean she was also experiencing some psychic phenomenon about his being in Denver. Still, the idea was upsetting.

His cell phone chirped. "Unknown Number" appeared on his screen, and he assumed it was Lotu. He touched the green "answer" button.

"Yeah," he said.

"Hi, baby." The voice was straining to reach a high pitch.

Emerson thought about hanging up, but before he could, the voice said, "I miss you, Emerson, my baby."

He couldn't tell if it was a man or woman, but his guess was it was a man imitating a woman, badly.

"Who is this?"

"This is your mommy, Kasa, baby. Don't you recognize me?"

Nonplussed, he started to disconnect the call, but heard, "Don't leave me again, Emerson. Why did you hurt me, Emerson? Why did you drive me to my death?"

This time he did hang up. He put the phone down and walked across the room quickly, distancing himself from it. Who in hell was that? What was going on? He felt more rattled than he should have from just a crank call.

Because it wasn't just a crank call. That person, probably a man, knew his name, his mother's name, and the fact that she had killed herself. Why on earth would someone assail him with this particularly mean, anonymous call? He sifted through the people who might want to do this, and while he dwelt on members of his father's family as possibilities, none of those he saw as a candidate was still alive. Maybe it was just some mean-spirited stranger who was following the trial and trolling Emerson. Although he wanted to just shake it off as nothing at all, the fact was the words burned into him like an electric prod, sizzling deep into one of his most vulnerable and protected places.

Courtney cried out in her sleep. He hurried into her room, pulled her gently to him and carried her out. She awoke.

"I saw him, that man," she mumbled. "There was blood."

"Shh," he said. "You're safe now." He sat on the couch, reached for the remote, put up the sound on the game so the room wasn't so quiet.

"But there was so much blood."

The poor kid. How often would she have to relive this memory, now that it had resurfaced? He couldn't imagine seeing his own mother killed like that. Courtney hadn't mentioned blood before, but he guessed there would have been plenty, when her mother was hit.

"Shh." He stroked her hair.

"But it was someone else," she said, not fully awake yet. "A lady." She was crying. "A lady and so much blood."

He figured it was just a nightmare, a fictional extension to a real memory. "Shh, it's okay now."

"No! I saw it." She was fully awake, looking at him urgently. "There was a lady, before he chased us. He was holding her, in a dark place, between the buildings, when we were lost. She was bleeding. And a bloody dragonfly."

"What do you mean? Is this real, Courtney? Are you sure it wasn't a nightmare?"

"No!" Her pale skin was streaked with tears, but she had

stopped crying, trying to get him to understand. "I think she was dead. I think he killed her. That's why he chased us. He knew we saw. That's why he hit my mom." Now the tears started again, so hard he wished he could take all that pain himself, if it would stop her from feeling it. "I'm so scared he's going to get us."

He held her and thought about what she said. Putting it together, it sounded like Courtney and her mother had somehow walked into a bad section of town, seen a man and a bloody woman in an alley, taken off running, chased by the man who was now in a car, and who hit her mother then sped off, leaving her on the brink of death, never to recover. And Courtney was left in a state of shock, memories creeping to the surface a year later.

He stared at the game without focusing. What was the truth and what wasn't? What if this guy was in Denver? A new urgency came over him, and he started to search the web.

He didn't find anything in the Springfield news or social media about an injured woman in an alley the night Courtney's mother was hit. But after some focused searching, he did find a report describing two teens discovering the body of an unidentified woman, stuffed in a refrigerator at the county landfill. She was too badly decomposed to determine the cause of death, but police identified her by her necklace. She was a runaway seventeen-year-old from Brownsburg, Indiana, who had recently started prostituting in Springfield, and she had been missing since roughly the time that Courtney's mother was killed. Locals speculated that the girl's pimp murdered and dumped her.

Police never connected the dead runaway with the hit and run. But had Courtney?

After his call with Emerson, Martin felt aroused. He didn't know why, and he didn't dwell on the reason. Something about imitating the dead mother of an unhappy man was just exciting. Maybe impersonating a woman turned him on. Maybe it was knowing that he'd hurt Emerson from a distance that did it. Maybe both. He didn't seek answers, he just enjoyed the feeling. Between that and the frightened waitress, taped up in the back seat, he was on top of the world.

Emerson knew the detectives would contact him, now that they'd found the second woman's body up near the trails where he had hit the hawk. He decided to save them the trouble and, the next morning before court, he went down to the investigation building.

When he walked into the third-floor reception area, Lotu and Sheen looked at him like cats that had found their mouse walking straight into their claws.

"Mr. Crandall! We were going to come see you. And you saved us the trouble."

"You've got to post that drawing."

"What drawing?"

"The composite sketch I gave you," said Emerson, exasperated that they seemed to have forgotten it again. "The man that Courtney said killed her mother in the hit-and-run."

"Why would we do that?" Lotu asked.

"She said he's here in Denver. If he is, someone might recognize him."

"Yeah, sure. Do you want the public to think we're crazy?" Sheen said. "We got no reason to think that guy even exists, let alone that he's in Denver. Didn't she have a dream or something?"

"Listen, last night Courtney regained another memory from that night. She said that before that man hit her mother with his car, they saw him in an alley with a bleeding woman."

Both detectives looked at him in mute surprise.

"Your daughter told you she saw the man who hit her mother with a car in an alley with a dead woman?" Lotu said.

"Maybe dead. Bleeding. Bits and pieces of that night have been coming back to her. She said she saw this guy in an alley with a lady who was bleeding. And look. This is from the Springfield newspaper. This girl went missing about the same time Courtney's mother was hit by the unidentified driver. They found her body at the landfill."

Now he even had Sheen's interest.

"She said he's here, in Denver. I keep wondering why she said that. I'm wondering if she saw him or something, without realizing it. I think you guys need to try to find him."

"How are we supposed to do that?" Sheen said.

"Use the drawing. Put it out on your website."

"And cause mass panic," Sheen said, but he took the article and started reading.

"Well, if he's the one who killed Annie, and he's here, you guys should be looking for him, especially considering this." He flicked the backside of the paper that Sheen was reading, making it snap loudly, surprising Sheen, who scowled at Emerson.

"What harm can publishing the drawing do?" Emerson said.

"I'll tell you what harm it can do," Lotu said. "We don't know anything about that Springfield situation. It would be irresponsible of us to release a drawing like that based on the description from the hazy memories of a little girl. You could find articles about dead prostitutes dumped in landfills in every state in the Union. The one you found near Springfield probably doesn't have anything to do with your daughter's dreams. We don't have any reason to think the guy who hit her mother is here, other than what you've told us, and you'll forgive me, but it's not much. Publishing that drawing would raise all kinds of false expectations in the public. It could be sending everyone on a wild goose chase. How'd you like to be some poor schlep that looks like that if we put out that drawing?"

"That poor schlep might be a killer."

"We'll consider it," Lotu said soothingly, and Emerson immediately knew that they wouldn't. "Now, why don't you have a seat? We wanted to ask you about a few things."

Emerson sat with a sigh. He could tell they weren't going to do anything with the drawing. Why had he bothered? It might be time to take matters into his own hands.

~37~

Lotu opened the email he'd received from Records. Well, well. Martin Pulga wasn't as squeaky clean as he presented himself. He was arrested on a battery charge in Dayton when he was twenty-three. It seemed he punched and strangled a prostitute over payment. She had him arrested, but the charges were reduced to solicitation of prostitution. Apparently, she left the area, because police couldn't locate her after her assault complaint. Lotu looked at the police photographs of the woman. She was young, with long dark hair and the sunken, jaundice pallor of an addict. The photos clearly showed the bruises on her face and neck. No one considered her disappearance unusual, back in Dayton. Addicts and sex workers were notoriously transient.

But still, where did she go? Why go through the risk of pressing charges, then disappear?

It was the photo of Martin himself that most interested Lotu. Without a beard and bangs, he was angular and hard, his bad complexion prominent, his neck short and strong. In the mug shot, the glowering heat of his expression showed a very different Pulga than the fussy insurance inspector they had met, with the eccentric hairdo. The two personas didn't match. That meant that what they saw was not necessarily the truth about Martin Pulga. He was someone who had more than one side. The one they had met was a friendly, responsible man with a good job and an apparent desire to please. But the other one, this dark counterpart, beat a prostitute in a squabble over money. When someone hid his dark side, it became harder to see what motivated him.

Sheen would argue that Emerson had a dark side too, as

evidenced by that rage they had witnessed. But a flash of unexpected fury wasn't the same as beating and strangling a woman. Emerson's record was clean. But besides the arrest, Lotu noticed that Martin was remanded to juvey when he was young. He would request those records, as well. He would also request that Martin come back in for a follow-up interview. And now, he had another face to look for in some of the recordings they had obtained during their investigation. Would he see Pulga in footage near Jonas' Beans and Greens, and Jack's Dogs? They already knew he visited the Salted Steak.

For now, he looked carefully at the photo of the old Martin Pulga. Maybe the real Martin Pulga. His face was familiar. But why?

He walked down the hall to the corner office, where his chief was reading something on his desktop. Lotu knocked twice on the doorframe, then stepped in.

"How's it going, Chief? Hey, I know staffing's tight, but I think it's time to put some additional night patrols on our restaurants – at least the ones where Emerson Crandall has eaten."

~38~

Emerson's neighbor, Mrs. Skate, looked through the peephole. She saw a workman with a spray tank waiting outside. She cracked the door.

"Yes?"

"Hi, I'm with Kelvin Pest Control. The building owner asked us to check for insects."

"Oh? Well, we don't have a problem with bugs."

"That's good, but one of the units reported roaches, so it's probably smart to have me do a little preventive spraying. This spray is organic, so it won't hurt people or pets."

She looked him over. His bearded face was badly scarred from acne, but he seemed friendly. His ID badge and company emblem were prominent, hanging from an orange lanyard that was bright against his slate gray coveralls.

"Well, okay, then, come on in."

"Thanks. If you can show me to the kitchen."

He chatted as he worked, talking about roaches and bed bugs and the like. She stayed with him, watching him spray here and there.

"That doesn't even have an odor," she observed, not realizing that Martin was just spraying water around the place. He didn't want to bother messing with actual chemicals for this reconnaissance trip.

"No, it's really good stuff. It won't bother you," he said. He finished quickly, then said goodbye. He went to Emerson's apartment next. It was locked, as he knew it would be, but he went around to the back and quickly opened the kitchen door, using a bump key. Picking locks was ridiculously easy. He slipped into the quiet, bright apartment and looked around, taking in the layout of the ground floor, then went upstairs. Emerson's room was first on the left. He skipped it and went to the little girl's. It had one window, about twenty feet up from the back alley. He noticed a small alarm device on it, which surprised him. The father was cautious. He debated for a moment, then removed the device and unlocked the window. He tested it. It slid opened easily, making a sucking, swishing noise. That probably couldn't be heard by a sleeping man. He opened the device and removed the batteries, then replaced them in the opposite direction, so the alarm would no longer work. This was risky, if the father noticed.

He went into the bathroom. This was the messiest room in the house, probably left in a hurry, its occupants rushing to get to school and court. There was an open bottle of kids' shampoo in the shower and one of men's body soap. Around the sink he saw a good quality, disposable razor and shaving cream, liquid soap, some barrettes, a hair brush. He picked up the brush and smelled it. It had a sweet, girlish sent that reminded him of Sissy. He pulled a couple of hairs from it and put one in his mouth, nibbling it.

He looked in the medicine cabinet and found little; a tube of antibiotic ointment, a small box of bandages. This place didn't feel like it was a real home, he noticed. Even this room didn't seem really lived in yet.

Satisfied that he understood what he might be facing should he choose this option, he went back downstairs, looking around.

He spotted a note on the refrigerator stating, "Babysitter," followed by a phone number. He added the number to his phone contacts, just in case. He then noticed a pile of papers on the kitchen table. Leafing through them, he found, to his horror, a drawing of his own face.

So, that's what he had seen on the detective's desk.

Martin's heart started pounding hard, causing blood to rush rhythmically through his ears in the quiet apartment. This was bad. It was very bad. He stepped to a wall mirror, held up the drawing. The artist had done a good job. Even with the beard covering the bottom half of his face, he was sure he could be identified by this picture. The girl had a phenomenal memory, he noted. Just like him. That's how Sissy would have been, too, if she had lived.

He wondered about the police detective with the drawing partly hidden on his desk. He remembered how he had adjusted his pile of papers to keep Martin from seeing them. Had they made the connection? Were they just toying with him? He had to make decisions, and fast. If this picture got out there, he would be recognized, quickly. Should he try changing his appearance again, or were the beard and bangs enough to stave off recognition?

He had planned to go through the pantomime of spraying other apartments, since he knew the old lady would be watching, but now he was so upset he just wanted to get away from there.

This was bad. It changed everything. He was out of time. He hated being rushed, but now he had no choice. He had to stop the girl before she could identify him, and then he had to get out of Denver.

"This is my last night shift for a while."

Angela used her fingernail to trace the swirl of dark hair around one of Emerson's nipples, kissed it and rolled onto her back. Her breasts were smooth and soft. He ran his hand over one of them in appreciation.

"Lucus was caught shoplifting last night," she said. "The police called me at work."

"Uh-oh."

"Yes. It's those so-called friends of his. They are a bad influence." She looked at the clock, sighed, rolled out from under the sheet. "So, I've decided to switch back to days, so I can be here after school and evenings. I have to help him refocus and make sure he's home, doing his homework, and not out stealing stuff from some crappy department store."

Emerson watched her round bottom jiggle slightly as she

walked toward the shower. If she switched to days, they would no longer be able to meet as easily, at least, for a while. He would either be in court or with Courtney, and she would be at work or with Lucus. He heard the shower start. Of course, he could get Mrs. Guevera to watch Courtney now and then, but she might not have an easy time finding help with a resentful seventeen-year-old.

He jumped up and slipped behind the shower curtain, sliding his hands over her flat, wet stomach and pulling her back into him so she could feel his growing arousal.

"Oh really?" she said, pressing back into him. "You're still hungry?"

"It might be my last meal for a while."

They made love in the soapy heat of the shower. Afterward, he used a big, white towel to dry her off, kissing the back of her neck, playfully tickling her ear with his tongue.

"To be honest, I sometimes lose my temper with him," she said, as they dressed. "I feel like I'm in a bad cycle, working during the times when he can get into trouble, then snapping at him for his stupid decisions. What else is a seventeen-year-old going to do? They all make bad decisions. That's why I have to be there."

She slid into a bright white bra and purple thong as he put his jeans back on, the damp towel still hanging around his neck.

"I feel like I just need to chill-out a little and be there, try to give him good guidance without being some evil authority or a best friend. I think he needs good parenting right now, and to do it, I have to be there. It's just so frustrating to always feel I'm chasing money just to keep us afloat, and then have him start doing these stupid things. I get so mad, but I have to stop being as big a jerk to him as he is being. I'm the grown-up, right?"

"Right," Emerson said, yanking his polo shirt over his head.

"Do you ever get mad like that, with Courtney?"

He looked out the window at the frosty street.

"No. Not with Courtney." It was true, he realized with relief.

Courtney was safe. His work on suppressing his rage had paid off so far, and she had never seen him flare up. To her, he was cheerful and warm, able to correct her with reason and kindness, and it was truly effortless, a testament to how well he had altered his tendency toward the fury that ravaged his early life.

He realized Angela was watching him. He turned and cocked an eyebrow, smiling.

"What?" he asked.

"I was just imagining you with your little girl. You are so sweet. I can't even imagine you losing your temper, not with anyone, let alone her."

He pulled her close and held her there, enjoying her soft warmth pressed against him, and knowing she would never realize how much her observation meant to him.

When he stepped out her front door, he did not notice the bearded man, seated in a dark car, parked across the street from Angela's apartment.

Angela pulled the ugly, maroon-colored dress over her head, then added the dark blue apron. She was expecting a busy night at work, thanks to both a university women's basketball tournament and an NBA game. Fans would be in town, hitting the diner before and after the games.

She stepped into the small living room of the tiny, two-bedroom apartment she shared with Lucus. He had arrived home from school about ten minutes after Emerson left and was now slumped in front of their laptop, focused on the screen. She was never subtle about examining what he was viewing online, and she looked over his shoulder. He shut the screen window quickly, but she caught a glimpse. It was a photo of a corpse, bloody, its stomach slashed open.

"What was that?" she said, shocked.

"Nothing." He was immediately defensive, shutting down.

"What was that?" She took him by the shoulder, making him look at her. He glanced up, then away, shrugging off her hand. His angry, dark eyes were cast down and the neatly shaped beard and mustache he was attempting to grow were sparse and patchy, betraying his youth.

"Cut it out. Nothing."

"Lucus, you tell me this minute what you were looking at."

He sighed, exaggeratedly. "It wasn't anything. Somebody leaked photos of the body they found over on the hill."

"Sarah Miller?" She felt her fury growing, tried to squelch it.

"Yeah."

"That isn't just a body. That is a dead woman. She had a name,

Sarah Miller. She had a life. She was a waitress, just like I am a waitress. She is not just some body for people to gape at, getting their kicks online."

"I know. I didn't mean it that way. Somebody just told me it was there, so I looked. It's not like I posted it."

He didn't look at her. She watched him for a moment, trying to calm down.

After a minute, she said, "Listen, Lucus. You have to be careful about things like this. People might start to become fascinated by the murderer. I think he probably gets off on that, on all the attention. He is a horrible, soulless person and he deserves to be despised, not to be the focus of everybody's attention."

He kept his head down.

"She wasn't just a hacked-up body. You think about how scared she was. Think about her family."

He glanced up, made eye contact for a moment, his face reddening slightly. She thought he might have understood. She was still upset but stopped talking. She'd let him think about it.

After a while, he said, "Mom? Are you afraid?"

She felt a wash of relief. She went to him, sat on the arm of his chair, draped her arm over his shoulder. She thought about the local frenzy over the murders. The whole city became fascinated and horrified by the discovery of the first corpse, especially when the rumors leaked about how it was mutilated and positioned. And that doll. It was all insane. Then, the second one was abducted, and her body found. Everyone in the area now focused on the news, waiting for updates.

When the third waitress disappeared after finishing her shift at Jack's Dogs, people really started getting scared, especially waitresses, and other shift workers. Police had increased patrols and warned them to be careful after dark, in empty parking lots and other desolate places. They also publicized what little footage was available of the man they believed abducted the second waitress from Jonas' Greens and Beans. The camera caught the waitress walking around the back of the restaurant, but her car was out of sight. Shortly thereafter, a man in the shadows crossed by the camera. It was impossible to identify him in the dark, pixilated footage, but it caused a collective chill in all late-night workers in the area.

"Yes, baby. I'm afraid."

"Do you want me to start picking you up?"

She was touched, and she felt a tear choke her throat shut for a moment. She swallowed and squeezed his shoulders. At last she said, "Thank you. But we are being safe. The other second shift waitress and I walk out together. We park under the lights, so we can see inside the cars and all around. We make sure we're locked in and safe before we drive away."

"Okay."

"Also, this is my last night shift for a while. I want to spend more time with you."

He sighed.

"Don't give me that. Shoplifting is enough reason."

"I told you." He was abruptly angry. "I didn't do that. It was Collin."

"Well, now you're stuck with me at night, so Collin can't get you in trouble."

She squeezed him again, then stood up. Time to go.

Customers filled all the booths that night at Buck's Spot. They even stood in a line, awaiting a table as long as forty-five minutes, during the height of the rush. Angela's section was filled from 4 to 7:30, then again after the basketball games, from 10 to midnight. She was so busy that she didn't really notice the single man who sat in a small, two-person booth near the counter. He had dark eyes, a sleek beard and bad skin, with long bangs spiked carefully down to his eyes. He seemed to watch every step she took. He wasn't friendly and had a bit of an attitude about the speed at which she served his meal, but she was going as fast as she could. He was trying to get a hot meal during the dessert rush. These were the worst kind, because she had to make the sundaes and milkshakes herself, and there was no way to do it fast. Just enough customers ordered hot food to prevent the cook from coming out to help. She and the other waitress, Dottie, had no choice but to muscle their way through, knowing it would end eventually. It meant low tips, because no one would be thrilled with the speed of service, no matter how sweet their smiles and apologies.

The grumpy, single man would just have to accept his fate, that he showed up at a bad time in an understaffed restaurant during a dessert rush. She kissed that tip goodbye altogether after noticing his expression when she finally brought him his hot roast beef sandwich with fries and gravy.

At last, the rush ended, and the third shift waitress showed up. Angela started her side work, filling salt and pepper shakers, ketchups, replacing mostly empty ice cream containers in the freezer up front. She sliced a new chocolate cake and set the pieces on small plates in a rotating, glass cooler, surreptitiously setting aside a slice to share with Dottie, for when they got a chance to sit down to roll silverware. Finally, the two of them sat in one of the now darkened dining sections and performed this task quickly, while chatting about the night and periodically forking sweet, frosting-heavy chocolate cake into their mouths. Inevitably, their conversation turned to the murders.

"They haven't found that woman yet, the one from Jack's," Dottie said.

"I pray for her," Angela said sadly.

"We'll walk out together," Dottie said, to reassure them, even though they both already knew the routine.

When they went out the back door, the cook was busy flipping eggs and French toast for a noisy table of tipsy college students. Angela and Dottie stayed together in the small parking lot, tucked in the rear of the restaurant, surrounded by trees and shrubs that shielded it from passersby. They called good-night and pulled out. But, before she got to the road, Angela realized her purse was still hanging behind the door of the employee's changing room. She backed up, stopped her car right outside the back door, put it in park with the engine still running and ran back inside. When she hurried back to the car, she didn't check the back seat.

Before she got it in gear, Martin leaned over the seat, clamped his hand over her mouth, closing his strong arm around her throat. She was unconscious before she could struggle.

~40~

Angela tried to fight as Martin dragged her from the car, but there was little she could do. Her feet were duct taped together and her hands were tightly bound behind her back. Once she succeeded in slipping out of his grasp, but she had no way to flee, and she fell into the snow.

"Cut it out," he said, and slapped her across the cheek. It hurt, shocking her. That slap told her he wasn't concerned about hurting her, not even giving it a single thought before he hit her, hard. Instead of causing her to stop fighting, though, the slap confirmed her fears. She knew who he was, and her only chance was to fight. She yanked away again, trying to get a good breath through her nose, since her mouth was taped. She fell on her side, straining against the tape, using her knees to push herself along.

Martin laughed harshly at her attempt.

"You look like a worm," he said. Then he broke her nose with his boot.

When she came-to, Angela's head pounded in pain. She couldn't remember where she was or how she got there. She lay on her side and realized her hands were taped down to her torso. Her ankles were still taped together. Her face was wet, maybe from saliva, and it hurt. As she regained awareness, she realized she was naked, lying on a hard, cold floor. She looked around, only with her eyes, because her head and neck hurt so much. Her vision was blurry. She saw she was in a rustic cabin. The walls were rough wood, the cross beams at the top were exposed and served as storage, holding tins and cans.

She moved her head slightly. What she saw next caused her to try to scream, but the tape over her mouth prevented it. She looked again, not sure she was really seeing it. It looked like the torso of a woman, bloodied, hacked and headless. The legs were cut off at the hips and were piled, together with the head, on the floor. Angela tried to scream again, tried to focus. The head was staring right at her, slack and pale. The eyes stared vacantly. Something was wrong with them. Then she realized it: No eyelids.

She now knew that some of the wetness she felt under her face was blood. It covered the floor where she was lying, along with other wet substances that she didn't want to think about.

She tried to get up, to move away. The pain in her head was intense.

"Don't bother," said a rough voice behind her. A boot pushed her in the back. "Just enjoy the view."

She lay still, her heart pounding. She was groggy, but terrified, and it was hard to breathe, with the tape on her mouth and her extremely painful, congested nose.

She heard the man walking behind her, now, back and forth. She heard him let out a strange, fretful, grunty whine. Then he started speaking.

"Get her," he snarled in a furious, guttural voice.

But then, another voice emerged from him, this one soft and gentle, childish.

"Sissy."

He appeared in her vision, lifting the severed head by the hair. She saw him carry it away, then, after a minute or so, she heard a hand saw.

Martin, naked except for his boots, barely noticed the new waitress on the floor. He was confused, divided on what to do next. He screwed the head tight in the vice and picked up the sharp bone saw. He was so upset, sawing through the head was easy, his adrenalin adding strength and fury to each stroke. When he finished, he loosened the vice and stuffed half the head in a black, plastic bag. He tossed the other half carelessly back on the floor, where it landed next to the other ones that had laid there, untouched, for several days. He then added the legs to the bag. He worked the torso into a second bag and made two fast trips to his car, putting the bags in his back seat.

He went back inside one more time and checked the new waitress's ties and the tape on her face. He added another strip of tape over her mouth and around the back of her head.

"You're staying here."

Finally, he rinsed his face and hands with bottled water and put on his clothes. He looked back at Angela.

"Shh," he said, then stomped out of the cabin. She heard a lock snap shut.

Things were just not right. He thought he would feel immense satisfaction at having Emerson's lover there, soon to experience his brilliance. But, he never had two women at one time. He was always methodical. He was good at making sure he finished one job before starting the next, at taking his time, savoring the whole process. Now, he had two. What if he mixed them up? It had to be just right. What was wrong with him? He wasn't even enjoying it.

He got in his car and started up the long, rough driveway as the first morning light turned everything gray. He had to get her. It was that girl that was messing him all up. He was consumed with the idea that she was going to identify him, at any time, soon. It could happen at any moment. She was ruining everything.

~41~

Jeff picked the restaurant, but he had never eaten there, so he couldn't have known how volatile the owner was. It was a small place, basically just a lunch counter for falafel, gyros and spanakopita. An old photo, on the wall near the register, showed a man shaking hands in front of a "Grand Opening" sign, together with that first dollar in a frame.

The same man now stood in front of them, older, scowling, his arms crossed over a round belly.

"Good afternoon," Jeff said, looking at him curiously.

Emerson had a bad feeling that he knew what was about to happen. It did.

"I won't serve him," the man said, his eyes shifting to Emerson then back to Jeff. "And if you're with him, I won't serve you."

Emerson felt his heart speed up, the blood quickly flushing his face red. The morning in court had gone badly for him, and this new agitation was impacting him more than it might have on a different day. Anger churned in his gut. He looked down and shut his eyes, taking a deep breath, forcing it back. Why was it appearing more often? A year ago, he would have shrugged this off so easily, laughed, teased the man, left the place. No big deal. People had their opinions and ignorance was rampant. Another shop owner would be happy to take their money.

But there it was, the fury, and the desire to unleash it. He tried to mentally seek a restful place, the deep woods on a steamy, summer afternoon, the buzz of a cicada — the sound of sunshine.

Jeff, unruffled and always ready for a debate, said keenly, "On what grounds are you refusing service?"

Emerson's attempt at calming himself wasn't working. Instead of going to his happy place, he imagined himself squeezing the man's neck until his face turned purple and his tongue and eyes popped out.

"On the grounds that I don't like cheats and I don't like murderers," said the man, his hairy arms crossed, old and pudgy, but determined, obviously a scrapper from way back.

So often, Emerson was able to imagine himself landing a blow on someone who agitated him, ending the thought with a smile, realigned and ready to be rational. But this time, he imagined himself hitting the man, again and again, watching his face turn into a bloody pulp at his hand.

"Well, since he's not cheating or killing anyone in your establishment, you don't have an actual reason to refuse service to him, and we'd like to order lunch," Jeff said, sitting on a round stool at the counter and starting to read the menu.

"Out," the man said.

Emerson stepped toward him. Jeff glanced up at him in surprise. When he saw Emerson's expression, he immediately jumped in front of him and put both hands on his shoulders.

"Let's go," he said.

But Emerson swiped his hands off him, still moving forward, his eyes fixed on the restaurant owner.

"Emerson!" Jeff said, grabbing his arm. Emerson shook him away like a bear shrugging off a wasp.

The restaurant owner looked surprised, a flash of fear crossing his face. But he uncrossed his arms and got ready. Another customer, a lean guy of about forty, who quietly observed the unfolding action, now stood and joined Jeff in front of Emerson.

"Easy, Mr. Crandall," he said calmly, resting a hand on Emerson's arm and letting his coat open to show a badge. "It's probably best to get out of here before you get arrested."

Emerson jerked his arm away, still focused on the restaurant owner.

"Emerson," Jeff said. "We're getting out of here, now. What's going to happen to Courtney if you get locked up again?"

The mention of Courtney caused Emerson to refocus on Jeff. Jeff didn't waste a second. He took Emerson's arm firmly and walked with him out the door and into the street.

Once down the sidewalk a few steps, Jeff said, "What in hell was that?"

Emerson drew a deep breath, let it out, leaned up against a building. He shut his eyes, opened them, looked at Jeff.

"I'm sorry."

"I never saw you like that."

Emerson didn't want to talk about it.

"It won't happen again," he said, feeling miserable, the adrenalin and dopamine from the rage now waning. "I'm really sorry, Jeff. Let's go to the hotdog place. That guy doesn't seem to have a problem with me."

Jeff didn't want to drop it. "Cripe, man. You were like the Hulk in there. I expected you to turn green and start jumping around in a pair of purple shorts."

Emerson snorted out a laugh, despite himself.

"'You wouldn't like me when I'm angry,'" he said.

"Yeah, no shit, Bruce Banner. You should channel that on the racquetball court. I wouldn't stand a chance."

"Thanks for the tip." They started down the sidewalk. "Do you think that plainclothes cop was following me?"

"Hope so. No better way to stop being a suspect."

They went into the hot dog place and had a filling lunch. But the incident weighed heavily on Emerson. He was afraid of what he might be turning into.

The woman in the picture was smiling, and it was her real smile, not the strained, fake one she sometimes pasted on for other photos. Holding her bright-eyed son appeared to be one of the few things that made Kasa Crandall truly happy. Emerson tried to feel comfort in that, but it brought all the guilt bubbling in his throat.

He decided to make the call. Although he had known she was out there, and even remembered her a little, he had avoided contacting his mother's best friend all these years. He was afraid of what she knew, of what she might tell him.

The phone rang, in a home somewhere near Seattle.

"Hello?" A woman's voice.

"Hi, this is Emerson Crandall. May I speak to Patty Mosher?"

There was a silence on the other end, the loaded type that filled him with dread and anticipation.

"Emerson. Wow."

"Hi Patty."

"Hi."

Another silence.

"I've been following your, uh, situation in Colorado."

He sighed. He knew she needed to hear the truth on this before she would talk to him.

"Yeah. Well, it's a terrible situation, and the press is enjoying painting me as a bad guy, but I'm not."

"Well, glad to hear it. I've kept an eye on you from a distance." She laughed self-consciously. "Kind of like a secret mother."

"You shouldn't have kept it a secret. I would've liked to know you sooner."

Another silence, so he went on.

"Anyway, even though I went to work with my father, I wasn't involved in any of the terrible things you've read about."

"I see."

"I didn't know what he was doing beyond what he presented to me, and it didn't include hurting people, using shoddy materials, all those things you've read."

"For your mother's sake, I believe you."

"Thank you." It was a bigger relief than he expected.

"So, what can I do for you?"

"Well, I have to ask you something. It's..." His breath caught unexpectedly, and he had to try again. "It's a big thing. But, I need to know. Did my mother say anything about why she did it?"

That full silence again.

"I mean," Emerson stumbled on. "I had been horrible, just before she left. I was really bad. And I broke a vase she really liked." He was alarmed to find himself choking up. And at how the words seemed to be those of a young boy, not the man Emerson had become.

"What on earth? Oh, no, Emerson! No!" She sounded shocked. "She loved you. You were everything to her. You could have done no wrong in her eyes."

"But she left." A tear leaked down his cheek, and he wiped it away. "She left, right after that."

"Oh, my lord." Realization sunk in for Patty, he could hear, and it was starting to for him, as well. "Have you been living with that idea all this time? Well, my love, let me help. That fear ends now."

"Really?"

"Your mother left because your father was a brute. He was cruel to her and to you. She knew she had to leave, so she could find a safe place, a place where she could bring you where he couldn't get to you, to either of you."

It made sense, but he was still surprised. "I didn't think of that."

"She was working with a lawyer, but your father cut her from their bank accounts and cancelled her credit cards. He told her that he would hire the best lawyers in the country and that she would never see you again."

Another tear fell, but this time, it was from relief. But a different kind of horror started to grip him. "Is that why..."

"She died?"

"She killed herself." It was still hard to imagine, to say the words.

There was another long pause.

"Emerson, I know that was the determination, but I was never wholly convinced that's what happened."

"What do you mean?"

"Yes, she was desperate. She knew he would be almost impossible to beat, but she was ready. She was determined to get you back from him and put the pieces in place so that you and she would never have to see him again."

"I had no idea."

"But that day, it's true, she had bad news from her lawyer. Your father had got hold of her mental health records. I knew about some of what went on back then, since a lot of it happened while we were roommates. She was wild at times, drugs, sex." She stopped. "I guess this must sound pretty strange, since she was your mother. Of course, not at that time."

"It's okay," he said, fascinated.

"She was a free spirit. And yes, she got into trouble with the law. And yes, she did attempt suicide in the past." Patty sighed. "But it was all part of Kasa being Kasa. She got mental help and it worked. She healed, graduated. She accepted a job at Cornell."

"What?"

"You didn't know? She was a scientist. She was going to research pathological biochemistry."

"No way." This was a shock. She had never had a career, that he remembered. The fact that she was once a scientist amazed and charmed him. It helped explain why he had chosen a career so different from his father's.

"It's true. But then she met Rexham, and things changed quickly." Her distaste was evident. "I actually lost touch with her not long after the wedding. He made sure of that. I believe he cut her off from anything she loved. At least, that's how it looked from my end."

"I believe it."

"Well, when she came here, it was just to get on her feet, to get away from him. Her plan was to get you, as I said. But that day, the day she died, he called and told her he was going to use everything against her, bring up her past, prove her unfit."

"Bastard."

"Yes. Well, she went out that day, and she was in a dark mood, there's no question. She was very upset. But I never thought she was upset enough to kill herself. I always thought it was an accident, or, well, I don't know."

"Or what?"

"Oh, it's probably completely wrong. But I never trusted Rexham. I wouldn't have put it past him to really hurt her. Like, permanently."

"Wow." He sat down. He tried to squelch his tears, but he could hear them in his voice.

"But let me tell you something. She loved you with all her heart. You literally could do no wrong in her mind. She wanted to spoil you until the end of time." A small laugh bubbled into Patty's firm tone. "So, you need to stop blaming yourself. If I had known you had that thought, I would've contacted you years ago. I just thought you were, well, you were with him."

"And just like him?"

"I was afraid of that, yes."

"Why wouldn't you think that? Sometimes I even think it, myself."

"I doubt it, now, after talking to you. I'm sorry I never reached out to you."

"What? You have nothing to be sorry about. It's just that I, I..." A little sob slipped through his words. Embarrassed, he forced it back. "I had been so mad. I was horrible. I was breaking things. I broke her vase." His words choked off again. He swallowed. "She was crying. I thought..." He couldn't finish.

"Oh, honey. You thought she left you over a little child's temper tantrum and a broken vase?"

Hearing those words made him realize how ludicrous it was. His mother wouldn't have left him over such a thing. No mother would. And now, hearing the truth, he realized that his fear, no, his certainty that his rage had driven her to leave and ultimately kill herself, was actually the very young and immature thought of a small boy. Back then, he had no way of understanding the complexities of his parents' struggles. But, because he never gained a greater understanding of what happened, that fear stayed with him, even as the rest of him grew and matured, amplifying and weighing him down as though he had thrown her over the cliff himself.

Now, it seemed so strange that his mother hadn't even mentioned his temper to Patty. Was it possible that it hadn't seemed abnormal to her? It occurred to him for the first time in his life that the rage he constantly suppressed, that he carried on his shoulders like a massive boulder, was, just possibly, not that aberrant. The revelation surprised him.

"She never even mentioned that vase," Patty added. "It wasn't important to her at all, obviously. You were important. She talked about you, how great you were, how kind and sweet and funny." He could tell Patty was crying, too. "She loved you with every cell, Emerson. I can tell you that as sure as there's a sun in the sky. Even though we don't see much of it, here in Seattle."

They both laughed, despite their tears. For him, the laughter came from his tremendous relief.

"It's a lot to hear," he said at last. "I think I need to go, to think about it. I can't thank you enough."

"You're welcome, Emerson. I only wish I had called you twenty years ago."

"You did nothing wrong. You've helped me, well, I can't even say how much you've helped me. Thanks again. Is it okay if I call you again? You know so much about her, and I know so little."

"Anytime. And if you are ever in Seattle, I'd love to meet you."

"I'd like that too. Well, thanks again."

When he hung up, he stayed seated, just thinking. A ray of light slipped across his face and into his eyes, the bright February sun tracing across the kitchen.

What he heard from Patty, and the relief it brought, were still sinking in. It would take time to fully integrate this new reality, but it was already helping. He stood up straight, and ascended the stairs, three at a time. He wanted to give his daughter a hug.

~42~

Sheen was finishing a list on the white board when Lotu joined him in the meeting room.

> *Kellerman*
> *Pro:*
> *Kellerman sues Emerson (motive)*
> *They have a public disagreement with threats (motive)*
> *Emerson's name badge in Kellerman's car (evidence)*
> *Murder weapon in Emerson's car (evidence)*
> *Con:*
> *Unidentified beard hair stuck on Kellerman's body*
> *Emerson's alibi solid*
> *Evidence too obvious – appears to be a plant*
>
> *Waitress Murders*
> *Pro:*
> *Murders start when he comes to area*
> *Has shown inappropriate violence (in interrogation and lunch counter)*
> *Appears covered in blood, after first murder and before body found, within a mile of body dump site*
> *Waitresses are abducted from restaurants where he ate (same day two times)*
> *Dates a waitress who is now missing.*
> *Injuries on bodies may be from two people, one strong, one weak. Maybe father and daughter?*
> *Con:*

No motive
No history of violence/arrests
Does not display typical personality disorders

Lotu read the lists, considering them carefully, as Sheen watched his face and waited.

"What lunch counter?"

"I told you. Churchman was in plain clothes. He helped stop Emerson from attacking the Greek guy in the restaurant."

"Oh, yeah." Lotu studied the board.

"That father/daughter comment is nuts."

"Yeah. I just threw it on there after it occurred to me. I don't really believe it."

Lotu thought about it. "I guess that video we got at Jonas' parking lot doesn't really come into play. It was too quick and dark, but it seemed like the guy was shorter and stockier than Emerson."

"I thought of that, but you really couldn't get anything from it. The long, heavy coat and hat, plus it was less than one second of footage."

Lotu continued considering the board.

"It's funny," he said at last. "If I weren't involved with these cases, I would look harder at Emerson for the waitress killings, based on your lists."

"That's what I'm saying."

"But you don't have a weighting on these facts. For instance, the unidentified beard hair gets a high weighting, with Kellerman. We know it's not Emerson's or Kellerman's. Take that plus the planted evidence and alibi, and I can't put that one on him, no matter that he has a motive."

"Yeah, I agree."

"The same goes for the waitress killings. The circumstances putting him near the waitresses – especially the dumping ground – seem fairly compelling, but his lack of a criminal history or a personality disorder outweigh that."

"He has shown some evidence of a personality disorder," Sheen said.

"Not the type of psychopathic shit we should be seeing. And I think we've pushed him enough to start seeing it, if it's there."

They studied the list in silence for a minute.

"So, tell me this," Sheen said. "Do you think there is enough on either of these to put the screws to him?"

"I'm not convinced, but I could go with trying to get more from him on the waitresses," Lotu said, with some reluctance.

"That's what I think, too," Sheen said.

Emerson heard a knock at the door. Courtney, watching television, yelled, "Daddy! Someone's at the door."

"Got it."

He went to the door and looked out the side window. Lotu and Sheen, this time with a uniformed woman standing behind them.

"Really?" he murmured to himself. So far, their showing up here had never resulted in anything good for him. Plus, they were not helping him, despite his requests about the composite drawing. He sighed and opened the door, stepping out and shutting it behind him. He just looked at them, waiting.

They looked back. They were looking at him differently, really looking hard. Their eyes went up and down his body, taking it in, lingering on his hands and throat. He frowned, waiting for their gaze to get back to his eyes. When they looked back at his face, he raised his eyebrows expectantly.

"Mr. Crandall," Lotu said. "We need to talk to you."

"I'm all ears."

"Can we come in?"

"My daughter is in there. She gets upset when she sees you, since you have a habit of taking me away, scaring her and generally disrupting her life."

"We brought Deputy Greene to help with your daughter," Lotu nodded at the deputy. She was dark-skinned, her black hair slicked back tightly under her deputy's hat, not a hair out of place. She nodded solemnly at him, her dark eyes guarded, but kind.

"What?" He was annoyed.

"Well, really, we need to take you to the station. We are providing Deputy Greene until your babysitter can arrive."

"What?" he said again, his heart beating harder. Deputy or not, leaving Courtney with this stranger for an unknown period was out of the question.

"Crandall," Sheen said suddenly, a challenge in his bloodshot gray eyes. "Your girlfriend is missing."

"Maddie?" he said, a bit of panic slipping into his voice.

"Who the hell is Maddie?" Sheen said. "We're talking about Angela Flores. The waitress from the Buck Stop."

Emerson leaned back against the door.

"It's him," he said, mostly to himself.

"Let's go. You can call the babysitter on the way and get her over here to replace Deputy Greene."

He did call Mrs. Guevera on the way, but not before sending Jeff a text.

"When did it happen?" he asked from the back seat. They didn't answer. Metal mesh separated him from them.

"What are you doing to find her?"

They said nothing. He hit the mesh with both palms.

"Cut it out," Sheen said.

"Tell me what's going on. Where is she?"

They said nothing, but led him to the familiar interrogation room, leaving him alone. This time, he was upset and not feeling at all cooperative. He was sweating, his heart still throbbing, worried mainly about Angela, but also about Courtney. He had to get her out of this city, out of this area. It wasn't good for her, what was happening here, what was happening to him. As soon as the criminal trial was over, they were leaving. He didn't know where. Anyplace but here.

Of course, that was assuming these two jamokes didn't throw him in jail.

Lotu and Sheen agreed that Lotu had to do the questioning, because he had a better relationship with Emerson. They were pretty sure Emerson would see through it if Sheen tried it. They had to bank on the small element of trust Emerson had in Lotu – that bit of trust Lotu was about to shatter.

"Ready?" Sheen asked.

Lotu grimaced and nodded, then reset his expression: Friendly, unassuming. They entered the room where Emerson was standing and glaring fixedly into the two-way mirror. There was no hint of movement behind it, but Lotu knew an officer had already started recording.

"Sit down, please, Emerson," Lotu said.

Emerson swung around, sighed deeply, slumped into one of the two, small, plastic chairs, running his hand slowly down his face. Lotu sat in the other one, moving it a bit closer to Emerson, but keeping a comfortable distance. There was no table between them, and the positioning was slightly awkward.

"So, here's the deal, Emerson. We need you to be honest with us about what you've been doing up in the canyon."

Emerson's expression changed to surprise. "The canyon? Why?"

"Just be honest with us. We know where you've been. What you've done. We know you must have a reason for it."

"What are you talking about?"

"You tell us, Emerson." Lotu kept his tone even and friendly.

"I have told you. I hike up there."

"Oh, sure. Hike. But that's not all, right?"

"Wrong. That's what I do."

Lotu inched his chair closer and Sheen stepped nearer to Emerson's side.

"Emerson, we have a witness."

They both watched his face keenly. They saw it go from confusion to guarded worry.

"A witness to what?"

"You tell us. You know as well as we do."

"No, I don't."

"It's a funny thing about the canyon. You feel like you're all alone up there, like you're the only person in the world. But in reality, there are people up there all the time. You might not see them, but they sure as hell saw you."

"Saw me what?"

Lotu was pretty sure it wasn't working. Emerson looked genuinely confused, a little angry. Lotu increased his intensity.

"Don't give me that, Crandall. You know damn well what."

It was the first time he'd ever raised his voice at Emerson, and Emerson showed the range of feelings Lotu expected: Anger, surprise, and was that a slight bit of fear? He kept the pressure on him.

"Come on, Emerson, you know what. Tell us what you were doing up there. We have a witness. They saw everything, so you might as well tell us. We just need you to fill in a couple details."

Emerson stood up abruptly. Sheen was ready, put a hand on his shoulder. "Sit down, Crandall." He pushed him back down, hard enough so Emerson could choose to fight or comply. After a moment, he chose to comply. At the same time, Lotu moved his chair closer, so they were inches apart, breaking all the rules of social distance.

"Come on, Emerson," he said. "We know what you did. We have evidence and a witness. You might as well admit it now."

"Admit what? Who is this witness? What did they say they saw?"

"You tell us. We already know. We know when you were at the restaurant, how you got her in the car. Shoot, we have half of it on tape. But we need a few details from you."

"I don't know what you're talking about."

"Yes, you do! Don't lie to us Emerson. We know everything you did up there, where you went, where you did it and what you did with the body." He was shouting, inches from Emerson's astonished face.

Emerson turned red from his neck to his forehead. His dark blue eyes showed shock, but also fear. Sheen and Lotu waited, the tense seconds silently ticking. Lotu's phone sounded, and he glanced at it.

"I have to take this, Emerson," he said. "It's our witness, the one who saw you up there. He said he was going to check his phone for photos. He's pretty sure he has one showing you up there, with her."

"Whoever it is, he's lying."

Lotu stood up. "Well, before we take a quick break, you tell me this: Why is Sarah Miller's blood in your car?"

Emerson stared at him, shocked. Lotu and Sheen left, going immediately to the observation room.

"What do you think?" Sheen said, quietly, as they watched him.

Emerson paced the room, his long legs taking him quickly from one side to the other. Usually interested in the mirror and who was behind it, this time he completely avoided it, running his hands through his dark hair. He was keyed up, no question. He checked his phone. He had not yet received a response from his lawyer, they knew, so this was their last chance.

"I can't tell," Lotu said.

"Are you kidding? Look at him. He's showing all the signs."

"My face would probably turn red and I'd be afraid if cops were saying these things to me, too. And look at him pace. I can guarantee you, he's not thinking up a story."

Sheen looked at Emerson glumly as Lotu's phone rang. It was Deputy Greene's number.

"Lotu."

"Hello, Sergeant. I just wanted to let you know something. I'm not saying it's anything, but I noticed one of those dolls at Emerson Crandall's place. I'm pretty sure it's the same one we've been seeing in the bodies of the murdered women."

"Really? Interesting."

"Of course, it was just an observation. I mean, we don't have a search warrant. But it's still in the box. Doesn't that seem a little strange, considering he has a daughter who would probably like to play with it?"

"Yeah, okay. Thanks for letting me know. You still there?"

"No, the babysitter arrived a few minutes ago."

"Alright, well, thanks for the call. Good observation."

He hung up and told Sheen about the doll.

"Add that one to my list," Sheen said.

"I bet there are a lot of those dolls in the homes of seven-year-old girls."

"Hah. Not in Creeley County. Anyone who buys that for their daughter now is automatically a sicko."

They thought about this as they watched Emerson, giving him a few more minutes to dwell on their questions, then went back inside.

"Here you go, Emerson.," Lotu handed him a cup of water and pulled up his chair. "Have a seat. We still need to talk to you."

Emerson took the water, drank it. He sat down and started tearing the paper cup into small pieces.

"Well, what do you say? How'd it get there? How'd her blood get in your car?" Lotu had no friendliness now.

"If it's there, it's a plant. Just like the label. Just like the knife."

"Oh, come on! We found it on the steering wheel. There are bloody fingerprints there."

Emerson just looked at him in confusion. "It's the hawk."

"It's not a hawk!" Lotu said loudly, with annoyance. "It's your fingerprints, Emerson. It's your fingerprints, clear as day, in that poor girl's blood."

"No."

"Yes."

Emerson crumpled the remains of the cup. It looked like he was shutting down.

"Where is she, Emerson? Come on, it's not too late. Tell us where Angela is. If she's still alive and you help us, it will go easier for you. We can help you. It's not too late." He softened his tone. "Come on, buddy. We know you didn't mean it. Sometimes, things just happen. Women, they'll get you all turned around, won't they? Just let us know where she is. We can help you out, if you just tell us where she is."

Worry crossed Emerson's face. His phone dinged. He looked at it.

"Put your phone down," Lotu said firmly.

Emerson read the phone, then looked at Lotu with a changed expression.

Lotu amped it back up. "Come on, Emerson. How do you explain it? How did her blood get in your car? How did your fingerprints, covered in Sarah Miller's blood, end up on that steering wheel? Where is Angela Flores?"

Emerson said nothing, just looked at Lotu with his mouth shut, his lips a thin line.

"Come on, Crandall. It's not going to help you to clam up now," Sheen said.

Lotu kept it up, questioning intensely, but Emerson said no more until there was a knock at the door, about thirty minutes later.

Lotu answered it and a woman on the other side said something quietly to him. Emerson glanced at Sheen, a tiny bit of satisfaction in his otherwise unhappy expression. Lotu mumbled to the woman and came back to his chair. He sat down heavily, looking annoyed, glancing at Sheen.

"Lawyer's here?" Sheen asked. Lotu nodded.

Jeff was shown in by the same woman.

"Detectives!" he said warmly. He was wearing a pair of khakis and a yellow polo shirt. "How nice to see you. Did you read him his rights?"

"He's not under arrest," Lotu said. "He's free to go."

"Oh really? It doesn't feel that way," Emerson said, standing up.

"We haven't arrested you at any point during any of our conversations," Lotu said. "Well, except for that assault, but as you know, we dropped those charges. Felony assault on an officer," he clarified, looking pointedly at Jeff.

"I didn't assault anyone. I tripped, and you guys went bananas," Emerson snapped.

Jeff touched Emerson's arm lightly, letting him know he should shut up, so he did.

"If my client is not under arrest, we'll go," Jeff said. "However, I would like to know why you're questioning him, and if it's in relation to a crime, what reason you have to question him in connection with it."

"We have reason to believe he spent a lot of time with a particular woman yesterday. A woman who is now missing," Lotu said. "She's a waitress, and we're concerned that she's been abducted by the same person who killed and mutilated two other waitresses and possibly abducted a third woman who's still missing."

Jeff looked at Emerson sharply. Emerson, still shocked by the interrogation, just looked back with a stunned expression.

"Read him his rights or we'll be going."

"We just need to know his timeline yesterday. We're not trying to pin anything on him. A woman is missing, and we want to know what he knows about her activities yesterday, whether he saw anything that could help us."

"I need to speak to my client alone."

The detectives looked irritable, starting to leave.

"If you don't mind, I'd like to speak to him in a room that

doesn't have a camera focused on him," Jeff said, nodding at the mirror. They led Emerson and Jeff across the hall, to a simple, little box of a room with a window and no mirrors.

As soon as the door shut, Emerson said, "They said they have my fingerprints in my car with Sarah Miller's blood on them! They said they have witnesses who saw me up in the canyon doing something."

Jeff looked mildly surprised, but only for a moment. Then he shook his head slightly. "They're lying, Emerson. Don't worry about it."

"What?" Emerson was startled, an emotion that quickly morphed into indignation. "Lying? They can't lie about something like that."

"They can lie about anything they want. They do it all the time." Jeff waited for this to sink in.

After thinking about it for a minute, Emerson heaved a big sigh. He rubbed his hands down his face, shook his head in disbelief. Finally, he looked up at Jeff, red-eyed and exhausted, and said, "I want to sue them. No, I want to punch them, but I'll settle for suing them."

Jeff chuckled. "One lawsuit at a time. Tell me about this waitress from yesterday. Did you spend time with her?"

Emerson filled Jeff in on his relationship with Angela.

When he was done, Jeff said, "Okay, well for now, we won't talk to them anymore. They don't have anything on you or they would've read you your rights. They're just on a fishing trip, hoping you'll say something that will either make you a real suspect or help them find her. It doesn't sound like you can help on that, since the last people to see her would've been the diners at the restaurant and her coworkers."

They called the detectives back in.

"My client has nothing to say," Jeff told them. "If you want to interrogate him, read him his rights."

Lotu sighed. "I'm very disappointed that he doesn't want to help find Miss Flores," he said, giving Emerson a reproachful expression that made Emerson feel terrible. He did want to help find Angela, but he trusted Jeff. And he no longer trusted Lotu, at all.

He just wanted to get out of Denver. But now, beside finishing the criminal trial, he was torn with anxiety about Angela.

~43~

Emerson was at the courthouse early the next morning. Jeff had rested the defense three days ago, and he and Jeff – along with the rest of Creeley County – were awaiting the jury verdict. It was taking longer than anyone expected, something Jeff assured him was a good sign.

"The longer it takes, the better it is for the defense," he said. "They may only nail you with one of the lesser charges, if any."

Emerson hadn't slept much and was exhausted. He had tracked down Angela's sister and asked if he could help, but she was cool toward him. He realized he didn't know enough about Angela to effectively help her family, anyway. It frustrated him, knowing she was out there somewhere, and he didn't know where to start looking to try to find her. Now, he was trapped at the courthouse, just waiting. His agitation was almost unbearable.

He couldn't help her from here, and his fear for her kept him in a state of constant tension. Not to mention that, despite his exhaustion, or maybe because of it, he dwelt on the idea that the man who killed Courtney's mother was still on the loose, and his daughter was having recurring dreams about him that terrified her, making her believe he was in Denver. Since the police weren't helping him at all on this topic, he decided he needed to push it further, on his own. Emerson wanted the guy found, and if he was in Denver, he wanted to get him off the street in case he was here to hurt Courtney.

His finger hovered over the website's "Post" button. He proofread his social media post one more time.

"Have you seen this man? He is wanted by police in a fatal hit-and-run incident in Springfield, Ohio, that left a young mother dead.

He may have moved to the Denver area. Contact me or the police if you have seen him."

He had already uploaded the photo of the drawing. He was ready to post on every one of Denver's news sites, as well as online community bulletin boards. He was trying to figure out what as-of-yet unknown consequences he would face for posting this, trying to decide if any of them were bad enough to keep him from hitting "enter." One was that Lotu and Sheen would be ticked off at him. They might even be able to charge him with something for doing it. But he doubted they would go to that extent, since they seemed keen to nail him for the waitress murders.

How could they possibly think Emerson could even kill someone, let alone kidnap, torture? The concept was so repellant to Emerson that he felt indignant they could even think it for a moment. However, he knew the detectives had seen that dark flash in Emerson, and he was sure that plain-clothes officer who saw him lose his temper in the restaurant had reported back to Lotu and Sheen. Maybe that's all it took to convince them that Emerson could kill someone. Even Emerson was afraid of that darkness within him.

He decided it was worth annoying the detectives to post this guy's face. If he had, at a minimum, killed Courtney's mother, it was worth finding him. If he was also possibly looking for Courtney, it was even more important to find him.

He tapped "Post," and let it loose.

Lala Orchard was playing a word game on her laptop with her granddaughter, who was home sick from school. She enjoyed it, especially because she and her granddaughter could "comment" back and forth to each other during the game. Mrs. Orchard had not fully embraced all the internet had to offer, but as her children and grandchildren showed her more of its uses, she gradually came to appreciate certain parts of it.

She could hear Martin downstairs, his heavy steps rattling the house slightly. He was an easy tenant so far, since he spent a lot of time at work or away. He had hurried through the front door a little while ago, a plastic grocery bag in his hand, not looking at her as he went by. He was usually charming, making sure that he stopped to politely ask her how she was, but this time he seemed upset, intent upon his task, whatever it was. Next, she heard him in the shower, then moving around the basement.

As she waited for Jasmine to take her turn, she opened the social media site her grandchildren had shown her. She followed several news stations on there. She was surprised to see a drawing of a man that looked a lot like Martin. She read the post carefully, noticing with shock that it was posted by Emerson Crandall himself, the man she had thrown out. The one who was about to learn if he would be found guilty in the trial against his father's company.

As she studied the photo and read the reason Emerson posted it, part of her attention now shifted to the lack of sounds from Martin, downstairs. After all his activity, he had grown silent.

There was no doubt about it. If you took off the beard and shortened his hair, that picture was a match for her tenant, right down to the acne scars. She did not want to contact the media, and she didn't trust the police. Contacting Emerson was out of the question. Instead, she hit the call button on her laptop, video-calling her granddaughter, a feature of the game.

"Hi, Nana!" She saw the lovely face of her thirteen-year-old Jasmine in a little window that appeared in a corner of the screen.

"Hello, baby."

"What's up? Calling to congratulate me because I'm winning? Or maybe, some trash talk?"

"No, honey. I'm wondering, is your daddy there?"

"Oh, I'll check. Is everything okay?"

"Yes, I just want to talk to him for a minute. I need to ask him about something." Mrs. Orchard regarded the intelligent, calm face of her granddaughter. "It's just, my tenant looks like the man they're showing on the news."

"What man?" Jasmine said. But as she saw the concern on her grandmother's face, she quickly said, "Okay, I'll get Daddy."

Just then, Mrs. Orchard heard something behind her. She turned slowly, almost afraid to look. Martin stood there, but he had changed. He had dyed his dark hair blond, but it was more than that. He had shaved his head high on either side, leaving only a strip of long, almost-white hair down the center, not quite a mohawk, but close. Weirdly, he had also shaved off his dark eyebrows, and the skin under them was lighter than the rest of his face, a crazy, clownish effect. He was wearing gray coveralls and an orange lanyard with an ID badge hung around his neck.

"Martin! What have you done?"

"What were you looking at?"

"What? I'm just playing a game with my granddaughter."

"Before that!" he yelled. He started to reach for the laptop when the face of her granddaughter reappeared.

"He's not here," Jasmine said, but then her face registered astonishment as she saw the strange man standing next to her grandmother. Martin immediately shut the video window and opened the social media news. He looked at the composite picture for a long time, as the laptop started ringing. "Jasmine calling" showed up in the corner of the screen.

"Martin, stop it. Let me answer that call."

But in one swift movement, he slammed the laptop closed and swung it around, hitting Mrs. Orchard solidly on the side of her head. She fell to the floor with the blow. He felt no pleasure in hitting her, but neither did he feel remorse. He smashed the laptop against the corner of the desk, dropped it and fled.

His window of opportunity to grab the girl was closing, and he had to hurry.

~44~

Lotu and Sheen were at their desks. Sheen was reviewing the forensic detective's initial report on the second body. Lotu was skimming video. Carlton, one of the police clerks, approached.

"Hey," Lotu said.

"How's it going?"

"What's up?"

"Well, I don't know if this is anything, but I took a call today from a woman who works at the toy store over on East."

"Yeah?"

"She said a guy came through her line to buy that doll, the same one you found with both bodies."

Lotu just looked at him. He didn't need to say it wasn't against the law to buy a doll.

"The thing was, she said the guy had a creepy vibe. I know it doesn't sound like anything, but I just thought I'd tell you. She said that she mentioned to the customer that the doll was the same one they had found with the body, and he just said that was the one he wanted, because it looked like his sister, and she would want it."

Sheen came over, listening.

"Yeah?" Lotu said. "So far, it just sounds like another random tip from someone with a good imagination."

"I know, but then she said he pulled out a photo of his sister to show her, and when she looked at it, she could tell it was old.. It was an actual, old-fashioned, developed photo, it was yellowed, and the whole scene looked old, the rug, the paneling. She said it all looked like it came from a different decade."

Lotu looked at him, this bit of information starting to sink in.

"The clerk said that there was no way the person in the photo was still a little girl. She would have to be an adult by now."

"So," Lotu said, almost to himself. "Why would he be buying her a doll?"

"Right," said Carlton.

"See if they have any video of him. Or a credit card."

"On it."

"Check this out," Lotu said.

Sheen looked over his shoulder at the video.

"Crandall and Kellerman outside the courtroom." Sheen recognized it. "So?"

"Check out the guy on the bench, looking at his phone."

"Can't see him too well. Oh, wait."

The man in the recording looked up briefly, then back down.

"No kidding," Sheen said, shocked. "Is that...?"

"Let's get Pulga back in here," Lotu said.

Martin went straight to Courtney's elementary school. As soon as the janitor had started out toward the bins, Martin slipped inside. He found the empty music room and, using the landline there, called Courtney's babysitter. He knew the caller ID at her end would show the school's number. On his cell phone, he was already prepared with the sound of school children that he had pulled from a random, online video, to make it hard for her to hear.

"Hello?" Mrs. Guevera said.

"Hi, it's Emerson."

"Oh, hello! It's hard to hear you."

"Sorry, I'm at Courtney's school, outside the gym. My phone died. They're getting ready for an assembly. I'm going to go to her spring concert then take her home."

"Oh, did court get out early?"

"Yeah, still waiting on a verdict."

"Okay."

"Talk to you later."

He then used a burner cell phone to call the school office. The number couldn't be traced to him.

"Eastwick Elementary."

"Hi, this is Emerson Crandall. I need to speak to Courtney. Can you bring her to the phone?"

"Is it an emergency, Mr. Crandall? We don't like to disturb them otherwise, but I could bring her a message."

"Yes. It's important that I speak to her."

"Okay, hold on for a few minutes while I locate her classroom and ask the teacher to send her to the office." The woman sounded put out by this simple request.

"Thank you." Bitch.

Martin needed this interaction to ensure the school wouldn't notice her missing. He slipped out from the empty music room and stood where he could see the office, as well as down two hallways. It wasn't long before he saw her coming. He stepped back into the room, waiting until she passed.

Courtney was feeling proud. Her teacher let her walk to the office by herself. That was a big deal for a second grader. Usually, a teacher went with them, not because it was a rule – it wasn't – but because some of the second graders had trouble getting places by themselves. When she got there, the secretary, who had watched her progress on the school video surveillance system, handed her the phone.

"Hello?"

"Hi Courtney, it's Jeff, your daddy's lawyer. Your daddy had to go back into court for a second and asked me to talk to you."

"Okay."

"He's going to pick you up early, today, okay? He'll be there soon."

"Okay."

"Okay then, you can put the school lady back on and go back to your classroom."

"Okay."

Courtney handed the phone to the school secretary and started to leave the office. She heard the secretary saying, "Okay then. Just a few minutes? Right."

Courtney walked out of the office. She was happy that her father was going to pick her up early, but also concerned, because she had a spelling quiz later. What would happen if she missed it? She turned the corner, into the hall that led back to her classroom. She didn't notice the shadowed figure, hiding in a dark doorway.

Suddenly, she was lifted in the air. Someone's hand was over her mouth and she was carried quickly down the hall, into the dark janitor's area where the furnaces were, and out the back door.

The school secretary was not watching the surveillance video at that moment. The security guard in the lobby, who had access to all the school's surveillance screens at the same time, was playing a game on his phone. Back at the Randall Security Company, the employees were watching lines of students change classes at the high and middle schools. No one saw the kidnapping, although one of the cameras recorded it.

Within a couple of minutes, the man who had taken her had taped her mouth shut, taped her wrists behind her back and her feet together and put a dark patch of some sort over her eyes. He set her in the back seat and put a blanket over her. Courtney couldn't scream. It was hard to breathe, especially since the car stank of cigarettes and something else, like the stinky parts of a grocery store. She squirmed around until she was in a better position. She was lying against something cold, hard and knobby. It was in a black plastic bag, and although she couldn't see what it was, she didn't like it. It terrified her.

The man drove for a while, seeming to go on worse and worse

roads. Then he pulled over. He got out and opened the back seat. He pulled the blanket off her and peeled away the eye patch, tearing hairs painfully from her brows. He looked at her for a moment. Courtney stared back. He looked familiar, but so strange. His dark eyes didn't seem to be able to focus on one thing. The shock of white-blond hair looked all wrong on his head. But suddenly, the image of that same scarred face rushed into Courtney's memory. It was him.

She tried to scream, to escape the car.

"Hush now," the man said mildly, pushing her back in place, not roughly. He was focused on the thing in the black plastic bag, with which he now struggled, dragging it out of the car. He shut and locked the door. Courtney sat up, watching. They were off the road in a remote area, partly snow covered, rocky, with weed stalks rattling in the cold wind.

The man fumbled with the slippery bag, then finally tore the plastic away impatiently. Courtney had trouble understanding what she was seeing at first. The pale thing was heavy and somewhat shapeless, but then she saw what looked like arms. Suddenly she understood, and she tried to scream again as she stared at the headless, legless woman's torso in the man's hands. The man set it down on a patch of snow and paced. Courtney watched with fear as he seemed to be talking to himself, shaking his head furiously. Finally, he seemed to make a decision, and he reached back toward the body. He dragged it about fifty yards away, spent time positioning it, then stood up and evaluated his work. He came back toward the car. He reached in for a second bag that Courtney had not noticed, yanked it out, and headed back to the torso. Courtney, petrified, watched him pull out the legs and place them carefully by the body. Then the head. Then, the doll.

She couldn't watch anymore, and worked her way back under the blanket, hiding.

After a while, the man got back in the driver's seat. He turned and yanked the blanket off Courtney for a moment, checking on her.

She didn't try to scream, knowing it was useless. He pushed the blanket back at her.

"Get back under that blanket," the man growled. Then his eyes became unfocused again. He looked at Courtney with confusion. "It's okay, Sissy," he said, unexpectedly gentle. "You're safe with me, Sissy. I'll protect you."

He tossed the blanket back over her head. Courtney didn't know what to make of this, and the strangeness of this statement only scared her more.

They drove for a while longer, their pace slowing as they bumped down a long, rough road. Finally, he stopped again. He opened the back door and picked up Courtney, carrying her to a little cabin. Inside, she was shocked to see a woman lying naked on the floor, which was covered with what Courtney thought was dried blood. The woman shifted slightly, looking up at Courtney from dark eyes that were nearly swollen shut. Her face was bruised and bloodied.

Courtney felt a surge of terror. Her throat closed. Her body felt like it was tingling with electrical impulses, telling her to run. It was hard to breathe. Tears flowed down her face.

The man put her down in a chair. He taped her legs to it with several layers of duct tape. She had never been constrained this way, and not being able to move frightened her even more.

"Don't cry," he said, angrily. He seemed to purposely avoid looking at her. He began to pace, muttering to himself. Now and then he would look at Courtney. One of these times, he said, with anguish, "Sissy! I won't let him hurt you." But then he started pacing again and said under his breath, "She has to die."

The woman on the floor watched him dully, now and then glancing at Courtney. Courtney could tell she was hurt and weak. Behind the woman, in the corner, she saw something she couldn't figure out. It looked like three, partial masks of women's faces, tossed in a pile, but so bloody and wet.

She didn't know what to do, so she shut her eyes and started calling out to her father, in her mind.

    Daddy, find me!

Hikers found the body of Sasha Kolomer, the waitress abducted from Jack's Dogs, soon after it was dumped. Lotu and Sheen arrived within thirty minutes of the call, a little after 11 a.m.

They grimly looked over the woman's remains, again positioned with the legs on either side, half her head missing, the other half tossed aside. The doll.

"Bastard thinks he's smart," Sheen said. Their officers had parked near Jack's Dogs the night she was abducted but left to respond to a report that a drunk was wandering through the Crestwood neighborhood, shooting a gun and pounding on doors. It took a while for the officers to sort it out and realize it was a false alarm. When they hurried back to Jack's, most of the staff had gone home, and the lone, remaining dishwasher was too new to know any of his coworker's names yet, let alone whether they had driven away safely.

"He is smart, but not that smart," Lotu said. Unfortunately, the killer was advancing his tactics better than they were. "We'll get him."

There was something about this scene that seemed rushed, less deliberate. The positioning wasn't as neat and symmetrical. The body's proximity to a road made it easier to find than the first two. Then, there was the fact that the killer had abducted Angela before dumping this body. Last time, he had waited to abduct his next victim until after he had dumped the previous one. So, things were a little different, hurried. Was it an indication that the killer was unraveling? Escalating? Maybe he just didn't have a real pattern.

The freshness of the site gave them hope that they might collect something useful. The forensic detective arrived and began a close, gloved-and-masked scrutiny of the scene. Among the bits of evidence he collected was a short, dark hair. Lotu asked that it be given priority on the rapid DNA analysis. It was in the lab and being evaluated by 2 p.m. This was when the Christmas and birthday gifts he showered on the lab personnel would pay off. Between the department's rapid DNA system and the good will he had garnered in the lab, he could expect results that night. He just hoped they would find a match.

Emerson was waiting in a claustrophobic room in the courthouse. Jeff still suspected that the jury had easily agreed on the theft charges, but that Emerson's fate was the subject of their lengthy deliberation.

"They may be trying to decide if you should be a scapegoat, basically. They might want to put a face to the crime, to have an actual, living person to blame for it." These were Jeff's words, delivered dryly, before he disappeared into the courthouse on some errand, the purpose of which he didn't mention.

Powerless in this part of his circumstances, Emerson scrolled restlessly through his phone. His composite-drawing photo was removed from social media within two hours of his posting it, probably by Lotu. Now, he was searching for murders in the Springfield area, to see if he could find anything else that would clue him in on the situation that Courtney had described.

He was distracted by an article that reviewed the psychology of serial killers, their feelings of inadequacy and desire to be admired.

"Bunch of narcissistic psychopaths," he muttered, wondering again how on earth the police here could suspect him of anything like that.

As he expanded his search, he started to find mention of several murders in Springfield, but then also in other places in the Heartland. Three prostitutes had been killed in Springfield, including the poor girl from Brownsburg. Two prostitutes and a waitress were killed in Milwaukee. It was the waitress that really caught his attention. The reporter for that story apparently had more time to dig into this one. Or more likely, waitresses merited slightly more attention than prostitutes. The reporter conveyed details of the waitress's death that the stories about the prostitutes didn't deliver, including the fact that the waitress was decapitated.

Emerson read through the story twice, and by the time he was almost done with the second reading, an alarm was sounding in his head. The decapitated woman was similar to the victims here. His stomach churned with anxiety about Angela. But there was something more that was bothering him about what he was reading. There was something there, just beyond his ability to make sense of it.

What if the night that Annie Hughes was hit by the car was the same one that young girl from Brownsburg was killed? Could she have been murdered in an alley, with the two events only a few blocks from each other? Courtney linked a bloody woman in an alley with her mother's death. The question was, were they really connected?

He thought about Courtney and the nightmares she was having. What had started them? In the year he had known her, she hadn't had that kind of dream until recently. Maybe it was just the timing, that it took a while for her shocked brain to start bringing the memories to the forefront. After all, first her mother was hit by the car, then Courtney stayed with a babysitter until it was clear her mother wasn't going to recover, at which point the babysitter deposited her with Emerson. After that, her mother died in hospital, and they abruptly moved to Colorado. Then of course, all the insanity occurred at the resort. He had tried to shield her, but it was impossible to keep her out of it completely. Now, here they were in another new place, with two moves in the past couple months, the police, the trial, jail. All of it must be shocking enough for a little girl. It certainly was for him, and he had a few more coping mechanisms. So maybe it was natural for her to start having those dreams at this point.

He suddenly remembered the odd comment Courtney had

made. What was it? A dragonfly? He started searching for news again about how police identified the corpse of the woman in Springfield – by her necklace. He checked the Brownsburg news, guessing that the local reporters would be more interested in details of the story, since that was the girl's home town. He was right. The newspaper detailed the family's devastation about their runaway daughter's death. And, yes, there it was. The Brownsburg news included a close-up picture of the necklace that helped identify the girl: A silver dragonfly.

Emerson stood up, paced the small room. So, he was right. The woman Courtney saw in the alley was the same one who was dumped at the landfill. Her memory was accurate, but she just hadn't been able to pull it all together, to make sense of it.

But why now? What had spurred these memories?

He sat down again and pulled up the image of the artist's drawing of the man. His face was hard, the eyes big and dark, smoldering with anger. He was frightening, and if he was the one who killed her mother, he understood why she kept dreaming of him. But was there another reason she was seeing him, now?

As he gazed at the drawing, something about it started to nag at him. The eyes. The rough skin, probably scars, from a rash, acne, or maybe chicken pocks. The alarm in his brain grew louder. The face was looking familiar, and not just because he looked at this drawing frequently. He was starting to think that he had seen it recently, on a real person.

He moved it to a photo app and pulled up the drawing tools. He started to draw a beard on the face, one that came high up the cheeks. He studied his work, and it still didn't look quite right, but it was close. He added long bangs that swept down over the eyes, a weird hair style that was too young for the face behind it.

Now he looked at it again, and the cogs started to click. He had seen that face, too. Where? He shut his eyes with the image still burned in his mind. At first, he couldn't remember, but then his brain abruptly started popping off the memories. That man he saw coming into Jonas' last week, when it was so crowded. It might have been him. And the one who passed by the window in downtown, when he and Jeff were meeting. He passed not once, but twice. Was that him? He thought it probably was. And in the park? At least, it looked like this guy, now that he had added the beard and hair. But how weird. And Courtney hadn't been with him during any of those times. Why was she seeing him in her dreams?

Then he remembered. It might have even been just before the nightmares had begun. They had seen him up in the hills that day, pulling out of the overgrown jeep trail that headed down toward a hunting cabin. Courtney had unexpectedly seemed scared, he remembered, and it was when she saw that driver. And they had exchanged a long look, that driver, Emerson, Courtney. To Emerson, it had just been a little strange to see a car appear in a spot that seemed so remote. But to Courtney, what had seeing that face stirred in her?

Nightmares. Memories.

He opened his eyes. Could it possibly be the same person? And if it was, who was he and what was he doing here? Why had he been nearby so often, both in Denver and in Creeley Junction? It was almost as if he were following Emerson.

It was then that the alarm in his head started clanging, and he finally realized why. Courtney hadn't just made the connection. Courtney was the connection. She had witnessed two murders that night, the prostitute's and her mother's, and now, the killer was coming for her.

Emerson jumped up. He had to protect his daughter. He stuck his phone in his pocket and left the room. Jeff was coming down the hall.

"Emerson, where are you going?"

"I have to get to Courtney!" Emerson said as he hurried down the steps to the first floor.

"But I have to talk to you. We might have a decision soon!"

He didn't wait for Jeff, who would just try to talk him out of this. "Tell the police. That serial killer is going after Courtney."

"What? Emerson! Come back! You're going to get us jailed for contempt."

But Emerson didn't stop.

~46~

Lotu sat at his desk, tired and disgruntled. He and Sheen were out most of the day, canvassing the area where the bodies were found, trying to find someone who had seen or heard anything that could help. Sheen rattled with nervous energy on a good day, and now was agitatedly scanning tip sheets, but not with any hope. Tips were pouring in, of course, but none particularly helpful. None of the residents around the dumping ground had seen or heard anything unusual. Social media had entertained itself with doll-themed images of all types, grisly, funny, sad. None of this got them any closer to identifying who was abducting, torturing and dismembering waitresses in Creeley County. To top it off, Pulga was nowhere to be found.

Lotu sipped his water, having reached his maximum load of caffeine for the day already. He used to drink coffee day and night and have no problem sleeping, but now in his fifties, the caffeine seemed to have a worse effect on him at night. He checked the time on his phone and saw it was nearing six – almost time to head home and let Oinky out. His cell phone rang. He looked at the number and immediately accepted the call.

"Detective Lotu?" Dominique, in the lab.

"Yeah. Hi, Dominique. What'cha got?"

"Well, unfortunately, there was a problem with the test. The sequencing starts off okay, but then gradually drops off. It may be a problem with the primer. I'm going to have to rerun it."

"What does that mean for me?"

"It's going take several hours to rerun," her young voice said.

"But I thought I'd call because I know you're in a hurry. Considering the problem with the primer, you need to take this information for what it's worth – from an incomplete sequencing. But what we do have shows several markers that match Emerson Crandall."

"Really?" He didn't know if he should feel glad or disappointed.

"Yes, but, as I said, we're still waiting to get complete results. So, I wouldn't get too excited yet. But I wanted to let you know that, so far, there is a chance that hair could've come from him."

"All right. Thanks. Let me know when you get the rest."

He clicked off the phone and stuck it in his pocket, looking over it at Sheen, his eyebrows raised, not really believing what he was just told.

"That hair," Lotu said. "Looks like it could be a match on Crandall."

Sheen looked as surprised as Lotu, but he took the news better. He grinned.

"Let's go get him."

Emerson was running.

"Nine-one-one. What is your emergency?"

"My daughter is missing."

"You said your daughter is missing?"

"Yes. My name is Emerson Crandall." He was trying to make sure he was clear, but not wanting to stop as he headed around the side of the school. "Her name is Courtney Crandall. I think she was abducted from her school."

"You say she was abducted from her school? Do you know who abducted her?"

"Yes. I think she was taken by the same person who's been killing those waitresses." Emerson scanned the back of the school for the smallest sign of Courtney.

"Sir? What is your location?"

"Eastwick Elementary."

He had already called the principal, and she was on her way to open the school to see if Courtney was, for some bizarre reason, still inside. For now, Emerson was running frantically around the school, calling her name. Mrs. Guevera, the babysitter, was there too, helping him search. She was horrified that she had been fooled by whomever had called her, pretending to be Emerson.

"It was so noisy!" she kept saying. "I thought it was you!"

After a few minutes, he saw Lotu and Sheen pulling up to the curb around the corner in their unmarked car. He went toward them, still holding the phone to his ear.

"Courtney's missing," he called to Lotu as he approached. "Abducted. It's the same guy, the same one who's been killing the waitresses."

To his surprise Sheen approached him quickly, gun drawn.

"Get down now, Crandall. Face down. Now!"

Emerson, still twenty yards away, stopped. It took a moment for him to realize that Lotu and Sheen were not here to help find Courtney, but to arrest him. It took him less time to decide that was not going to happen. He turned and ducked back around the building's corner as a Lakewood police car screeched up.

Lotu and Sheen shouted his name, telling him to stop and immediately chasing. He felt a rush of terror as he wondered if they would shoot.

Younger and fitter, he outpaced them easily. This was the last thing he needed. He had to find Courtney and didn't even know where to look, other than in the school. But he wasn't about to let these two guys take him in when she was out there somewhere, maybe in the clutches of the killer.

He made it back around the school to Maddie's car and took off, driving he didn't know where, trying to think where Courtney could be. He prayed that the principal would search the school, despite all this new confusion, with the police chasing Emerson. He knew they would be after him in a moment. He needed to check the apartment, but he guessed they would be there, too. He got there quickly and parked in the lot of the neighboring building, pulled a hoodie up over his head and walked in the shadows toward his building. Sure enough, a white patrol car was pulling up to his apartment. The cops got out and pounded on the door. He held his breath, hoping that Courtney's little head would appear in the doorway. The apartment remained dark. The police pounded again, then kicked the door in.

He waited in the shadows until they reemerged, talking into their radios. Obviously, they had not found Courtney. He saw his neighbor, Demond, stick his head out his door, then duck back in. The deputies noticed him, though, and immediately approached his apartment. They knocked, and he answered, speaking to them for a few minutes. Then the deputies drove into the darkest corner of the parking lot, turning off their car.

Shoot, they were watching his apartment.

Emerson ducked behind the privacy fence at the back of the lot and made his way to Demond's back door, his heart pounding. He knocked quietly. It took a few tries before Demond figured out he was there.

"Hey, man!" Demond said, apprehensive. "The cops are looking for you."

"I know. They're parked in the corner of the lot. That's why I came to the back. I'm really sorry. I know it looks weird. Listen, my daughter is missing, and I need a car they won't recognize to try to find her. Any chance I can borrow yours?"

"I'm supposed to call them the minute I see you."

Emerson stared at him for a moment, wondering if he had badly misjudged him. Then his neighbor smiled.

"Shoot, man, I'm not going to call them. You can't borrow my car. I need to get to work later, but you can use my mother's. She never drives. Come on in."

He stepped into the apartment, which was just like Maddie's, but much more lived-in looking, with soft furniture and fleecy, Denver Broncos blankets and pillows tossed here and there. Demond's mother was watching a game show on television.

"Hello, Mrs. Skate," Emerson said.

"Hello, honey," she said, lighting up a little when she saw him.

"Emerson needs to borrow your car, okay, Mama?"

"Of course."

Demond returned with the keys.

"Here you go. It's the green Lumina."

"It's sea foam, not green," Mrs. Skate said.

"Where is it?" Emerson asked.

"It's out back. They can't see you out there." Demond went to the kitchen window and hit a button on the key fob. Headlights in the back lot flashed briefly.

"That's great," Emerson said. "Thanks a lot. I really appreciate it."

"I hope you find her."

"Find who?" Mrs. Skate said.

"My daughter is missing," Emerson said. "I think she was abducted."

"Oh, no!"

"Can you keep your eye out, and if she happens to come home, let me know right away?"

"Of course! Did you issue an Amber Alert?" she asked.

"No!" He was horrified he hadn't thought of it. "I will, somehow. Thanks again."

He took the key and headed toward the car, stumbling through a shrubby ditch instead of using the sidewalk. Before starting, he went into his social media account on his phone, and posted his own alert, including a photo of Courtney. He posted it with everyone he knew and asked them to share it. After a moment of consideration, he added the altered drawing of the man Courtney had identified, the one that included the drawn-on beard and hair. Then he called the local news and told them about her and directed them to his alert on social media. Since he was already notorious in the area, local reporters were eager to relay the information that his daughter was missing. Then he left a voice message for Mrs. Guevera, asking her to make sure she asked the police to issue the official Amber Alert.

Finally, he texted Jeff and told him briefly what was going on. His phone started to ring immediately with Jeff's number, but he declined the call and powered down his phone. The police probably were tracing the cell ping, by now. He knew he should talk to Jeff, but his lawyer would likely try to talk him out of trying to find Courtney, to let the police handle it. He was not in the mood to be talked out of anything by Jeff. On the other hand, he didn't want to leave the phone off for too long, in case she tried to call, but he figured he would at least put some distance between himself and his last cell phone signal, hoping to gain some breathing room, to think and look for Courtney.

He found a colorful ski hat in the passenger seat and put it on. It might help disguise him and look less suspicious than a black hoodie. He drove through the dark street in the sea-foam green sedan, his scattered brain trying to form a plan. Stopping at an intersection, he gazed into the night. Snowflakes flittered silently in his car headlights as a storm slunk over the area.

He had a feeling he knew where to go. It was his only chance, the only possibility for him. But he could be so wrong. It was such a risk. If he was wrong, it would take him miles away. And could he even remember which narrow, mountain road they were on that day they saw the bearded man appear on that rough, overgrown drive?

Think, Emerson. Which day was it? Where were they going? It was a hike. His brain gradually fed him the view of the trail head, where they had parked to go for a walk. He dragged his memory backward from there, to the spot where they saw the man, and from there, back to the nearest intersection, and the route sign. He saw it.

He remembered. He headed toward the canyon. It was a

longshot, but the only one he had. If she wasn't there, he might not ever find her.

~47~

Courtney fought to keep her eyes open. She couldn't believe her body was trying to fall asleep now, of all times. Taped to a chair, teetering on the bloody floor next to a battered woman with a terrifying killer moving about the room, she needed to stay awake. But she was exhausted, and before she could stop it her head nodded forward, and she tumbled into sleep.

She didn't know how long she had slept when an anguished wail awakened her. She opened her eyes to see the man bending over the woman. He was holding a knife, running it along her torso.

Courtney screamed through the tape on her mouth.

The man jumped, surprised, and swung around toward her. She screamed again as he came at her with the knife. He pressed it into her throat.

"You!" he yelled at her. "You can't watch this! You have to die!"

Tears rolled down her face. She looked into his crazy eyes, powerless.

Suddenly, his expression changed. He seemed to be seeing something new.

"Sissy?" he said softly. "Sissy? Is that you?"

Courtney realized he was seeing someone else when he looked at her. Whoever this "Sissy" was, his mistaking Courtney for her seemed like a good thing. She nodded.

"Oh, Sissy!" he said, suddenly hugging her. "Oh, Sissy! I've missed you so much!"

He leaned back and looked at her. "Oh, poor Sissy. What did they do to you?" He gently pulled the tape off her mouth and hands, but her legs were still attached to the chair.

Courtney moved her jaw. It felt much better.

"Are you ready, Sissy? Here's your knife." He held out a small, sharp knife. Courtney didn't want to take it, shaking her head and staring at it.

"What's wrong, Sissy? It's your turn. Show me where to cut, the way you always do."

"No!" she shouted, surprising him.

The sound of her voice seemed to snap him back to reality. He looked at her differently.

"What do you think you're doing?" he snarled. "You're not Sissy. Stop pretending to be her. I'll deal with you next."

He looked at the woman on the floor, then said to Courtney, "You can't watch this!"

He turned her chair. The last thing she saw before she turned were the terrified eyes of the weakened woman, who now looked slightly familiar, despite her injuries. Courtney was so scared. What was he going to do to her?

"Sissy? Come on out, Sissy," she heard the man say. She heard him pacing.

"Sissy?" His voice was changing again. It became soft, and it almost sounded like he was crying.

"Oh, Sissy, there you are. No, don't worry about that girl. I'll take care of her. She won't see you. Here you go. Here's your knife. Show me where I should cut. Here, I'll help you. You know I'll help you."

Courtney heard the woman scream through her tape gag and shut her eyes, tears dripping out of them, terrified. When she opened them, she thought she saw a movement outside. She looked at the window. All she saw was the blackness of the night, snowflakes reflecting the dim, cabin lights. She heard the man behind her, still talking to "Sissy," and the woman shrieking. She was afraid to try to look around at the man, and she kept looking outside. Suddenly, her father's face peered around the edge of the window. His head and shoulders were dusted in snow and he was wearing a silly hat she'd never seen before. He had his finger over his mouth in a "Shh" gesture, his eyes fiercely intent on his message to her.

She was so happy that she tried to lunge toward him, toppling the chair, since she was still taped to it. But he shook his head and disappeared around the edge of the window.

"What are you doing?" the man growled. Courtney knew he was looking at her. She didn't move, holding her breath. He came over to her, yanked her back into the chair, upright.

"How did you get the tape off?" he demanded, then spotted the ball of duct tape he had left by her chair just minutes before.

Thinking fast, Courtney said, "Don't you remember? It's me. Sissy."

He looked at her in confusion. Then he bent down near her face.

"You're not Sissy," he said in a way that terrified her to her core. "Sissy's over there, cutting that whore. You are that girl, the daughter of that woman who saw me in Springfield. You can identify me. You have to die."

"No! It's me! It's your Sissy!" Courtney said, crying.

"Shut up!" He slapped her, not very hard, but hard enough to surprise her.

Emerson took a chance, looking in the window again. He wanted to see where the killer was before he entered, so he could plan his first few moves. They had to count. It only took a moment to take in the scene: The man, leaning over Courtney, yelling at her and fumbling with a roll of duct tape. Angela, naked, bound, her face swollen and bruised, her neck showing a small cut.

Please let her be alive, he thought.

The man leaning over Courtney stood up as though distracted. He looked at Angela and started talking. Emerson could hear his voice, but not his words. He seemed to be speaking to someone. He slowly crossed the room toward Angela, smiling at the air, holding out a little knife as though offering it to someone. But there was no one else there.

Totally insane, Emerson thought, and extremely dangerous. He took a moment to picture his next move.

Emerson tightened his grip on the ax he found on the wood pile near the cabin. He stepped through the door quietly and swung the blade at the back of the man's neck. At the same time, the man, whose instincts must have been on edge, swung around. He managed to move out of the way in time, and he lunged at Emerson, knocking the ax out of his hand, the long knife aimed at Emerson's stomach.

Emerson dodged back. He spotted a shotgun leaning against the wall and lunged for it. The killer came after him, and Emerson swung the shaft of the gun up, knocking the hand that held the knife. Then he brought the gun back down, hitting the man on the head, but it was not a solid strike. The man rolled away, grabbing the knife and, in a flash, held it against Courtney's throat. He swiftly positioned himself behind her.

Emerson felt a surge of fear prickling through every nerve. He pointed the shotgun at the man.

"That gun is loaded with two and three-quarter inch, number one buckshot," the man said. "At that distance, you could shoot me right through your little girl. But you would blast a three-inch hole in her head while doing it."

Emerson still pointed the gun at him. "Get away from her."

They glared at each other, the cabin silent as no one seemed to breathe.

Then Martin said, "I tell you what. I'll cut her tape, and then she can go to you, and I'll just leave."

"Okay, cut her loose."

Martin swiftly cut the tape at Courtney's feet, completely releasing her binding. But then he picked her up, pressing the knife to her throat again.

"Daddy!" she said.

"Shut up!" Martin said. "Now you listen, Daddy. I'm going to leave, and I'm taking this one with me. You are going to count to one thousand before doing anything, or I'll leave little pieces of her spread along the trail for the ravens."

He backed toward the door, holding Courtney in front of him. She struggled, and he dug the knife into her throat.

"Cut it out," the killer warned.

"Daddy!"

"I'll come for you, Courtney, don't worry."

"That would be very stupid."

They went through the cabin door. Emerson stepped to the window. Martin immediately appeared in it, still holding the knife at Courtney's neck, hard enough that if she struggled, it would cut her.

"Back off," he said through the glass.

Emerson stepped back. "All right," he said, lowering the gun.

Martin walked backward. Emerson knew he would leave tracks, but he was afraid that as soon as he was away from the cottage, the man would kill Courtney and run. Angela moaned weakly, on the floor behind him. He knew he should get Angela out of there and try to summon help. But his impulse was to run after Courtney.

"Go." It was Angela. She was sitting up, the word sounding garbled through her swollen mouth. "Cut me loose and go. I'll get help."

He picked up one of the knives, swiftly cutting through the tape at her hands and legs. Her face was badly bruised, but she stood with only a little help.

"Are you sure?"

"Yes! Go get Courtney." She was already reaching for her clothes.

He gave her his phone. "Drive out of here until you get a cell. Then use my phone to call Detective Lotu and tell him to get up here.

He's in my contacts. My phone's passcode is 0317." Courtney's birth month and day. "Remember, March 17. St. Patrick's Day. Got it?"

"Yes. Go find her."

Feeling a surge of both relief and anxiety, he nodded and ran out the door, following the killer's tracks.

~48~

Lotu and Sheen were at Emerson's apartment, looking in his car. The snow was falling steadily now, small, urgent flakes, getting in their eyes. They were trying to decide where to go next, when Lotu had the impulse to check Emerson's social media pages. Emerson's public posts were, well, interesting lately, especially when he posted that drawing – causing all hell to break loose with the public. Maybe he had added something new that might give them information.

He immediately saw Emerson's alert about Courtney, but he was most interested in the altered police artist's sketch, with its drawn-in beard and bangs. He recognized it, now. He pressed his palm against his face, covering one eye, shutting the other, groaning.

"What's wrong?" Sheen asked.

"You dummy!" He meant himself.

"What?"

"Look." He handed the phone to Sheen.

Sheen squinted at the drawing, using his fingers to make it bigger. He looked back at Lotu.

"Yeah," he said.

"Pulga, right?"

"Yeah."

Lotu's phone rang.

"Lotu."

"We just got a hit on his phone." It was Randall Nixon, who was commanding this incident back at the station.

"Where?"

"It's up at Ram Horn Canyon, Route 7."

"What the hell's he doing way up there?"

"I can't tell from here."

"All right, we'll start out that way. If anybody's closer, get them going."

"Will do. Hey, I got something else."

Lotu beckoned to Sheen.

"Pinged Crandall's phone, up by the canyon," he said to Sheen as they headed to the car. He put the phone on speaker and started the engine.

"Go ahead."

"There's an old lady in the hospital. Lives over in Lakewood. She said her tenant was the one who put her in the ER. She said he looks just like that composite Crandall slipped out on social media, except that the last time she saw him, he had dyed his hair blond and shaved off his eyebrows. She said when he saw her looking at the picture on the computer, he attacked her. Her granddaughter saw him, too. She had been talking to her on the computer."

Lotu and Sheen looked at each other in concern.

"And get this, Crandall and his daughter had stayed at that same apartment before this guy moved in."

"Okay," Lotu said. "Is the old lady going to be okay?"

"Hope so. It was a nasty blow and she's seventy-six. Cracked her skull. But at least she was talking."

"Okay. Anything else?"

"That's it."

"Thanks."

Lotu clicked the phone off. It immediately rang again.

Sheen answered it and put it on speaker.

"Go ahead."

"Lotu? This is Dominique, from the lab."

"Yeah, good. Whatcha' got?"

"That sample you gave me? The hair?"

"Yeah," Sheen said, impatiently.

"Well, I hope I didn't mess you up. It definitely has markers that match Emerson Crandall, like I said, except for one thing."

"What?"

"The person who left this hair is female."

"What the hell?" Sheen just stared at Lotu.

"Are you sure? That doesn't make sense," Lotu said.

"Well, it's a fact. Also, how old did you say your subject is?"

"He's thirty-three."

"Yeah, well, this DNA came from a child."

"Oh crap," Sheen said as this sunk in. It meant Emerson's daughter had somehow been near that body, or the killer had one of her hairs on him when he dumped it.

"Thanks, Dominque," Lotu said, his gut tightening with anxiety. "Gotta go."

Lotu and Sheen looked at each other, realizing what this meant. That hair could have come loose and attached to the killer if he had carried the girl, or if she shared the same space as the corpse.

Sheen put the magnetic light on the top of their car as Lotu hit the siren and the gas. He turned the car around and headed toward the canyon, going as fast as he dared through the snowy, residential streets.

Sheen punched numbers on the phone.

"Terry? Sheen. Listen, that Crandall girl, we think her father might've been right. We think it's possible she has been abducted by the killer. Get some more units out there and start that Amber Alert."

He clicked off the phone.

"Crap," he said again.

Then they both were silent, staring ahead, snowflakes reflecting in the headlights, blowing back toward the car, making it seem as if they were speeding through a white tunnel of light. They finally saw the last of the city lights as they started up the canyon highway.

~49~

Martin had not gone far. He waited in the woods to see what Emerson would do. Of course, Martin would kill him. He was glad to see the other car leave, because he intended to use his own to get out of there, and that one had blocked it. He knew he would be able to pull this off. He had to get rid of them all, of course, but he was convinced his powers were above those of most men. He wasn't worried. He knew what he could do.

The funny thing was that, to Martin, it was obvious that Emerson did not know what he, Emerson, should be able to do. Martin had seen the rage, sure, and it had worried him. But obviously, Emerson had not learned to harness the power of that anger. If he had, Martin might be dead now.

He planned his next steps. He would start with this girl. No drama, just a swift slice across the throat. He would do that now. He braced himself for the act, but when he glanced down, he realized he was holding his little sister. Tears filled his eyes.

"What am I doing? I almost hurt you." He hugged her tightly. "I'll never hurt you. I'll protect you forever."

That's when Emerson stepped out of the woods and hit him in the back of the head with the shaft of the shotgun. Martin collapsed as Emerson yanked Courtney out of his arms. Emerson started to run with her, but he dropped the gun. He didn't stop as he hurried to the car. They were almost there when he heard the first blast. He dove to the ground, landing in a drift, shoulder first, rolling to protect Courtney.

"Run to the car, go around that way!" he said to Courtney. "Stay behind trees as much as you can."

She took off as fast as she could, which was not fast at all. He could hear Martin coming up behind them. Emerson followed Courtney, getting to the car and jumping behind the steering wheel. Then he realized he didn't have the keys. He searched frantically, on the floor, behind the visor. Martin stepped out of the woods, pointing the gun at him. He was grinning.

"Courtney," Emerson said quietly, "I'm going to get out and try to talk to him. When I do, you slip out the back door and run. Stay low at first so he doesn't notice, but as soon as you get a little ways away, run to the road and go as fast as you can down the hill. The police will be coming soon. When you see them, go with them."

"But I want to stay with you."

"I'll be right behind you. In fact, I hope I'm driving this car. But don't come to the car unless you know it's me. Got it?"

"Yes." Her voice was small and scared.

"Okay, wait until he's looking the other way. Got it?"

"Yes."

Emerson slipped out of the car, leaving the driver's door open so the killer wouldn't notice the light coming on when the back door opened.

"Hey, buddy," he said quietly, in a warm, friendly voice, "can we talk about this for a second?"

The killer raised the gun at Emerson's head. Emerson's legs were shaking, a startling indication of his true fear, but he continued his approach.

"Sure," Martin said, sarcastic. "I'd love to hear from you how it feels to know I'm going to kill your little girl. After I kill you."

Emerson hoped that Courtney was leaving, and at the same time, he tried to think of something that might slow this guy down, maybe even stop him. His mind was surging with adrenalin and completely devoid of any ideas. He said the first thing that popped in his head.

"I'm Emerson."

"I know who you are, dickhead."

Martin noticed movement in the woods.

"Hey!" he yelled. "Stop!"

He fired toward the movement. Emerson let the adrenalin take control and leaped at Martin, driving him sideways, the gun knocked loose and landing behind him. Emerson got in one good blow to his cheek before Martin pulled out the knife. Emerson pressed closer, grabbing the hand that held the knife. But, while Emerson was strong, he lacked the fighting sophistication that Martin had honed. Martin rolled them both in the snow until he was sitting up over Emerson. He grabbed his arm and twisted it painfully, forcing Emerson to turn away to prevent it from snapping. Martin shoved Emerson's face in the snow, positioning the knife point by his carotid artery, holding him down with the weight of his body, his face pressed near Emerson's ear.

"Here we go then," Martin said, calmly. "I'm going to tear this knife through your artery here. Just like I did Kellerman. I can't believe you're not in jail for that one. Then I'm going after your little girl. I won't even bother to get out of the car. I'll just run her down, same as I did her mommy."

Emerson struggled, and felt the knife poke harder.

"Let me finish. This is half the fun," the killer said. "You told her to run to the road, right? Well, I'll find her, squash her like a bunny. You really screwed up, you know? Just like with your mother, the one you drove to suicide."

Emerson tensed more, in surprise. Martin laughed. "Oh, yeah. I know all about you and your dead mommy. Then I'll catch up with your girlfriend and finish her off. I won't be able to do what I really wanted to do to her, because I know you have the police coming."

Martin's voice suddenly changed weirdly, loud, deep and frightening. "That whore! But you first. And yes, I really am that good."

Emerson felt the knife tip puncture his skin. He jerked his

head away. The knife stayed against his neck, but he dislodged Martin's hand slightly. Martin shoved back, pressing Emerson's face through the snow to the frozen ground beneath it.

For a moment, the anxiety and fear surging through Emerson overwhelmed him. He felt weak and cold, the snow on his face draining his warmth and strength, Martin's knee in his back paralyzing him. The knife. The blood. It was becoming a blur.

"Give it up." Martin's whisper near his ear was almost soothing. Emerson could feel his beard stubble and smell his hot, rank breath. "Just let it go."

Emerson might have considered it for a moment, but then, something else in him took charge. That fiery rage in his guts frothed, finally finding the right opening to blast to the surface. This time, instead of fighting it, Emerson unleashed it. His furious adrenalin surge through his exhausted muscles.

He abruptly heaved himself up, catching Martin off guard, throwing him off his back, following him over, the leverage of his long legs holding them both steady.

"Not today, asshole," Emerson said. The menace in the tone sounded like it came from someone else.

He engulfed Martin from behind, squeezing him in place. Martin had never experienced anyone as big and fit as Emerson fighting back. His victims were always smaller and weaker, by design. Emerson shoved him down, pressing Martin's face and shoulders with one arm, his other hand on Martin's, holding the knife. Emerson squeezed his forearm on Martin's neck as he tried to break his hold on the blade. He felt teeth closing on his arm. Emerson jerked it away and drove his thumb into Martin's eye. Martin's grip loosened on the knife, and Emerson grabbed it. He was wearing leather gloves, but the sharp steel still cut his hand. Martin yanked, and the knife flipped away, leaving a red trail as it disappeared into the snow.

Emerson brought his palm up fast, slamming the heel of his hand into Martin's nose, driving it up. The painful blow knocked the man backward. Emerson was up quickly, and he kicked him under the chin. He could see that Martin went unconscious, but it might only last a moment. He pulled the keys out of the killer's coat pocket. He figured he had just enough time to get to the car and drive out of there before Martin revived.

He started to go, but then stopped. He looked back at the limp figure. In a fragment of a second, he considered another option. Instead of leaving, he bent and found the knife, picking it up with his torn glove. He watched Martin struggling to regain his senses.

It would only take two strides. He would drive the blade into Martin's left, carotid artery, twisting it hard, feeling a resistance of sinew against steel. So easily, the man who tortured and killed those women, who kidnapped Courtney, would fall, and never hurt anyone again.

Emerson made his decision. He stepped to Martin's car, reached into the passenger seat for the roll of duct tape, then went for him.

Martin, still on his stomach, rubbed his face with one hand, the blood from his nose streaking his fingers. His eyes flickered, then opened. He saw Emerson and took a moment to remember what was going on. Before he could start the fight again, Emerson placed his knee on Martin's neck. Yanking Martin's hands back, Emerson worked quickly before the killer revived enough to understand what he was doing. The cold tape resisted his fingers, but Emerson managed to secure Martin's wrists together.

Martin grunted and tried to pull his hands away, kicking his legs to get free. Emerson grabbed one ankle, wound a band of tape around it, then fought Martin to press his feet together. It was sloppy work, but he managed to get the feet bound. Martin struggled.

"Let me go," he said, his words muffled against the ground.

Ignoring him, Emerson taped together Martin's knees. Finally, he ran the tape between his feet and hands, so they were bound tight behind his back. In this position, it would be almost impossible to get up. Just to be sure, Emerson wrapped a length of tape around his neck, then attached it to his wrists. Now, if he pulled too much, he'd cut off his own air.

"Please," Martin mumbled, trying to get his tongue to work after being knocked out. "Let me go. I promise I won't hurt your daughter."

The words only served to stoke Emerson's anger. Maybe he had made the wrong decision. He picked up the knife. Still kneeling on Martin, he set it against the throbbing artery in his neck. He pressed the point into his skin, watching it pushing the flesh, anticipating how much force it would take.

"Please," Martin said. "I don't want to die."

Emerson thought of the women he'd tortured and killed, and how easy this should be. Why didn't he do it?

He tilted his head, face to the sky, letting the flakes gently tickle his sweaty skin. Other than their heavy breathing, the night was silent. After all this, how could it be so cool and quiet? It felt the same as when he was a little boy, walking with his mother on a winter night, his mittened hand holding hers. He remembered leaning back, just like this, to feel the snow on his face, as she smiled down at him, laughing at the pureness of the moment and at her young son's discovering the magic of a silent, wintery evening.

He pressed Martin's face with his palm roughly, using it to shove himself up. Martin cried out under the weight, then coughed, and rolled to his side, looking at Emerson standing over him.

"What are you doing? Let me go, please. Please, Emerson. Don't leave me out here. I'll freeze to death. Please."

He could kick him in the face, or break some ribs, maybe hit him in the teeth with something hard and metal.

"Please, don't leave me here. Please, Emerson. What would your mother think if she knew you'd left me out here to freeze to death?"

Emerson bent down to him, pressing his face close, holding the knife so near to Martin's nose he could probably smell Emerson's blood on it.

"Don't make me change my mind."

He traced the sharp blade down Martin's cheek, just enough to open the skin. Martin screamed, a high-pitched, pathetic wail, as the white slit filled with blood. Emerson pulled the knife back.

"My daughter."

"What?"

"My daughter, not my mother. She's the only reason I didn't tear open your artery and let you bleed out in the snow."

Emerson stood. He threw the knife toward the cabin. It rattled against the door and fell, landing on the step where the police could easily find it.

He felt spent, but he couldn't stop. Courtney was out there somewhere, growing colder and wetter, and he had to find her before the freezing, mountain night claimed her.

He could hear Martin pleading for him to come back. As he moved farther away, the sound faded. But before he was out of hearing, he thought he could hear Martin laughing, a jarring dissonance in the otherwise silent, winter woods.

The temperature dropped as the snowstorm intensified. Courtney couldn't find the road. Somehow, she got turned around and was trying to scramble through a thick patch of pines and deep snow. The ground was covered with buried branches, rocks and holes, causing her to trip and fall. She was so tired, hungry, thirsty and cold, but knew she had to get to the road. She climbed up over the trunk of a fallen tree but slipped, falling face-first on the other side. The snow went into her shirt, packing around her neck, and it was so icy it burned. She needed to rest. She wished she had a drink.

Squirming under the log, she huddled in a spot where the snow was thin and tried to clean the ice out of her shirt. Her hand was wet and numb, and she couldn't do much with it. She put some snow in her mouth, and it tasted pretty good, so she ate some more. But it was making her even colder, so she stopped.

Now, she realized how wet her clothes were. Her sweat had soaked her shirt. The damp clothes felt terrible next to her skin, and she started shivering. She was sleepy, too, so she shut her eyes. She was amazed to hear the snowflakes hitting last fall's leaves with a rustling tinkle as she fell asleep.

Lotu and Sheen saw the light green Chevy in a snowbank up ahead. They pulled over and approached cautiously, guns in hand. There was no movement inside. Lotu shone his bright flashlight inside the car and was surprised to see a woman slumped over the steering wheel. Her face was severely bruised, but he was pretty sure he knew who she was.

"Angela?" he called, knocking on the glass as Sheen checked the back seat, found it empty and nodded at Lotu.

"Angela, is that you?"

He tried to open the door, but it was locked. Sheen solved this problem quickly by putting the butt of his flashlight through the passenger-side window and pressing the "unlock" button. Lotu open the door.

"Angela, you with us?" He felt her neck, relieved to find a pulse. He nodded at Sheen, who was already calling for an ambulance.

A patrol car pulled up, and Lotu and Sheen drove on, leaving Angela in the hands of the deputy.

By now, the road was covered with a couple of inches of new snow, but it looked as though someone had driven on it recently. They decided to take a chance. After about a mile, they saw headlights.

Emerson had abandoned the car, leaving it running.

"Courtney!" he yelled. "Courtney!"

Using Angela's phone flashlight, he walked back up the drive, edged the woods, hoping to find the spot where she entered. The snow would soon cover any tracks, and he had to be efficient and fast. She wouldn't last long in these dropping temperatures, probably already wet, working her little legs hard to get through the stiff and unforgiving underbrush.

He found a spot where the snow was disturbed. It might be tracks. He looked closely under the phone's light that reflected blue off the new snow. God, how did trackers do this? He couldn't be sure, but it looked like a path might have been disturbed in a line through the woods, now covered lightly. He had to decide, and once again, faced knowing that if he chose wrong, he could go on a wild goose chase, and Courtney would die. Well, he was lucky once. He had to try it again. He plunged after the vanishing path, the phone's flashlight beam already dimming from the steady drain on its battery.

As he went, he tripped over unseen branches, tumbling down, pulling himself up, surging on. He was still traveling on adrenalin, but that was starting to wane, and with every step his soggy boots felt heavier, clumsier, his clothes wetter with each stumble and fall.

If he was following her path, she had stayed in the woods, not going to the road as he instructed. It was very possible that he was now just following a deer's trail, not his daughter's. But he understood that a little kid might have trouble finding the road that was just yards away. The trail seemed to push through the tangled limbs of a fallen tree and he decided it might be Courtney's, because he doubted a deer would do that, as he couldn't even fit through there. He dragged his heavy feet around the downed pine, stumbling and sliding on its branches. On the other side, he tried to find her trail again, but to his dismay, he couldn't locate it. Either the snow had covered it completely by now, or he had gotten off track by having to detour.

"Courtney!" he yelled. He tried to climb over a large branch, not quite making it, falling again, heavily, knocking the back of his neck on something hard. He stayed down for just a moment, his body yearning for this brief respite at the same time as he knew urgently that he needed to get out of the cold woods. He was tired, felt desperate, not completely losing hope yet, but fighting the seedling of doubt that he would find her.

He heard a car driving slowly on the road, saw flickers of its headlights through the dark woods. That gave him new hope, that he wasn't totally alone out here.

"Hey!" he yelled toward the car.

Still on the ground, he shone the dim beam around, trying to see a trail. All he could find was the disturbance he'd made when he slipped, bringing down a shower of snow from the branches. His light flickered on what looked like a small lump of wet clothing under the log. He recognized the clothes that covered his daughter, just as his flashlight dimmed to black.

"Courtney!" He crawled to the log in the darkness, reached for her, pulled her out like an unwieldy, wet sack of sticks. She was loose and pliable, her head flopping back as he pulled her against him. He put his hand on her forehead. Her skin seemed so cold. He felt her neck, holding his breath, barely able to hold his own finger still, his heart was throbbing so hard. But then, he felt it: A small, fluttering pulse.

He let his breath out in a gasp of relief. He unzipped his coat and, holding her carefully, zipped it around them both, so she was snuggled against him like a baby kangaroo. Then he started back toward the car lights on the road.

"Hey!" he yelled again.

He now noticed the bright blue and white flash of a police light bar, parked next to the car Emerson had taken from the cabin, idling in the middle of the road. In the last few yards before he left the woods, he could see Sheen looking around, shifting his weight back and forth anxiously, while Lotu examined the car. They both looked up in surprise when he emerged from the woods, guns ready.

Lotu relaxed slightly when he realized the figure clamoring

from the woods was Emerson.

"I hope that's your daughter you're holding under your coat," Lotu said, noticing with concern that Emerson was covered in blood.

"Yeah," Emerson carried her to the car. "I have to take her to the hospital."

"Not in that car," Sheen said. While they were waiting, they had run the plates and learned it belonged to Martin Pulga. The chagrin they felt from this final revelation had intensified their desire to find Emerson and his daughter alive.

"Get in here," Lotu said, opening the back door to his car. "I promise, we won't lock you in."

It was warm inside, and Emerson gently laid Courtney on the seat, taking off his coat and tucking it around her.

"Turn that heat up," he said. Lotu obliged.

A second cruiser came toward them, emergency lights strobing brightly against the falling snow and woods, followed shortly by a third.

"Let's go," Emerson said. "Take me now or I'm driving myself."

"Okay, okay," Lotu said. "Can you quickly tell us what happened? Just the highlights. We can get the details later."

"Just tell the deputy to take a right down that driveway. He'll see what happened soon enough."

"What do you mean?"

"He should probably hurry, unless you don't care if that psycho freezes to death. I certainly don't."

Hearing this, Lotu and Sheen switched Emerson and Courtney to the patrol car, sent them in the direction of the closest hospital, and headed up to the cabin themselves.

Their headlights fell on the hog-tied form of Martin Pulga, the shock of newly dyed, blond hair hanging wet and frozen over one glaring eye. He struggled against the tape.

"That crazy fucker tried to kill me," he said as they approached.

"He left me here to die. I want to press charges. I want him arrested."

"Yeah, we feel real sorry for you." Lotu paused to take a photo of Martin for their records, then cut the tape and jerked him to his feet, pulling him to their car and stuffing him in the back seat.

As they started to back up the long drive, they heard Martin crying in the back seat. Lotu and Sheen exchanged a disgusted glance.

After a few minutes, Martin said quietly, "You two inept morons never would've caught me."

~50~

Courtney slept soundly, an IV of saline dripping slowly into her arm. The ER doctor had assured Emerson she would be fine, but they had moved her to the pediatric room for the night, for observation. Now, a late-night nurse stopped in to check on her, tapping the IV bag and scanning a thermometer across Courtney's forehead.

"She's doing great," the nurse said.

"Good," Emerson said. "How is the woman, Angela Flores? She would have come in a little while before us."

"Are you a relative?"

"No. We're, uh ... " He looked at the nurse. "Connected."

Then he realized it was more than that.

"I mean, she's my girlfriend."

"Well, if you're not a relative, I can't tell you anything." She glanced toward the empty hallway, then looked back at him, stepping closer, conspiratorially. "But I will, off-the-record, tell you that she's in bad shape and needs surgery, but she'll recover. At least, physically."

So, she was there. He would find her.

"That's good," he said. "Thanks for telling me."

She nodded, then looked at Courtney. "This little one is going to be fine. She just needs rest." She headed toward the door. "It's late. You might want to get some rest yourself."

With Courtney in a deep sleep, he left to look for Angela. He found her name outside a room on the second floor and ducked in. Her face was barely recognizable, her eyes black and swollen, her nose broken. Her cheek bone looked damaged and he wondered if she was going to need surgery to fix it. She slept heavily, sedated.

She had been abducted by one of the most dangerously insane men he had ever heard of, but she'd survived. Many others had not. How was she going to cope now?

Before leaving her room, he found his phone in her coat pocket. Then he went back to Courtney's room and stretched out on a cushioned bench, a feature of the children's rooms considerately placed for parents. Within minutes, he was asleep.

At 8:30, he was awakened by a combination of his phone ringing and Courtney telling him his phone was ringing. He grinned at her, happy to hear her sounding normal.

He looked at the number. Jeff.

"Hey," Emerson said.

"Hey yourself, you jerk. What the hell is going on?"

"Sorry. I'll tell you when I see you."

"Well, that better be in thirty minutes, in a suit, in the court. We have a decision."

Emerson barely made it. He slipped in next to Jeff just as the bailiff called in the jury. He watched their perplexed faces as they looked back at him. Despite the suit, he was bruised and scraped, and he must look shocking. He couldn't tell what they had decided from the serious looks on their faces. His stomach knotted.

"Ladies and gentlemen of the jury, we have an announcement," the judge said.

Emerson looked at Jeff in surprise. Jeff ignored him, staring expectantly at the judge.

"This morning, a plea agreement was reached by representatives from the plaintiffs and the defense. Therefore, the jury is now dismissed. Thank you for your important service. The bailiff will escort the jury from the court."

Emerson stared at the departing jury.

"What's going on?" he whispered to Jeff.

"While you went AWOL, I've still been here, doing my job," Jeff whispered back.

Once the jury was gone, the judge resumed. "The plea is as follows: The defense, Crandall Enterprises, pleads guilty to the charges of theft. However, in exchange, the defendant's representative, Emerson Rexham Berit Crandall, pleads not guilty to all charges. Is that correct?"

"Yes, your honor," Jeff said.

"And is this plea bargain accepted by the plaintiffs?"

"Yes, your honor," said Maddie's lawyer. The lawyers representing the investors and the state added their consent.

"Then, with this plea bargain offered and accepted, this case is now closed. The sentencing hearing will be held in approximately thirty days, on a date for which you will all receive ample notice. This court is dismissed."

"All rise," shouted the bailiff.

Already standing, Emerson felt his legs grow weak. After the judge left, he sat down heavily in the stiff wooden chair. The plaintiffs' lawyers commenced shaking everyone's hands, including Emerson's, which he accepted in a daze.

Jeff glanced at Emerson and smiled as he started briskly packing files in his heavy leather briefcase. Finally, he said, "I was coming to tell you last night, but you ran out of here before I could."

"But, how?" Emerson finally said. "I didn't even know it was still an option."

"Oh sure, any time before the jury's decision, as long as the judge is okay with it, and she was. What happened was the jury was taking so long to make a decision. The plaintiffs' representatives got worried. A guilty verdict didn't seem like such a slam dunk anymore. They all needed that to be able to move on to their civil suits. That's where the real money will be. Once they started getting cold feet, they were more interested in accepting our plea. I never took it off the table, you know."

"So, it's what we wanted?"

"Yes!" Jeff was both exalted and exasperated. "You told me you didn't care what happened to Crandall Enterprises, as long as you were exonerated. That was my initial offer. But back then, they didn't want to let you off. Well, Miss Cunningham's lawyer was in favor of it from the beginning, but the investors were out for blood, and you were the only warm body to get it from."

"Maddie's lawyer?" Emerson felt an unexpected surge of happiness.

"But when the jury was taking so long, they started worrying they were going to lose their guilty verdict, so I reminded them of our plea offer. I still liked it, because for my part, I wasn't one-hundred percent convinced the jury was going to let you off the hook."

It finally sank in. Emerson stood up and offered his hand to Jeff. They grinned, shaking hands vigorously and then clapping each other in a hug. Emerson sighed again and stood up straight. The load he had carried on his back for the last few months slid off like an old skin. He sucked in another big breath and let it out in a short laugh of relief.

Emerson sat next to Angela on a daybed on the front porch of her sister's house. Even though it was cold outside, the sun streamed in the glass on all sides, bringing warmth. She ended up needing a metal plate where Martin broke her cheekbone and the orbital bone under her eye and was in the hospital five days.

Her face was bandaged.

"Hey," he said.

"Hey," she said, accepting his gentle kiss on her forehead.

He didn't ask how she was doing. He could guess how she was doing, and it wasn't good. He sat next to her, holding her hand quietly for a minute. Finally, he said, "What do you want to do now?"

She sighed. Tears slid out of her unbandaged eye and

dampened the bandage on the other one.

"I decided I'm going to San Diego, to stay with my parents," she said. "My son isn't too happy about it, but I think it will be better for both of us, for a while. He can finish high school there, hopefully get his grades up and get into a decent college."

"Oh? Yeah, that would be good for him," Emerson said. "And you, I think."

She sniffled. He carefully blotted her eye with his sleeve.

"I just need to get out of here for a while. I mean, I liked it here, but now..." She sighed a shuddering, teary sigh.

"I know," he said, rubbing her back.

"I'm sorry," she said.

"Hey," he said. "You have nothing to be sorry about. Why did you say that?"

"I just like you, and I wish...I don't know."

"I like you."

"But it's too complicated now."

"I know."

"Oh, I'm sorry. I meant to congratulate you on the trial. I'm really happy for you." She started to cry harder.

"Hey." He held her, being careful not to touch her injuries.

"I just don't feel like being with anybody, I mean, in a relationship. That man." She gulped, trying to stop crying, failing, reaching for a tissue. "I'm just..." She wiped her face. "I'm just messed up."

"It'll take time, but you're strong." He rested his cheek lightly against her hair.

After a while, they said good-bye.

~51~

As the teen who bought Maddie's car drove off, Emerson looked at the cashier's check with satisfaction. He had sold the car for $1,500 more than Maddie expected. The $7,500 check represented three times what he currently had in his bank account, which was finally unfrozen, and his car, released. Unfortunately, the court had claimed that most of the balance of his meager account was Crandall Enterprises' money and thus owed to the creditors, and that had depleted what was already a scarily low balance. He kept the black car and what the court considered to be sixty days' worth of child care expenses. A pittance.

He and Courtney were almost ready to go. He decided that they would give Washington a try. The Apple Tortrix was staging an assault on fruit trees west of Seattle, and that type of invasive insect was right up his alley. The FDA was setting up an extensive grant program for research aimed at combatting it. Emerson thought he had a good chance of spearheading a study, and he was planning to start his PhD.

It would not be a high-paying gig, though, and this worried him. He needed to provide enough for Courtney. Well, he had to start somewhere. He smiled ruefully to himself, realizing this exact concern was what caused him to take the high-paying job with his father last spring.

Look how that ended up.

He picked up his cell and made an appointment with Maddy's lawyer for later that day. Before then, he had to clean up the apartment and finish packing.

He had just dumped some cardboard in the recyclables bin at the apartment when Lotu pulled up. Emerson leaned down to look at him as Lotu pressed the button that opened the passenger-side window.

"What's up?"

"Brought you a coffee." Lotu held up a to-go cup. "Join me?"

Emerson opened the passenger door and climbed in, accepting the cup. They faced the canal, looking out at a man trying to fly a kite, a boy running along with him. He sipped the coffee, waiting for Lotu to say something.

"So, this guy, Martin Pulga," Lotu said. "He's a major whack job."

"No kidding."

"I got his records from Springfield. His mother, she was a waitress." Lotu let that sink in, then went on. "And she was a heroin addict, but not just that. She was really messed up in the head. The father was unknown. Probably some junkie."

The kite twirled tightly in the air behind the man and dove abruptly into the mud.

"Apparently, she didn't want a son. She wanted a daughter. The social workers investigated her once, after she sent him to school dressed as a girl. His hair was long, tied in pigtails. Wore a little party dress. Mama said she was just letting him express his true self, so they went all PC and backed off."

Emerson looked at Lotu.

"Bad decision," Lotu went on. "She started going out with a real creep. One night they got all tweaked out, and the guy decided, since the mother was so determined to make Martin into a girl, he was going to treat him like he treated girls."

Emerson sucked in his breath, looked away, back out at the pair on the bank of the canal, who were running again with the kite.

"He raped him. Seven years old. The mother was so high, she just passed out while it was happening."

Emerson said nothing.

"Finally, the school noticed he wasn't showing up and sent the cops. By then, the boyfriend was gone, and the mother off somewhere. The boy had cut off his long hair. He told the cops the man had killed his sister." Lotu watched the pair with the kite. "He's got to let more string out."

"What happened?"

"Well, first, they tried to find the sister. Finally, they realized there was no sister. Martin was the sister."

Emerson pictured it and felt sick about the little boy that Martin had been.

"They put him in a group home, charged the mother. I made some calls. He was already done. Hurting other kids, getting in trouble. I'm sure his lawyer will hire a shrink, so maybe we'll find out more. Not that I really care, at this point."

"Do they know when he first killed someone?"

"No." Lotu sighed. "He probably started on prostitutes, street people. Like the one your little girl saw him with. Anyway, we have what we need."

Emerson had heard enough and reached for the door handle.

"We might need you to testify, if he decides to plead not guilty."

Emerson remembered pressing the knife against Martin's throat. What would be different now, if he had followed that impulse, up there near the cabin?

"Well, I'm not sticking around."

"Where you headed?"

"I haven't decided," Emerson lied. "But it will be far away from here."

"Text me. We might need you."

"Why? You want me to do your job for you, again?" He felt Lotu's eyes on him and turned to cast him a challenging look. "This would be a good time for an apology."

Lotu flashed that disarming smile. "You don't realize everything that comes our way during an investigation. We do what we do to stop criminals from hurting more people."

"Things that come your way? Like an accurate drawing of the actual serial killer, for instance?"

Lotu looked through the windshield. "Yeah. That was a miss."

Emerson sipped the coffee. "That it, then?"

"Yeah."

"All right." He opened the door, climbed out, heading for the apartment. Lotu cruised past him, giving him a wave.

Emerson imagined the contents of the envelope one more time before opening it. It was from Maddie, left for him at her lawyer's office. Earlier that day, when he dropped off the check there, the plump receptionist surprised him by handing him the bulgy, little envelope.

"I was asked to give this to you," she said. "It's from Maddie Cunningham."

Now, several hours later and with Courtney asleep, he examined it. Was it a confession of love? He enjoyed the thought, but the envelope didn't even have his name on it, so why would it be anything that personal? It was probably some weird, biologic sample she wanted him to take to the university.

He finally opened it. It contained a short, handwritten note and something wrapped in tissue and tucked in a small plastic bag.

"Hi, Emerson," the note said. "I'm guessing you could use something like this right about now. All is well on my project. Say hi to Courtney for me. Go Pampas Cat. M."

He tore open the little packet. To his astonishment, a clear, pink stone dropped out, falling with a sharp tap onto the table. He picked it up and examined it. It was about the size of a cranberry and rough. He could see it had beautiful color and clarity, even in its uncut state – a lovely and sizable pink diamond.

He thought about it for a moment. Well, well. This certainly changed things. What impulse caused her to give it to him, he wondered. Was it an offbeat way to admit she liked him? A "thank you" for helping her in the past? Maybe it was simply a small share of the diamond vein they had discovered together, on her land?

Whatever the reason, it was a pretty damned nice gift.

The next day, he and Courtney pulled out of the apartment lot for the last time. He was still heading toward Seattle, but they were going to detour to San Francisco first. With a quick Web search, he had found an auction house there, renowned for its gem sales, where he would learn what that diamond was worth. He planned to place it in their next jewelry sale.

As they headed out of town on Route 6, Emerson felt light and cheerful. He joked with Courtney, telling her corny riddles that caused her to alternate between rolling her eyes in disgust and giggling uncontrollably.

He was leaving Colorado, and an extraordinary year, behind. He remembered the person he was when he moved to Stony Valley with his daughter, still a stranger back then. In thinking about that version of himself, he saw a younger, more naïve and much more trusting person. Something in the past few months had changed all that. Something about being hunted by the police and about learning his mother's true circumstances had changed him. Something about his decision to leave Martin's pulsing skin intact under the steel of his knife instead of driving the blade into his artery, that had changed him, too. The rage he tried so hard to suppress had fought back, abruptly emerging, but he had controlled it. Emerson finally realized he didn't always have to deny that fury. He could harness its power.

And that could come in handy.

Pulling on to Route 70, he pointed the car toward the Continental Divide. He never looked back.

The End

Note from the author:

I hope you enjoyed *For Sissy*. If you did, please remember to leave a positive review at the site from which you purchased it. Positive reviews help others find and enjoy this book.

Read on for a preview of its terrifying prequel, *The Crandall Haunting*. In this paranormal suspense novel, Emerson meets Courtney, and they encounter murder and revenge that lead to the collapse of the Crandall Resort.

For information about me and my work, please visit my webpage, www.ahgilbert.com, and sign up for updates.

Thanks for choosing *For Sissy*!

– A.H. Gilbert

The Crandall Haunting

Chapter 1
Colorado, 1897

The diamonds didn't start the trouble. The possibility of diamonds did.

The possibility of diamonds brought Silas to this dark, hot house, his searching hands in a desk drawer, the muzzle of a pistol pressing against his temple.

"What are you looking for?" said a husky, male voice behind him. Silas realized it was Asa, the rancher who owned this house. And he knew that things were about to go bad.

Silas could tell that Asa hadn't noticed Lonnie, standing on the dark stairs. Lonnie had time to take aim. There was a quick flash, a loud crack and Asa fell forward into Silas, splattering him with blood.

"The woman!" Silas said, shoving aside Asa's limp body. Lonnie headed to the bedroom, gun still ready, while Silas stepped through the puddling blood and followed.

Mayla, in bed, had pulled a pistol from under the pillow. But the dim moonlight shone on her, while Lonnie and Silas were shielded by the home's inner darkness. She didn't have time to aim, and Lonnie was ready. His bullet penetrated her head, blasting it open and spattering the pillows with blood and brains.

"Damn, Silas!" Lonnie whispered, horrified. They crept toward her, unable to take their eyes off the sight. Silas fumbled for the room's lantern, found it, lit it, held it out toward her. The light cast feebly white, and long shadows stretched across the bed. The woman's face was gone, her head a pulpy mass.

"Oh, Jesus, Silas."

267

They looked, spellbound by the horror. Silas' thoughts flitted back to earlier in the day, when they had stealthily watched that woman. She had bustled around the chicken coop, gathering eggs and cheerfully scolding the annoyed hens. Lonnie's rifle had blasted that life away, leaving a hot, headless mess. Silas felt his stomach heave, his heart pound. Then his attention was distracted by a bit of pink cloth, mostly hidden by the bloody pillow.

"What's that?"

"What?"

"There."

Silas jabbed a finger at it.

Lonnie tucked the rifle against his body, still pointing it at the woman, as if she might come back to life. He reached out with his other hand, keeping as far back as he could, pulling at the piece of silk. It was a small bag, closed with a drawstring. When he almost had it free, the woman's body slipped, falling toward his arm. Blood gushed out, over his hand, soaking the little bag.

He yelled and yanked his arm away, dropping the bag on the floor. It landed with a thud and a shimmering pink stone slipped out, glittering in the white lantern light.

"Oh Lord, Silas," Lonnie whispered.

"Pick it up. Let's go."

Lonnie grabbed the bag, shoving the stones back inside and tightening the drawstring.

"Wait. Look." Silas nodded at the woman's neck. A large, pink diamond dangled there, mounted on a heart-shaped pendant, wet with blood. Lonnie held his breath, then reached out and gingerly lifted the pendant. The woman's body started a slow descent, slipping out of the bed. It hit the bedside table, toppling onto its shoulders, the rest of the body following, sinking to the floor, blood pooling beneath it. Silas fought back the urge to be sick.

"We got to go," Lonnie said. "What if someone heard?"

"No one could have heard." Silas remembered the miles of distance to the nearest home.

"Someone could have heard."

They hurried through the front room. Silas paused to check Asa's body, and found another large pendant under his nightshirt. It was a diamond, set in silver wire, hanging from a leather tie.

So, it was all true, the stories of the diamonds. Now he knew.

He tried yanking the pendant, but the leather was too strong and Asa's body jerked forward, his head snapping back weirdly. Silas used his knife to slice the leather.

"Go," he said.

They slipped out of the house and mounted their horses. They started fast, trying to put plenty of distance between themselves and the carnage. The moonlight was bright, and they had no trouble seeing the road. But as they topped a hill and started down the other side, they saw dark storm clouds rapidly crossing the moon, rolling toward them over the valley. This surprised them, and they pulled their horses to a halt. They didn't want to be stuck on the prairie when a big storm hit.

"Did you have any idea there was a storm coming?" Lonnie said.

"No."

Their horses, blowing hard, put their heads up, looking toward the storm, ears alert. They snorted and jigged on the road, unable to hold their feet still. Lightning flashed and, at the same time, a crack of thunder rumbled across the mesa. Lonnie's horse reared straight up and turned quickly, catching Lonnie off guard. He fell, hitting Silas' horse as he went. Silas's horse bucked twice, dumping Silas, hard, on the road, stunning him for a moment. By the time Silas could sit up, the clatter of the horses' hooves was far in the distance. The storm continued to pour in around them, and big, heavy rain drops struck them like ice. As bright as it had been just minutes before, it was now dark. Silas couldn't see Lonnie.

"Silas? You OK? You there?"

"Here."

Silas crawled forward, his head throbbing, and now shivering in the sudden cold. He reached out, trying to find Lonnie. His hand closed over what he thought was Lonnie's arm.

"Here," he said again, squeezing.

"Where?"

Silas was startled. Lonnie's voice sounded ten feet from him. He squinted through the heavy rain, trying to see what he was holding. Through the darkness, he thought he saw someone, or something, rising up next to him. A scream started deep in Silas' chest. He tried to release the icy thing he was holding, but his hand was clamped on. He could not get it free. He sat back and kicked out, screaming.

"Silas?" Lonnie whispered, his voice tight with fear. "What's happening?"

Silas was staring in horror at his hand, still locked on what seemed to be an arm. Straining his eyes in the darkness, he saw his hand was turning white and hardening like ice. The crackling ice traveled up his arm as he screamed, trying to push away with his feet. Then the cold traveled up over his shoulder to his neck, where it spread down his body. It crept up his face, freezing him, hardening him, his scream abruptly silenced.

"Silas!" Lonnie stumbled toward him, tripping on Silas' body, now hard and cold. "Silas!"

Lonnie thought he saw movement, and looking up, he saw a dark and shadowy figure rise up before him. He gasped and tried to stand, tried to run, but something caught him in mid-stride and burned him with intense cold. His scream turned into a ghastly gurgle, and he fell on the road, clattering like a block of wood. The hardened bodies of the two men continued to change, now drying, becoming a fine gray powder, blowing this way and that in the gusting wind, until no trace remained.

The bloody pink bag had fallen from Lonnie's shirt and hit the ground, spilling its contents across the wet dirt. The diamonds sparkled in the last flickers of lightning as the storm rolled over the horizon.

When the sheriff and his men investigated the murders, no one was entirely sure of the motive. It seemed robbery was probably the intent, but both corpses were found with their diamond necklaces in place, and the pink bag of diamonds was tucked under Mayla's pillow. How could the robbers possibly have missed them?

Chapter 2
Present Day; Syracuse, New York

Emerson's cell phone chirped as he finished his fiftieth push-up. Good excuse. He was going to add ten more today, but instead, he pushed himself up with a grunt and found the phone.

"Hello?"

"Hi, Emerson, is that you? Well, of course it's you. What a silly question. Who else would answer your phone, using your voice?"

"Hi Gary." His partner.

"Well, I've got some bad news." Gary was uncharacteristically direct.

Emerson took four strides to the refrigerator that rattled in the tiny indentation he called the kitchen.

"Let's hear it." He tucked the phone against his ear with his shoulder and opened the refrigerator, reaching for the carton of orange drink.

"We're canceled."

He paused, carton halfway to his lips.

"What does that mean?"

"We're done, man. The Aggies canceled our funding. They said they have to reallocate their funds to the Asian Longhorned Beetle, which, to quote, 'is rapidly becoming an epidemic in virtually all varieties of maple in Massachusetts.' As well as attacking the ash and poplar, I might note."

"I know what the Asian Longhorned Beetle is."

"Apparently the Asian Longhorned Beetle is considered to be of greater importance than the hemlock looper."

Emerson put the carton down and stepped to the window. A plump, dark woman was walking a fluffy white dog across the street. It pulled on the leash, lunging against its harness to get its nose to the base of a light pole. The woman didn't notice its frantic tugging, and she dragged the frustrated creature along easily at the end of an orange leash as she talked into a cell phone. Emerson watched her dully, a distant gaze in his dark blue eyes, his thoughts darting around Gary's news. It was bad.

"Can we appeal the decision? I mean, they pretty much guaranteed us another two years."

"I suppose we can write to someone. The board, the committee, the president, the Royal Canadian Mounted Police. But you know how stubborn Aunt Aggie is when she makes a decision."

"Aunt Aggie" was one of Gary's many nicknames for the U.S. Department of Agriculture, which funded their research.

"So what do we do, just turn off the lights and lock the lab?" Emerson ran one long hand across his forehead and into his dark hair, which hadn't seen barber's clippers in a few months.

He noticed a rusty hatchback pulling into a "no parking" zone across the street. The driver, a middle-aged woman, turned to the child in the seat next to her, taking hold of the young girl and hugging her.

"Well, we could stage a protest, let the loopers loose," Gary was saying. "That would show them. Do they have any hemlocks on the grounds of the Department of Agriculture in D.C.? Maybe we could fling some loopers at the President's motorcade. Can you imagine the coverage? The news coverage, I mean, not the coverage of the motorcade with loopers. Hey! We could get sympathy donations from the anti's and professional protesters. No, wait, they're always broke."

Emerson turned away from the window as Gary prattled on. They would actually probably have to kill the loopers, an odd thought, after he had worked with the little, striped caterpillars for so long.

"Maybe we could ask the Saudis," Gary was saying.

"Alright, Gary," Emerson cut in. "I've got to think. I'll talk to you later."

"Sorry."

"Me too."

"Bye."

Emerson sat on the bed. He hadn't yet folded it back into a couch.

Great. No more money for their research also meant no more income for him, meager as it was, just enough to keep this cheap studio in a questionable neighborhood, barely enough to keep gas in his ailing, 12-year-old car. Enough to buy imitation orange juice, but not real orange juice. He couldn't say they were close to finding a way to eradicate the looper, but they were definitely making progress. This sudden change made his last two years of work seem, well, useless.

Useless. He had heard that word so often. The image of his smirking father wedged its way into any fleeting optimism he tried to muster. While Emerson was in college, his father never missed a chance to harangue him about his choice of majors, although, admittedly, he did help pay for it. To his father, biology was only useful if it led to medical school. Its leading his only child to a solitary, low-income life in a lab full of insects was, to his father, a complete waste of time and money. To his father, it made no sense to work so hard at anything that didn't involve a big financial payoff or notoriety, or best of all, both. Any conversation they had attempted in recent years revolved around his father trying to belittle and bully Emerson into forgoing this work and, instead, coming to work with him. The concept repelled Emerson as much as it enthralled his father, who longed to have his son working by his side. Now Emerson was about to become destitute, with funding hard to find, but he still couldn't tolerate the idea of going to work with his father. The thought made him feel almost physically ill. He would have to be nothing less than desperate to do it. Emerson couldn't imagine ever getting to that point. Even a job waiting tables or serving burgers would be better than that. He could just hear his father's disgust if he heard that his master's-degreed son was working in a fast food restaurant.

Hell, it would probably pay better than his research grant.

He sighed and stood, stepping toward the shower, which was set, with a sink and toilet, in an alcove off the kitchen. A plastic, accordion-style door separated it from the rest of the room. Just then he thought he heard a quiet tapping on his door, two little knocks. He froze, naked, and listened.

Tap-tap.

"Just a minute."

He rummaged in his dirty clothes hamper for a pair of shorts. Stepping to the door, he put his eye to the peephole. He could see the top of a small head.

"Who is it?"

"It's me," said a little voice, almost too quiet to hear.

Emerson pulled back the chain and turned the deadbolt. He opened the door to see a girl about three feet high with straight, dark brown hair and deep blue eyes. She looked up at him with an expression of mingled curiosity and fear. A lanky six-foot-two, he towered over this little person. He scratched the hair at his chest absently as he looked back at her.

"What can I do for you?" he said, not quite knowing how to address a little kid.

She took a deep breath, stared at his knees and spoke as though she were reciting something she had memorized. "My name is Courtney. I'm seven. I'm in second grade. You're my father."

That stated, she glanced up at him shyly and then looked back at his knees. As her words sunk in, a woman appeared in the doorway. She bore an overall rumpled appearance, with a tired, middle-aged face. Her body was soft and pudgy, bulgy under a baggy, long-sleeved T-shirt and sweatpants.

"Are you Emerson?" she said.

"Yes," he said.

"The bug guy?"

"Yeah, you could say that. What's going on?"

She thrust a pink, child-size knapsack in his hands. "This girl is yours. Her mother was in an accident and can't take care of her. She's in a coma. Hit and run," she added, anger flitting across her face.

"What?" He heard her words, but they didn't make sense.

"I brought her all the way here for you, because she's a good kid and she has a good mother. But that's all I'm doing. I've got too much." Her face was sad, and utterly exhausted. Then she looked at him with a hardened expression and said, "Ask the child. She has all the information for you."

Her eyes rested for a moment on the girl. Then she said, "Good bye."

She hurried down the hallway and out the front door with surprising speed.

Emerson looked at the little girl, who was staring back at him. He heard a car engine start and he hurried to the window to see the hatchback pulling away from the curb. He tried to open the window, but it was painted shut, as he already knew.

"Hey!" he yelled, slapping the glass as the car disappeared down Fourth Street. "Hey! Stop!"

"Can I come in?" Courtney asked quietly, glancing uneasily down the dank and dingy hallway. Muffled shouting came from one of the other apartments, and the hallway stank of old fried food and cigarettes.

"No!" he said, feeling panicky, stepping back to the girl.

"My mother said if I ever met you, I should show you this."

She held up a glossy, color photo. He took it, frowning. It showed a group of people on the dock of a lake. They were holding cans of cheap beer and smiling. He was one of them, and he had his arm around a woman.

He remembered that day. It was a graduation party, a small group of the science students, celebrating the end of their college careers. They had earned their degrees and were preparing to start jobs. Barry Ross had invited them to his Dad's cabin on Loon Lake, up in the Adirondacks.

He gazed at the woman in his arm. He remembered her, too. Annie Hughes, a sweet, smart botanist who had been in some of his classes over the previous couple years, and who surprised everyone that weekend by revealing a delightful, bikini-clad body. Since she was normally hidden in baggy shirts and loose jeans, Emerson would never have guessed that she could be so appealing. Apparently she liked him pretty well, too, because they ended up making love several times over the course of that weekend, in the lake, in the woods, in the tent. It was sweet, and fun, but it didn't last beyond those intense, forty-eight hours. She was slated to start research on the Aleutian Islands the next week. He was coming to Syracuse to work on a study aimed at preventing the emerald ash beetle from spreading into New York. They sent a couple e-mails and had tracked each other on social media for a while. But they both seemed to know that it was just one of those goofy, horny episodes that was never meant to be anything else.

Except, apparently, it had become something else, and that something else was standing in his doorway, now looking like she was about to cry.

He watched her with consternation. Emerson's total experience with children was limited to conducting school field trips at the nature preserve. Watching her eyes fill up with tears, he knew he needed to stave off her crisis so he could focus on his own. He drew on what he could.

"Want to see a really cool bug?"

The girl looked at him in surprise, then nodded.

"Come on."

She stepped through the door and he closed it behind her. He showed her a lighted glass terrarium atop a pressboard stand. "Can you see the bug?"

She looked intently through the glass. He watched her dark blue eyes examine mossy sticks, leaves and rocks as she turned her head this way and that to see under objects.

"Where is it?"

"I'll give you a hint. It looks like a stick."

She continued to look, but, after a moment, said, "I can't see it!"

"Look up."

A long, greenish brown bug was perched upside down on the screen covering the terrarium. It was four inches long, no thicker than a cocktail straw and had long legs with knobby joints.

"I see it!" she said. "That's a bug?"

"It's called a walking stick."

"Why does it look like a stick?"

"For camouflage. It looks just like a stick so birds won't see it. That way it won't get eaten."

She looked back at the bug in wonder.

"What's its name?"

"I haven't thought of one yet. Maybe you can think of one. I'll be right back. I have to make a phone call while you're thinking of a name."

He set down the knapsack and looked up the phone number to the police and punched it on his phone. He looked back at the little girl who was watching the bug and thinking hard, her almost-black hair falling across her pale cheek. On impulse, he stopped the call and went to his closet. Reaching up, he pulled out a worn photo album. In its first few pages, he found what he was looking for, his kindergarten photo. He looked at the photo and back at Courtney's thin face with those deep blue eyes surrounded by long, dark lashes. His face was different now, of course, with his straight nose, long arching brows and angled jaw, but still, there was no doubt about it. They could have been brother and sister. Or father and daughter. He felt weak. He sat down heavily on the bed.

A daughter!

If he called the police, what would happen? They would try to find that woman, maybe, and the girl's mother, and the girl would be sent to temporary foster care. That was probably the best solution, he thought. Then his mind abruptly bounced across memories of news stories of foster parents starving their children, keeping them in closets, abusing them. Surely, they weren't all like that?

The girl noticed his intense gaze.

"You could call him Sticky," she said.

"Sticky?"

"Uh-huh."

"That's a good name. OK, from now on, she's Sticky."

"She?" Courtney grinned, showing tiny, slightly uneven white teeth. Braces as a teenager, he thought, same as me. He realized he needed more information before he could figure out what to do.

"Courtney, where do live? What's the name of the town where your mom is?"

Courtney looked down. Her lip trembled. He got up from the couch and went to the kitchen. He pulled out a chair at his Formica table that he had found at the Good Will store.

"Here you go. Have a seat."

She sat. He reached for the orange drink, deciding she wouldn't suffer from a few of his germs, from his habit of drinking out of the container, and poured her a cup.

"I had to come here, with Lois." she said, her voice sad. Then apparently remembering something, she went back for her small knapsack, unzipped a pouch and pulled out a large, tan envelope. Handing it to him, she sat down again.

"That's from her."

He looked at the envelope with apprehension. On the front, "Open in case of emergency," was written in large, red block letters. It had already been opened, and now he pulled out the contents. The first document was apparently this girl's birth certificate, with a social security card clipped to it. He read the birth certificate and felt a surge of adrenalin when he saw his own name on the line for "father."

He stared at it so long that Courtney said, "There's a letter for you, too."

It was in a plain white envelope with "Emerson" on it in small, round cursive. He unfolded the single sheet of lined paper, dated a year earlier, and started to read.

Dear Emerson,

I hoped you would never have to read this note, but if you are, it's because something has happened to me, something that is preventing me from taking care of Courtney, so here goes:

Courtney is our daughter. I know you'll see it, just looking at her. And I gave her your last name. Don't ask me why I didn't tell you. I just didn't think it was fair to force you into this, once I made my decision to have her. You were just starting out, too, and you didn't ask for this.

But now, if you are reading this, it's because I don't have anyone else I can trust to take her. I know it isn't fair, and I'm sorry for that. But I couldn't bear to see her go to foster care. One of the reasons I am so messed up is because I spent my childhood with some really bad foster families. PLEASE DON'T DO IT TO HER.

I know that you and I didn't stay close, but I also know you are a good, gentle man. I have followed your research, and you are doing important work.

Courtney is the sweetest girl, with a big heart and incredible curiosity, and she is so smart. Please, please keep her safe. Thank you, Emerson. Thank you.

Sincerely,
Annie Hughes.

Emerson's stomach tied itself in tighter knots with every line he read. He put the letter down and shuffled quickly through the few remaining documents. He paused over another note that listed his name and current address as Courtney's custodian in the event that Annie was unable to care of her. He had moved here a couple years ago. She really had been keeping tabs on him. The packet even included a photo of him, taken from a news article when he received the looper grant. The bug guy.

It was so weird to think this had all been going on without his knowing – the baby, Annie's careful planning, her keeping his address current in these documents. But why the heck had she kept this a secret from him?

He stuffed everything back in the envelope and went to the little girl. Kneeling on the floor, he put his hands on her shoulders.

"Courtney? Where's your Mom?"

Her eyes got wide and round. Bright orange drink stained the skin above her upper lip.

"Where does she live?" he said, more urgently, panic creeping into his voice. "Who is Lois? Courtney!"

He gave her a little shake.

Tears burbled out of her eyes and ran down her face as she stared at him. He pulled his hands away from her.

"I'm sorry. I didn't mean to scare you."

She jumped up from the chair and ran to the door, trying

futilely to open it, not able to reach the deadbolt. Emerson was horrified.

"I'm sorry," he said. "It's OK."

He went over to her and kneeled down again.

"No!" She yelled, giving him a furious, useless shove. "Go away! I want my Mom!"

She dissolved into sobs, clutching her knapsack. He tried to hold her, but she cried louder and fought him off. He jumped up and walked to the window, picked up his phone, put it back down. He turned to his laptop and punched in Annie's name, starting a search, but not really knowing if it would produce any magic, useful information or a solution. He focused intently on this endeavor for a few minutes but didn't get far before Courtney's quiet crying snapped him back to the room and the physical facts in front of him, mainly, a real girl, huddled miserably on the floor like some soggy pile of pink and purple rags. He sat down next to her, his back against the wall.

It was too much. His research. This kid. What in hell was he supposed to do now?

End Preview

Want more? Find **The Crandall Haunting** *on Amazon.*

About the Author: A.H. Gilbert

www.ahgilbert.com

Listening: Podcasts

Brain Science; Hidden Brain; Horses in the Morning; Listen Money Matters; Locked Up Abroad; Love + Radio; My Dad Wrote a Porno; Mysterious Universe; No Such Thing as a Fish; On Being with Krista Tippet; Savage Love cast; Sword and Scale; Ted Radio Hour; The Dough Roller Money; The Guardian's Science Weekly; The Moth; The New Yorker: Fiction; The Vanished Podcast; True Crime All the Time (and TCAT Unsolved); Unfictional; Writing Excuses

Listening: Music

Leonard Cohen; Grace Vanderwaal, Annie Clark (aka St. Vincent); Tom Waits

Doing

Photographing insects & nature; Horseback riding; Hiking; Golf

Binge Watching

Better Call Saul; Chopped; Stranger Things; The Fall; The Forest (The French series, with subtitle); *The Killing; The Walking Dead*

Recent Reads:

Right Behind You, by Lisa Gardner; *The Good House,* by Ann Leary; *The Road,* by Cormac McCarty; *The Girl with All the Gifts,* by M.R. Carey; *John Dies at the End,* by David Wong; *The Dry,* by Jane Harper; *All the Birds Singing,* by Evie Wyld; *Confession of a Serial Killer: The Untold Story of Dennis Rader,* by Katherine Ramsland

www.ingramcontent.com/pod-product-compliance
Lightning Source LLC
Chambersburg PA
CBHW061546170626
46811CB00001B/113